POLARIS

ALSO BY TODD TUCKER

Zulu Five Oscar
Collapse Depth
Ghost Sub
Over and Under
Shooting a Mammoth

POLARIS

TODD
TUCKER

Thomas Dunne Books   📖. Martin's Press   New York

THOMAS DUNNE BOOKS.
An imprint of St. Martin's Press.

POLARIS. Copyright © 2016 by St. Martin's Press, LLC. All rights reserved. Printed in the United States of America. For information, address St. Martin's Press, 175 Fifth Avenue, New York, N.Y. 10010.

Based on a concept by Todd Tucker and Jay Piscopo.

www.thomasdunnebooks.com
www.stmartins.com

Designed by Steven Seighman

The Library of Congress Cataloging-in-Publication Data is available upon request.

ISBN 978-1-250-06978-8 (hardcover)
ISBN 978-1-4668-7842-6 (e-book)

Our books may be purchased in bulk for promotional, educational, or business use. Please contact your local bookseller or the Macmillan Corporate and Premium Sales Department at 1-800-221-7945, extension 5442, or by e-mail at MacmillanSpecialMarkets@macmillan.com.

First Edition: June 2016

10 9 8 7 6 5 4 3 2 1

To Pamela

I must confess that my imagination, in spite even of spurring, refuses to see any sort of submarine doing anything but suffocate its crew and founder at sea.

—H. G. WELLS, *ANTICIPATIONS*, 1901

BOOK
ONE

WELCOME ABOARD THE USS *POLARIS*

A Legacy of Freedom

The officers and men of the USS *Polaris* extend to you a sincere WELCOME. It is our pleasure to have you as our guests. As your hosts, we hope that your visit on board will be informative, interesting, and enjoyable.

Watchstanders will be happy to answer any questions you may have as long as they do not interfere with assigned duties.

EMERGENCIES

Should any emergency situation arise, alarms will be sounded and the word will be passed. You are requested to STAND FAST, BUT CLEAR of all passageways and operating areas. Do not obstruct ladders, hatches, or watertight doors. Allow ship's personnel to perform required action without interference. Members of the ship's company will explain the situation as soon as possible.

OPERATION OF SHIP'S EQUIPMENT

Do not operate equipment or switches, position any valves, or enter any posted areas without prior approval from ship's force to do so. Observe posted precautions and procedures in all operations.

SECURITY

Certain aspects of the ship's operational characteristics and certain areas of the ship are classified. The Radio Room, Sonar Room, Navigation Center, Missile Control Central, and the Engine Room are classified areas.

CHAPTER ONE

He sensed the pain before opening his eyes. Slowly he regained consciousness. It was dark and loud, his eyes stung from smoke, and his ears rang from the multiple discordant alarms that rang just outside the door. His face was pressed against a steel floor. He rolled over onto his back and looked upward, trying to get his bearings and let the splitting pain in his head subside, but there was nothing to see, just more steel, pipes, and cables. He felt a momentary panic, afraid that he'd been swallowed whole by a giant machine.

He sat up, felt something heavy in his hand. He was startled to see he held a nine-millimeter pistol.

He slowly pulled himself to his feet, waiting for the disorientation to pass. *Where am I?* He saw the sweeping arc of a yellow alarm light through the crack in the door. Several kinds of smoke combined in the air he inhaled: the sharp ozone of electrical fire, the sour tang of gunpowder. He shook his head, but the disorientation didn't pass.

He made his way to a small metal sink at the end of the bunks. The sink was made to fold into the wall. Reluctantly putting the gun down, he pushed a button, and a narrow stream of cold water ran out. He filled his hands with the frigid water and buried his face in them, savoring the coldness that snapped him awake. For the first time, he looked into the mirror that was above the sink.

A bumper sticker, cracked and faded, had been pasted across the top: POLARIS: A LEGACY OF FREEDOM. The silhouettes of two submarines faced each other in the background, one very old, he somehow knew, with a flat missile deck and a boxy tower, and one very new and much larger. A big, modern submarine. The submarine he was aboard.

Focusing suddenly on his own reflection, he saw he was in the blue uniform of a submarine officer, a nametag embroidered onto his chest: HAMLIN.

Only then did he notice the gash above his left eye, caked in blood.

He heard hard, quick footsteps outside the door, hurried climbing down a metal ladder, but somehow sensed he wasn't ready to venture outside the stateroom yet. He desperately wanted some idea of what was going on first. Taking the gun back off the sink, he turned and faced the darkness.

The bunks were made with military precision, a contrast to the papers that had been thrown around the rest of the room. Military documents stamped SECRET combined with personal effects on the floor: photos of girlfriends, of dogs, handwritten letters in pastel-colored envelopes. For the first time Hamlin became aware of movement, a slight rolling at his feet; the ship was under way. Where it was going, and where it came from, remained a mystery. At least to him. A battery-powered battle lantern was affixed to the overhead. He found the switch and turned it on. Its single beam of light crossed the room, landing on the form of a person, sitting, head slumped forward.

Pete raised the gun, startled. "Hey!" he said. No response.

He stepped forward just as the ship rolled again, and the body fell over, revealing a stark, lifeless face, a hole in the middle of his forehead. The light of the battle lantern reflected a thick streak of gore on the bulkhead where he'd been leaning.

Hamlin read his nametag: RAMIREZ. He felt a stab of sadness and knew somehow that Ramirez had been his friend, even though he didn't remember him. He stepped back and felt a growing sense of horror as the dead man stared at him accusingly, and he felt the weight of the gun in his hand.

Someone grabbed his shoulder from behind.

He whipped around, gun raised.

It was a strikingly beautiful woman wearing a uniform like his, but with oak leaves embroidered on her collar. Her nametag read MOODY. She had a wound, too, a torn sleeve that revealed a gash on her upper arm, and she looked breathless with exhaustion. Unlike Hamlin, though, she seemed to know exactly what was going on. Also unlike Hamlin, she seemed exhilarated.

"Jesus, Hamlin, relax. It's me."

Slowly he lowered the gun.

She stepped past him into the stateroom and looked at Ramirez. Amazed, she looked back at Pete, and then back at the corpse again.

"Is he dead?"

Pete nodded.

She knelt down, searched his pockets, looked at the papers that had fallen from his desk onto the floor. "Good. You stopped him before he did any more damage."

Satisfied with her search of the body, she stood and looked at Hamlin quizzically. "Are you okay?"

"I'm . . . really not sure."

She stepped toward him and looked him in the eye. "I'm

sorry you had to do this," she said. "Truly. But you did the right thing. You might have saved the ship. And—you'll never have to prove your loyalty to me again."

They both looked down at the body a final time.

"Let's go," she finally said. "We're not out of the woods yet."

CHAPTER TWO

"The control room is secure," she said as they walked briskly through the narrow passageway. "Along with missile control. The good guys are back in charge now." She was moving fast, a natural athlete riding a charge of adrenaline.

"Good," said Hamlin. He somehow knew they were moving forward in the ship, but little else seemed familiar to him. He felt the comforting weight of the pistol in his pocket as they moved.

They stopped at a motor generator room, scarred heavily with streaks of black soot and charred insulation. A heavy layer of smoke clung to the overhead, and thick gray foam dripped from every surface.

"The automatic extinguishers kicked in immediately, put the fire out. But both motor generators are trashed. We've switched all the vital loads, but there are some lighting busses we can't reenergize. There are parts of the ship that are dark, parts of the ship that are cold, and probably will be for a while. Especially with our engineer—" She pointed back toward his stateroom. "—gone."

Hamlin started to reach out to touch the damp wall when Moody grabbed his hand with surprising force.

"You know better than that," she said. "We haven't overhauled this yet, might still be energized and dangerous. We can't lose you now."

He put his hand down.

"Are you hurt?" she asked.

He shook his head. He thought better of telling her about the complete amnesia that seemed to have befallen him. "My head," he said truthfully. "It's killing me."

She reached up and touched his forehead with surprising tenderness. "The bastard got you good," she said. "We'll get that bandaged up. When we can."

They walked by the radio room, where a half dozen computer monitors blinked and an acrid smell hung thick in the air. "He started with radio," said Moody. "Took out communications before he did anything else. It's completely wrecked, we'll be lucky to get any of it working."

As they continued forward they came upon a room that Hamlin knew was sonar. They approached a screen.

Moody pointed at a symbol, an upside down V in the center of the screen. "Our shadow. No change. We've made their job easy today, with all the noise we've been making. No change in range, about one nautical mile behind us, as always."

She hit some buttons on the screen, and the display changed, a banner reading DRONE CLOUD appearing at the top of the screen. The thought of drones resonated with Pete; he knew that once he'd had deep familiarity with them. Along with all his memories, that was gone, but it left a shadow of dread inside him.

"Normal," she said. "Medium density. Direct overpasses every fifteen minutes or so." They continued walking.

"Propulsion is in good shape," she continued after a mo-

ment. "I think that was probably going to be his next stop, before you got him. The screw is still turning and the lights are
still burning. Most of the lights, anyway."

Hamlin had a sudden vivid memory of close-quarters
fighting: fists, blood, and screams. His head hurt with the
memory.

They were nearing the control room, Hamlin knew. Immediately aft of it was an escape trunk, a large steel egg with
beveled ends that was designed to allow an emergency escape
from a crippled submarine. The bottom of the trunk penetrated from the overhead. Its access hatch at the very bottom
was open, its ladder cast aside.

"You need to see this," she said. "We converted the forward
escape trunk into a makeshift brig. There's actually a procedure for that, believe it or not."

Hamlin stepped beneath the trunk.

"Be careful," she said. "He's dangerous."

Hamlin looked up and saw that a heavy steel grid had
been affixed to the bottom of the trunk, fastened by heavy
bolts on the outside. He could also see the soles of two shoes
on the grid above his head, a pair of standard-issue Navy ox-
fords.

Suddenly the prisoner looked down, between his legs,
and saw Hamlin. He immediately threw himself to his hands
and knees.

"Pete!" he said. "Thank god you're here!"

His face was dirty and his eyes were frantic, but Pete thought
he recognized something just as he had in Ramirez: a friend.

"Finn," he said, surprising himself with the memory of a
name.

"You've got to get me out of here!"

Suddenly Moody stepped to Pete's side, into the view of the
prisoner.

McCallister's face darkened. "Moody? Pete, why are you with her?"

"That's right, McCallister, he's with me. And you're in there, trapped like the animal you are."

"*Pete!*" The intensity of his shouting made Hamlin wince. "You've got to get away from her!"

"Shut up, McCallister," she said.

"She's going to destroy us all!"

Moody suddenly pushed Pete aside and pulled something from her pocket. She pointed it up at the steel grid and fired it.

An electric blue arc jumped from her hands to the steel grid that McCallister knelt upon. Sparks shot across the chamber. McCallister howled and tried to jump away from the pain, but there was nowhere to hide inside the metal cell. He screamed and bounced off the sides of it in agony as Moody held her finger down on the trigger, a grim smile on her face.

When she finally relented, McCallister collapsed to the grid, his face pressed against it, breathless, almost unconscious. A thin stream of drool escaped his mouth and fell between Moody and Hamlin.

"I guess you're done talking now," she said, reholstering the Taser.

McCallister muttered in pain. "Pete . . ." he said. "Help me. . . ."

"Ignore him," said Moody. "He's a traitor."

WELCOME ABOARD THE USS *POLARIS*

A Legacy of Freedom

BIOGRAPHY OF OUR COMMANDING OFFICER: CAPTAIN FINNEGAN "FINN" MCCALLISTER

Captain McCallister is a native of Dennison, Ohio, and is the son of Mr. and Mrs. Finnegan McCallister, Sr. He received his commission in June 2009 upon graduation from the United States Naval Academy. Following graduation, he received Nuclear Power and Submarine Training.

Captain McCallister reported to the USS *Alabama* (SSBN 731) in December 2010. He served in division officer assignments prior to transfer in June 2013 to Naval Ballistic Missile School. Subsequently he was assigned to the USS *Seawolf* (SSN 21) from October 2013 to October 2015. Captain McCallister attended the Submarine Officer Advanced Course (SOAC) from October 2015 to March 2016 before reporting to the USS *Newport News* (SSN 750) as engineer for a three-year tour.

Starting in March 2019, Captain McCallister took a series of roles within Naval Sea Systems Command to design and build the new class of *Polaris* submarines.

Working at the right hand of Admiral Wesley Stewart, the father of the *Polaris* program, he was an integral part of the team that designed the weapons suite as well as the long-life nuclear fueling program designed to increase the duration of submarines.

Captain McCallister assumed command of the USS *Polaris* in May 2027. He remained in command as the *Polaris* was assigned to support the Alliance in 2029.

Captain McCallister's personal decorations include the Legion of Merit with a Gold Star, the Alliance Bronze Star, Meritorious Service Medal with a Gold Star, Navy Commendation Medal with three Gold Stars, and the Navy Achievement Medal with two Gold Stars.

CHAPTER THREE

Hana Moody and Pete Hamlin climbed a short ladder into the control room. Standing on the conn was a muscular lieutenant who was studying a green sonar console. He jumped to his feet when they entered.

"Commander Moody!" he said, clearly ecstatic to see her. His biceps bulged in his uniform sleeves and he practically leapt toward them. He was attracted to Moody, it was obvious. But as he started talking, it was evident to Hamlin that he craved her approval as much as he craved her body.

"Were you worried, Holmes? Think I can't handle a few mutineers? And look what I found," she said, waving her hand at Pete.

"Glad you could help out," said Holmes with a sneer. "Now that the fighting's done."

"He did his share," she said. "He killed Ramirez."

"What?" said Frank, shocked.

"I saw the body myself," she said. "Got him in the head, killed him with one shot." Moody reached up and for the second time touched Pete's wounded head. "So it looks like he was in the fight at least as much as you were."

Stung by the words, Holmes glared at Pete. "Looks like he was kicking your ass before you got to his gun."

Pete shook his head, waiting for the memory to come back to him. "Maybe so," he said.

Frank sneered at Pete's lack of a comeback.

Moody guided Pete over to the computer screen where Holmes had been staring.

"Still there?" she said.

"Still," said Holmes. "Always one to two miles behind us. Never maneuvering too close, never completely drifting away. I'm sure it was easy for them to track us during the fight, god knows there was plenty of noise."

Hana turned toward Pete. "We still don't know if she's friend or foe, no way to tell. If she's a Typhon boat, they're still not making their move."

Typhon. The word jolted Hamlin. He knew that Typhon was their enemy, one of the few distinct memories to return to him. But was the word an acronym of a foreign slogan? Part of a phrase made pronounceable for English speakers? A slur against all those who would kill them? Pete strained to remember but wasn't sure he'd ever known.

"But if it's Typhon, they made no move to attack us during the mutiny," she continued.

"We should attack them first!" said Holmes.

Moody sighed impatiently. "What if that's an Alliance boat? And they somehow got word about the mutiny? They may just be trying to determine if the mutiny succeeded or not, ready to blow us out of the water if they think we're in the hands of the enemy."

"Not if we get her first."

"And then we've got every submarine out here after us:

Alliance and Typhon. Stick to driving, Frank, and leave the thinking to us."

Holmes turned red at the insult. "Hey, hotshot," he said to Pete. "Why don't you take the conn for a while? I've been up here for hours."

Moody looked at them both, and nodded in approval.

"Sure," said Hamlin, unsure what to do next. He stepped toward Frank, hoping that some knowledge of the task at hand would materialize. At least the mechanics of how to take the watch. But nothing came to him.

"Would you like to know our course and speed?" said Holmes after a moment, mocking him.

"Of course," said Hamlin.

"Ship is on course two-four-zero, twelve knots, depth seven hundred feet," he said. "Rigged for general emergency. The port nonvital bus is deenergized because of the fire in the motor generators. I'm guessing about half our lights are out. Sierra One, our shadow, is still behind us, about one mile abaft."

"OK," Hamlin responded.

Holmes looked at him in disbelief. "Did you just say 'OK'?!" He looked to Moody for affirmation, and then back at Hamlin. "How about, 'I am ready to relieve you'? That's the customary phrase at this point."

"I am ready to relieve you," he said.

"No, you're not," said Moody, stepping forward suddenly. She looked him up and down impatiently. "You're hurt worse than you look, aren't you?"

"Maybe," said Hamlin.

Holmes sighed loudly in disgust.

Suddenly Moody turned and slapped Holmes across the face, stunning them all. "I'll relieve you, Frank, how's that? Go belowdecks and eat, or read a comic book, or whatever it is you do in your free time, you weak son of a bitch."

Holmes trembled in rage and shame.

"Go!" she said. "Now! I relieve you! I have the deck and the conn."

Holmes stormed out of the control room, leaving the two of them standing there.

She stared at Pete with concern. "You always were tough," she said. "Don't risk the ship on it."

"Yes, ma'am."

She looked around to verify that no one else was in the control room, and leaned in. "I love it when you call me that," she whispered in his ear.

She then stepped back. "Now get yourself to sick bay, Hamlin, and pull yourself together."

He waited a moment before responding. "Yes, ma'am."

Moody exhaled deeply as Hamlin walked out of the control room. Could she trust him? She'd seen the gun in his hand, seen Ramirez dead at his feet. Still, he seemed off, perhaps hurt worse than it appeared. She would ask the doctor after he'd had a chance to look him over; maybe he'd medicate him with something. If the drugs were good enough, maybe they could all use a dose. For now, she knew only the next step in the patrol order, the one thing the captain had shared with her, and he'd done that only when he had to. But it was a doozy: they were going to drive through the old Pacific degaussing range. Ever since she found that out, she'd been trying to figure out what it meant for the rest of their mission.

And she could only guess, because no one would tell her.

But now Hamlin wouldn't have any choice. He would have to show her the complete patrol order so they could fulfill the mission. And Hamlin should trust her, shouldn't he? She'd thwarted those two traitors, one of whom Pete himself had killed.

From the beginning, she hadn't known what to make of him. Maybe it was a natural by-product of him being on the ship the least amount of time—a few weeks, when Frank, the next-newest crew member, had been onboard for two solid years, never stepping outside the hull that entire time. They all knew each other like one big dysfunctional family, living in a house with no windows that they could never leave.

But it was more than that: Pete was opaque. He wasn't quite Alliance, and he wasn't quite Navy. But the simple fact was now she had to trust him.

And surely he could see that she had only one goal: the mission. And beyond that, the Alliance. It was all a big joke to McCallister and Ramirez, always had been, a punch line. The Alliance officers like her and Frank, with their coloring-book training and their in-depth knowledge of Alliance dogma. Moody could debate them into the ground about international politics. Unfortunately, on a submarine that had been on patrol for far too long, that was much less important than being able to keep a main feed pump working, or the generators going. At least in Captain McCallister's eyes.

But that's why she was here; that's why the Alliance had put her onboard, made her second-in-command. Because she believed in the mission with the same kind of purity Ramirez had tried to get out of his roaring evaporators. From the cold murk of the ocean that surrounded them, he could produce water a thousand times cleaner than anything available on land, a requirement for his nuclear power plant. That's what was required with ideology, too; it had to be even purer at sea than anywhere else, to hold up under the relentless pressure that constantly tested them all. Ramirez had never believed that, and neither had the captain. But now: she was in charge.

She looked down at the display and checked again for the two undeniable realities in their ocean at the present time: the next step of their mission, represented by the two bright, straight lines of the degaussing range fifty miles ahead. The lines were superimposed electronically on the screen, essentially drawn on by the computer. It was a motionless, silent structure that was invisible to their sonar, or anyone else's. The bright lines on the screen conveyed certainty, but they were just the coordinates they'd inputted, a visual representation of where the range was supposed to be.

The upside-down V behind them on the screen represented less certainty, but was at least the result of real acoustic information, the thin but steady stream of noise that came to them from their shadow, the other submarine that had dogged them for days. Despite what she told Frank, she was certain she was a Typhon boat, based not only on her menacing posture but also on that noise: she was too loud to be an Alliance boat. A modern Alliance craft in their baffles like that would be silent and invisible. She sat down on the small foldout seat in front of the console, fiddled with the range, and realized for the first time how exhausted she was.

It was hard to believe that just three years earlier she'd been a high school teacher. Business and Econ, her only responsibility a roomful of disinterested eleventh graders in Oak Lawn, Illinois. It was a working-class area, the kind of area that the military had always fed on: patriotic kids without a lot of options. So when the war heated up, Oak Lawn sent its share to all three services, and Ms. Moody was one of the teachers who encouraged them, making her a friend to the recruiters that periodically swept through the halls giving away ARMY OF ONE T-shirts and promises of upward mobility, college tuition, and adventure.

At first, like most of the teachers, she was conflicted about sending the kids away. Even though she believed deeply that it was the right thing, she knew many of them would end up in harm's way, and some of them would end up hurt, or even dead. Many of the teachers quietly discouraged kids from joining for just that reason, although they soon learned to keep their mouths shut about any doubts they had. Teachers were public employees, and public employees who were labeled as unpatriotic soon found their careers limited. Especially as the enemy had one success after another in the Pacific, and the war seemed to close in on them all.

But as time went on, Moody began to actually envy those kids. The war consumed all the media, and it was clear, as the Alliance coalesced in a last-ditch effort to defeat Typhon, that democracy itself was at stake. Many of her former students were in the fight, doing something about it. They would come back to school occasionally, with their uniforms and their ribbons, and sometimes even with their wounds, and she could see it in their eyes: their lives had purpose in a way that hers did not. Meanwhile she continued to count textbooks and teach supply and demand, the Laffer curve, and price elasticity.

Finally, one day, a Navy recruiter lingered in her room after giving the standard pitch to her kids, and they struck up a conversation about officer programs. She fit the criteria, he enthusiastically told her: she was young, single, a college graduate. She found herself surprised as she listened, surprised at how right it all felt. She gave herself one more day to think about it, and then she drove down to the recruiting office, sandwiched between the Department of Motor Vehicles and a Laundromat, and volunteered to be a US Naval Officer. Over the next few days, she filled out a stack of forms with her personal information, took a short medical exam and a basic math test. The fantasy grew in her mind with each step: military glory, exotic ports of call, her own return to Oak Lawn in uniform, an example to all.

One week later, the Navy rejected her.

The embarrassed recruiter was flabbergasted. He tried his best to assuage her, afraid it would turn her against the entire recruiting program, of which she had become Oak Lawn High School's biggest supporter. He attributed it to an unusually good month for officer program recruiting, her lack of a technical degree, some kind of glitch in her application. He asked her repeatedly if perhaps she had something dark in her past that would have come to light in the initial background check, perhaps a youthful DUI or a shoplifting arrest. He finally left her alone in her classroom when it became clear that she now regarded his shoulder boards and ribbons as an insult, a reminder of her rejection.

For two weeks she simmered about it. The school year ended, and she resigned herself to a life in her small classroom, perhaps inspiring her students toward adventure, or maybe even glory, but never tasting it herself. Perhaps after the war and retirement, she thought, she could take a budget trip to Europe and see Rome or Paris.

Then one day as she sat at her desk in an empty classroom, compiling another semester of grades, a stranger walked into her room.

"Ms. Moody?" he said with a smile. "I'm Chad Walker. I'm a recruiter with the Alliance." He handed her a business card that had no rank or title, just a name, phone number, and email address. And he wore no uniform, just a tasteful dark suit. She invited him to sit down. He somehow managed to look perfectly comfortable in the undersized desk–chair combo right in front of her.

The Alliance needed officers, too, he told her. Men and

women who would work alongside the traditional military. People like her were desperately needed. "And I believe," he said, looking her right in the eye, "that you would thrive as a military officer."

"Would I have a military rank?" she asked. "A normal uniform? Could I do any job in the military?"

Walker answered yes to all her questions. You'll have all the same opportunities as a traditional military officer, he assured her. The war effort, and recent legislation, guarantees it.

"So what's the difference between being an officer in the Alliance and being an officer in the regular Navy?"

Barely any difference at all, he said with a chuckle. If you ascend high enough, you would eventually end up working at Alliance headquarters, rather than at the Pentagon. But in the trenches, you'll be a military officer, with the same privileges and responsibilities.

She said yes before he left her classroom.

There was a background check again, and another skills test. While the Navy had asked her math questions, the Alliance asked her political questions, and she wasn't always sure what answer they wanted to hear. Did she always vote? Had she ever run for office? Could she name the five original member countries of the Alliance? Could she name its current commander? Did she believe that every nation could function as a democracy? She sweated over the answers, desperate not to feel the sting of rejection again.

Two weeks after her physical, she got a congratulatory letter and her orders. She would begin basic orientation at the Alliance Training Center in the countryside west of Baltimore in one month. The orders contained a list of items she was to bring with her to training, and what not to bring: "minimal" cosmetics were allowed. Playing cards were not. The congratulatory letter was from the Alliance Commander, whose name, she saw, she had gotten incorrect on the entrance exam. She resigned from the Oak Lawn school district the next day.

Chad Walker was right about one thing: Moody did thrive as a military officer. She found an athleticism she never knew she had during training, excelling on the obstacle course, the daily runs, and the hand-to-hand combat sessions. She learned to her surprise that she was still a very good swimmer, her best sport in high school, cutting through the water so efficiently that she lost herself in the process, swimming laps until she lost count and had to pull herself exhausted up the ladder. The order and rigor of military life came easily to her; she was one of those people the military has always coveted, a person who found great comfort in being part of a system.

"Systems" was a keyword in her Alliance training, a shorthand for the simplified block diagrams they used to explain everything. The entire submarine was reduced to three blocks labeled CONTROL, WEAPONS, and PROPULSION. Turn a page and propulsion was reduced to blocks of PRIMARY and SECONDARY. One more page and the primary system was turned into blocks of NUCLEAR REACTOR, MAIN COOLANT PUMPS, and STEAM GENERATORS. Occasionally they would drag in an actual engineer who would show them photographs of pumps, breakers, and pipes, but it all looked drab and undramatic, indistinguishable blobs covered in wires and lime-green insulation, objects whose appearance seemed unworthy of their exalted positions and titles on the block diagrams. The reactor itself, the holy grail of the ship, the block that touched in some way every other block of every other diagram, looked like a large steel trash can penetrated by a dozen ordinary-looking pipes. After studying its characteristics and the nearly magical process of nuclear fission, seeing what a real reactor looked like filled Moody with the exact same flavor of disappointment she'd felt when she lost her virginity.

All the block diagrams were compiled in a softcover book that they were encouraged to take notes on, and it was universally referred to, by teachers and students, as "the engineering coloring book."

The philosophy of the Alliance was treated similarly, in a separate coloring book: broad outlines in a neat, digestible framework. The pre-Alliance world was shown as a jumble of democratic nations, represented by small- and medium-sized blocks—the United States, Britain, Canada—all jumbled on a page, their energies directed in different directions, friendly but tragically unorganized. Opposing them, on the opposite page, was a large, unified block that contained inside it the allied nations of Typhon. Ominously, they were lined up neatly inside the Typhon block, and the lines of their individual borders were dissolving, as if Typhon were feeding on them to gain strength against the peaceful, unorganized nations it preyed upon.

On the next page, though, the Alliance was born: a giant dotted line that surrounded the friendly countries, which had suddenly lined up neatly to face their enemies in the Typhon block. Moody gathered that because the Alliance nations kept their solid borders intact despite their overarching block, they were still free and independent, just better organized to fight their enemy. Twice during their political course, they got word from their instructors that allegiances had shifted. An Alliance nation shifted to Typhon, and a Typhon nation shifted to the Alliance, and they were instructed to scratch out and hand-draw them in their updated positions on the appropriate pages of the coloring book.

She excelled at every stage of training, graduating number one in her class, and was given her choice of orders. She chose *Polaris*, the most advanced submarine in the fleet.

Once onboard, she soon found out that Chad, her recruiter, wasn't right about everything. She was not indistinguishable from other military officers. In fact, since their uniforms were all the same, it was generally the first thing officers asked each other at the officers' club, or the Navy Exchange, or the base gym while making small talk. And it was clear that when you answered "Alliance," this was somehow a second-class status. Over beers, some regular officers would even confide in her, often while trying to romance her, that while they weren't talking about *her,* of course, everybody knew that the Alliance officers were generally men and women who'd been rejected by the regular military. The Alliance recruiters got lists of every reject, which became their feeding ground. The highest compliment that anyone could pay an Alliance officer was that they *probably* could have made it as a regular. This was a compliment that, to Moody's disgust, the Alliance officers even paid to each other.

It all just made her work harder, volunteer for every tough position, and pounce on it with a giant chip on her shoulder. On the *Polaris,* she attacked her qualifications and was promoted twice in a year. After two more years of impeccable fitness reports, and setting a squadron record for the physical fitness test, she was promoted to second-in-command. She got another personalized letter from the Alliance Commander, and oak leaves for her uniform. They had a real dinner in the wardroom to mark the occasion, with a roast beef that Ramirez had found in the darkest recesses of the deep freeze, served with respectable gravy and a loaf of fresh bread that was downright good. After the meal, Captain McCallister pinned the oak leaves on her collar and told her that he was delighted to have her as his Executive Officer.

Just a week later, she stepped into the galley to get a cup of coffee before taking the watch. The coffeepot was full and fresh, and the wardroom door was closed, indicating that someone was having a conversation that they didn't want overheard. She filled her cup and stood silently for just a minute, her curiosity piqued.

"So that's the way it is?" She could hear Ramirez through the door.

"She's worked hard," said McCallister. "As hard as any officer I've ever known. She deserves this. I would have made her my XO regardless."

"I don't work hard, Captain?"

"I need you in engineering. She's not qualified to run that plant, and you know that."

"So I'm too qualified to be XO?"

"Stop whining," said the captain, not without affection in his voice. "You're a fine officer, you'll get your chance."

"If I can't get promoted on this boat, I'll never get promoted. They'll never let me off. That's the curse of an engineer."

There was a pause; then the captain spoke quietly. "Everything OK with Tracy?"

"Fine," said Ramirez. "I get letters every mail call, filled with pictures. I send letters every mail call. We're great at this now, we've mastered it."

"Are you worried?"

"Worried that we might just be good at this: being a couple that never actually sees each other."

"There's a war on," said the captain. "That's the world we live in. And we're all beholden to the needs of the Navy."

"The needs of the Navy?" asked Ramirez. "Or the needs of the Alliance?"

"Tell yourself whatever you need to tell yourself to keep this submarine running and to fulfill our mission. I personally don't give a shit if you do it for the Alliance or if you do it for the Navy."

"Did you have to promote her, Captain? Did somebody tell you to?"

There was a long pause as the captain considered his answer. "Yes," he said. "It's been encouraged for some time now: they want Alliance officers in command positions. But the guidance was widely ignored. So they formalized it. Every boat gets a Number Two from the Alliance."

"So Moody is a token."

"Would you rather have Frank Holmes as your XO?"

They paused for a moment; Hana pictured them drinking their coffee, the easy camaraderie they would never share with her.

Ramirez finally spoke. "To think, they told me an engineering degree would be good for my career."

"Yeah?" said the captain. "They told me I'd be fighting Russians."

"Commander Moody?"

She was snapped awake by the appearance of Frank Holmes, that muscular, dogmatic, slightly dense incarnation of the Alliance officer stereotype.

"Sorry," she said. "I think I fell asleep for a second."

"About earlier . . ."

"Forget it," she said with a wave of her hand.

"Do you want a relief, ma'am? Hit the rack for a few minutes?"

It was incredibly tempting, but her eyes drifted down to the screen in front of her, where they had inched closer to the degaussing range, and their shadow had stayed, maddeningly, the same distance away.

"No," she said. "No time. Find Hamlin. I sent him to medical a few minutes ago to get fixed up. Tell him to slap a Band-

Aid on his head and to meet me in the wardroom so we can talk about what's next."

Frank snapped to attention with ridiculous precision. "Aye, aye, Captain."

He spun on his heel and walked down the ladder to find Hamlin.

CHAPTER FOUR

Two miles away, on the Typhon submarine, Commander Jennifer Carlson listened to the recording from sonar. Her second-in-command, Lieutenant Banach, stood next to her. She pushed a button, and listened again.

"Any ideas?" she asked Banach.

He shrugged. "It's loud." He spoke with the thick accent of his native province, and he'd learned to speak in short direct sentences to avoid confusion.

She nodded back. "Thank you for that penetrating analysis, Lieutenant."

Carlson was the purest killer Typhon had, in any branch of the military. On the first day of the war, three long years earlier, she'd sunk two Alliance warships in the South China Sea: a guided missile cruiser, and a destroyer that was sent to destroy her. Afterward, she'd steamed among the wreckage, taking photographs through the scope, looking at what they'd done with their two torpedoes, and acquired a taste for killing that had never been sated. She didn't believe in politics, diplomacy, or anything that Military Intelligence told her. She wasn't even all that fond of nuclear power, which kept her highly engineered killing machine moving through the water. She believed only in torpedoes, missiles, and, when thing got really tight, bullets. She believed in angles of attack, ranges, and keeping her baffles clear. Because she was pure, the crew adored her.

She hit play again.

"You're right," she said. "It *is* loud."

In fact, for them to hear noise from an Alliance submarine with their crude sensors, it had to be deafening. "I hear hatches slamming shut, depth changing, alarms. Maybe even a gunshot."

"Impossible," said Banach. "They carry no small arms onboard *Polaris*-class boats."

"Well, they also say that *Polaris*-class boats are silent, so I guess you can't believe everything you read."

"Do you think our man onboard is taking over? Giving us a signal that the mutiny is complete?"

"No," she said, "unfortunately. They are still submerged, still cruising. Maybe it was a failed attempt."

"Such weakness," he said. "Our crew could easily overpower us if they chose to mutiny."

"True, they are armed to the teeth, and extremely bored."

"What shall we do?"

"Stay on it," she said. "Same range. They don't seemed inclined to shoot us at the moment. We should have some contact soon from our spy; if he's still alive, maybe he'll fill us in."

"Aye, Captain."

She put the headphones on and listened again, let her imagination go to work on the noise. Banach hadn't learned it yet, but on a ship with no windows and very limited sensors, an imagination was a vital military asset. She pictured the submarine in front of her, and tried to picture the chaos within. She badly wanted to shoot them, and they were there for the taking. But she'd learned from her experience with the airplane; it was better to shoot somebody on their return from Eris Island, not on their journey there. Take out the vessel *and* their precious cargo.

The temptation was great because she needed to kill an enemy submarine; it was a gap in her résumé. She'd come close once, very close, in an episode that was now taught to midshipmen in her home country, and celebrated on military holidays.

It was in those early days off Eris Island, one year into the war, when they were watching the drones take off endlessly through the scope. Initially they'd tried to count them all, but it proved impossible. Instead they tried to count how many took off in an hour, and then counted the hours. A few times the drones had seemed to notice her scope, and they quickly submerged, moved to a different sector, and resumed their surveillance of the island. Other than the drones, they had the ocean around Eris to themselves. No Allied ship came anywhere near them.

Carlson sent messages to fleet headquarters. They replied indifferently, asking pointedly if she had plans to surveil any targets of military value. Then the drones began dropping their little bombs on their surface ships, and the commodore asked her why she hadn't sent more thorough reports about the drone menace.

At some point, a daring Allied submarine commander decided to take a peek at the waters around the island as well— perhaps looking for her, perhaps just equally curious about the business at Eris Island. He was able to completely sneak up on them. The Allied submarine service had made a cult out of silence, and her primitive sonar couldn't have detected a submarine that was twice as loud. Her submarine was designed to be durable and cheap, so they could manufacture them in vast quantities and overwhelm the enemy. This might have been helpful to the commodore, who commanded twenty-six boats, but it did little good to Carlson, who had only one. Banach was in control when the enemy attacked.

"Torpedo in the water!" he shouted into the intercom. By the time she ran into control, Banach was already turning sharply toward the unmistakable sound of muzzle doors opening and a torpedo hurtling toward them.

"Launch the countermeasures!" he said, and suddenly the sound of the screaming torpedoes was replaced by a wall of noise pumped in the water via their noisemakers, shot out of both signal ejectors, one on each side of the Typhon boat.

Carlson looked at the sonar display while Banach tried to save the ship. Their countermeasures appeared to be working; the torpedoes were peeling away.

"Ready bearing and shoot!" he said, sending a bearing to fire control. The enemy ship, of course, far more sophisticated than theirs, remained silent. The only datum they had for her location was the sound of the torpedo being launched. They were two people shooting at each other in a dark room, firing at the muzzle flash.

There was a rumble beneath her feet, a loud *whoosh* of air, and her ears popped as her submarine fired her torpedo.

"Torpedo is in high speed!" said Banach.

"Very well," said Carlson. That left them just four torpedoes.

She looked at sonar. The enemy torpedoes were behind them now, drawn to the noise of the countermeasures. But the Alliance weapons were steerable and could turn back, as long as there was a man alive on the Alliance boat.

"Fire another?" asked Banach.

She was contemplating just that when they heard an explosion to starboard.

"They're hit!" said Banach. Carlson watched the display.

For a few moments, they listened for the telltale sounds of a submarine dying: tanks exploding, the gush of flooding, the desperate roar of an emergency blow system. But nothing came.

"They're still alive," she said. She heard something, though, hull popping as the enemy ascended. "But she's going shallow. They must be hurt."

"To fight the flooding," said Banach. "Shall we finish her off?"

Carlson nodded. "Not now," she said. "We might not have to."

The wounded ship was noisy, undoubtedly busy trying to save herself. Carlson maneuvered them away from her, to disguise their position, but the Alliance boat seemed like the fight, at least temporarily, had gone out of her. "Take us to PD," she said. "Let's see if we can take a look."

Banach complied and drove the ship carefully upward. Carlson raised the scope right on the bearing of the Alliance submarine. She was making so much noise now, she was impossible to miss, the pumps working to get water off her, men hammering on pipes trying to staunch the flood. She took a quick sweep around, verified there were no drones on top of them. It was clear, for the moment. The drones were like that, they had learned, could come and go with the randomness of a rain squall. She trained the ship's single eye back on the bearing where she knew the enemy ship was fighting for her life.

"I see her," she said. "I see the scope." There it was, like a pencil sticking straight out of the water, a small V behind it as it moved slowly forward.

"Why aren't they surfacing?" said Banach. "Do they think we don't know where they are?"

"That can't be it," said Carlson. "They're making too much noise. They really should surface if the flooding is as bad as it sounds. Of course, I'll shoot them if they do."

Suddenly a drone caught her eye on the horizon, sweeping lazily across the water, searching.

"I see," she said.

"Captain?"

"They're afraid of the drones, just like we are."

"Drones will attack their own?"

"They will attack anything, they are the dogs of war."

"So what shall we do?"

She had an idea. "Tell me, Banach, how many of those inflatable lifeboats do we have?"

The question startled him, and he had to think. "Three."

"And what is the direction of the current?"

Banach went to the chart, did some calculations, and told her. "Just three knots, running southwest."

"Tell our sergeant to prepare to launch one of those life rafts from torpedo tube number three."

"Can I explain to him why?"

"I'd rather not say," said Carlson. "In case it doesn't work."

She positioned the boat carefully so the wounded enemy with its periscope was down-current. She thought about timing, watched the random drones that were still in the sky, not having spotted either scope. She wanted to be close enough that by the time the drones spotted the raft, it was directly on top of the enemy, right on its scope ideally. If the drones got to the raft too early, it would be a waste. And then she would have to leave because the drones would eventually spot her scope. Doing the rough math in her head, she crept to about six hundred yards until she finally gave the order.

"Deploy the boat," she said. She heard the clank of the hatch, the rumble of the torpedo tube ejecting its contents.

"The lifeboat is deployed," said Banach, taking the report on his headphones as she watched through the scope.

A few seconds later it popped to the surface, a bright orange bundle. Immediately it began to inflate and unfold, growing to full size in seconds. It appeared motionless, but Carlson could see that it was in fact moving with the gentle current toward the enemy's periscope. It looked almost comical, a big orange tent bobbing happily upon the sea. Triangular panels on the outside had a metallic sheen—radar reflectors, designed to make it highly visible to rescuers. She couldn't take her eyes off it.

After all, it was designed to be seen.

And soon enough the drones saw it.

The first drone flew directly over it at high speed. Carlson panicked for a moment; it was too early. But the drone didn't drop its bomb; instead it flew high into the sky. Alerting its brothers, she realized.

A swarm of four came in, flying at high speed and in a direct line. By now, the bright orange boat was directly against the enemy scope.

When the first bomb landed, the lifeboat simply evaporated, like an exploding balloon. Tiny pieces of orange fabric littered the ocean around them like confetti. The more substantial parts of the raft remained afloat, in a pool around the scope, and the drones poured their bombs upon them.

Whether a drone targeted the scope, or it was just a lucky shot that missed the life raft's detritus, Carlson didn't know. But the bomb landed directly atop the scope, shattering it, sending smoke and sparks into the sky. Too late, the enemy captain lowered it, undoubtedly with new fires and flooding to combat.

"Shall we finish her off with a torpedo?" said Banach.

"No," said Carlson, although it pained her. She wanted to preserve her remaining four torpedoes. "They are damaged beyond repair. She is out of the fight. Even if she doesn't sink."

"Very good, Captain," he said. The enemy ship was making a racket as she pulled away, damaged and clinging to life. Carlson could hear alarms onboard from her ship's hydrophones—the enemy's overworked pumps—and she imagined the screaming of burned men inside.

"Everything OK, Captain?" Banach had caught her in her reverie.

"Yes," she said.

"You look angry."

She nodded. In fact, she was. She knew she'd done the right thing in not finishing her off, in conserving those last four torpedoes, not using another on a ship that was already crippled beyond repair. They were the same four torpedoes that she still possessed, and it was looking like they might very well need them for the fight ahead. But it galled her that the Alliance submarine had gotten away with her life. Galled her that somewhere a submarine captain was sitting in an officers' club, telling the story of his close call, his escape, his survival.

CHAPTER FIVE

Pete walked away from the control room, still trying to gain his bearings—and to recall some memories of what had happened to the *Polaris,* and his role in it. He climbed down a ladder as he headed aft to avoid McCallister, locked in a steel cage one level above.

Exiting the forward compartment through a watertight hatch, he stepped into the missile compartment: two parallel rows of missile tubes stretching into the distance like a forest of steel trees. There were few signs of the mutiny in here, save for a wisp of smoke that followed him from the forward compartment and the darkness caused by the partial power outage. But there were signs everywhere of a ship that had been stretched to its limit. A shower room, wedged between two missile tubes, was taped off with a sign: OUT OF COMMISSION. The floor was dusty and the stalls had no curtains. Next to it were two nine-man bunk rooms that were dark, their metal racks bare of any mattresses. It looked like the ship had been designed to carry far more men than she had now, and that she had been reduced, even before the mutiny, to the bare minimum complement. The few lights that remained energized blinked and buzzed, and the air smelled dank, like somewhere below him a bilge needed to be pumped. The *Polaris,* like her crew, had been at sea far too long.

He reached the end of the missiles and came upon two massive machines that were covered in indicators and dials. One had a large red tag hanging from a breaker that read OUT OF COMMISSION. Its twin looked functional, but wasn't energized. Pete looked it over for a minute and found a small sign: OXYGEN GENERATORS. Behind the amnesia, his engineer's mind went to work, looking at the dials and indicators, and soon enough put together a rough picture of how the machines functioned. They took the one natural resource that the submarine had access to in unlimited quantities: water. They placed a large voltage across that and tore the water molecules into their constituent parts: hydrogen and oxygen.

While the machine was turned off, a monitoring panel remained lit—a small diagram of the ship with a digital indicator for each of the three main compartments: forward compartment, missile compartment, and engine room. A selector knob allowed him to choose different attributes to measure: oxygen, carbon monoxide, and carbon dioxide. The oxygen level of the engine room and missile compartment was 20 percent—the number was in green, leading Pete to believe that was in the acceptable range. The forward compartment reading was lower and in bright red: 14 percent. Perhaps a result of the fire? The panel showed an open valve between the oxygen banks and each compartment, and Pete pictured an outlet somewhere dispensing the invisible, odorless air that they all needed to survive. But the oxygen banks, he saw, were severely depleted. One was completely empty, and the second was at less than one-quarter capacity. Could anyone onboard make that machine run and create new oxygen? Anyone who wasn't locked in an escape trunk? He continued aft.

Pete surprised himself by arriving at medical. It seemed like a lot of his memories were like that, trapped right below the surface. If someone had asked him how to find medical, he never could have described it. But wandering through the ship, thinking about everything else, he had found his way there.

The door was unlocked. He found a light switch but it did nothing when he flipped it. In the darkness, he could see locked glass cabinets containing gauze and bandages. He tried the doors, hoping he might procure some industrial-grade painkillers, but they were all locked, and despite the chaos that seemed to have descended upon the *Polaris,* he was reluctant to break into them and violate the thin glass and tiny locks that guarded them.

He walked farther into the room and began opening drawers until he found a thick roll of gauze and a pair of scissors. He started to fumble with the gauze but dropped it, and it rolled across the floor.

As he bent over to pick it up, he heard movement from the corner, and he flinched just enough to avoid a massive blow. It hit him on the shoulder rather than on his head, where it likely would have cracked his skull.

He rolled onto his back and quickly kicked the implement out of his attacker's hands—it was a small fire extinguisher. His attacker looked briefly like he wanted to say something, but Pete gave him no time. He sprang to his feet, punched his assailant quickly—twice in the kidneys—then threw him to the ground and put him in a merciless choke hold.

He felt the man tapping his arm, trying to speak. He let the pressure off his throat just enough.

"Pete . . ." he gasped. "It's me . . . Doc Haggerty."

The name was familiar enough that Pete let him go, but he threw him to the ground and stood up, still unsure if he was friend or foe. He felt the gun in his pocket and resolved to use it if necessary.

"Jesus," he said, rubbing his throat. "You nearly killed me." He started to get up, but thought better of it, and sat on the deck while Pete looked him over.

"Who are you?" he said.

The man chuckled at first, but then saw he was serious. "Jesus, Peter. I'm John Haggerty. Ship's doctor. Your friend!"

Vague memories went through Pete's mind as he looked him over: the dark beard, the intelligent eyes, the professorial glasses. He seemed familiar enough that he reached down to help the doctor to his feet. The doctor warily took his hand.

"I'm sorry," he said.

"No, *I'm* sorry," said Haggerty. "I didn't know what else to do when the mutiny started, so I came back here to guard my little domain."

Pete nodded. "Trying to fix this," he said, pointing to the gash on his head.

The doctor looked at him quizzically, and then went to work, skillfully binding up his wound. He looked Pete closely in the eye as he worked. "Do you want to tell me what happened?"

Pete decided that the time had come to trust someone. And this was the ship's doctor apparently—maybe he could help. He took a deep breath.

"I don't remember anything," he said. "I woke up in a stateroom with this cut on my head, and a gun in my hand."

"A gun?"

Pete nodded, and hesitated. "I think I shot Ramirez."

The doctor took a moment to take this in, watching Pete carefully as he did.

"You really don't remember anything?"

Pete nodded.

"You could easily have some short-term amnesia—brought on by that blow to the head. Or, maybe, the trauma of killing your friend. Your memories will probably come back with time. And with rest."

"How much of either of those am I likely to get?"

He nodded. "Good point." He looked Pete over hard as he finished, snipping the tape that held the gauze in place. "So you don't remember our orders? Your mission?"

"Nothing," said Hamlin.

The doctor sighed and leaned heavily against the wall. "Where do I start? You came here a month ago, sealed orders in hand. When you showed the captain, he brought me in— thought I might be able to help, given the nature of the mission."

"Which is?"

"You really don't remember, do you?"

"I wouldn't be asking you if I did."

"You carry the fate of the Alliance—and maybe the whole world—on your shoulders."

"And now I don't remember a thing. Great."

The doctor nodded grimly, and seemed ready to speak, when loud footsteps came down the passageway. Frank Holmes appeared at the door.

"You're needed forward," he said to Pete. He ignored the doctor. "Captain Moody wants us both in the wardroom, now."

"What about me?" said the doctor.

Frank smirked. "She didn't say anything about you. You can stay here."

Without another word, he turned on his heel and walked away.

Hamlin turned to Haggerty. "I guess I should go."

He nodded in agreement. Just as Pete walked out, he stopped him. "Pete . . ."

"Yes?"

"Don't tell anybody what you've told me. Trust *no* one."

Pete nodded at that, and followed the sound of Frank's footsteps ahead of him. As he did, a thought crossed his mind. *Why would the captain assign a doctor to help me?*

WELCOME ABOARD THE USS *POLARIS*

A Legacy of Freedom

COMMAND HISTORY

The USS *Polaris* is the first *Polaris*-class submarine, and the first ship to bear that name. She was named for the *Polaris* missile, the first submarine-launched nuclear missile, in honor of the contribution that weapon made to world peace during the Cold War.

The keel was laid on October 14, 2020, and the crew was formed in July 2023. On May 19, 2024, Irene Gilchrist, wife of the Honorable James Gilchrist, United States Representative from New York, christened the *Polaris* during launching ceremonies held in Groton, Connecticut.

Builders' sea trials were conducted between February and April 2025. Each sea trial set a record for efficiency, and the ship was delivered sixty-eight days early.

On May 25, 2025, USS *Polaris* was commissioned at Naval Underwater Systems Center, New London, Connecticut.

The ship then commenced shakedown operations and underwent shipwide inspections. The crew completed a

Demonstration and Shakedown Operation (DASO), and launched the ship's first C-6 missile. In April 2026, the ship conducted its first strategic deterrent patrol.

In fall of 2028, the USS *Polaris* spearheaded a program to assist the community near its homeport in educating local schoolchildren on water-quality issues. "Water for Life," as this program was christened, has become a landmark project involving local, county, and state agencies in a major cleanup of the area watershed.

On May 29, 2029, operational control of the USS *Polaris* was given to the Alliance, to aid in their mission of supporting democracy around the world.

CHAPTER SIX

Hamlin walked into the wardroom just behind Holmes. On the table was a pitcher of slightly gray-looking reconstituted milk and a dozen tiny boxes of cereal in a metal mixing bowl. Moody was waiting at the head of the table: the captain's chair.

"Gentlemen," she said. "We've got some time before we get to the degaussing range. Wanted to get a quick status update. Frank?"

"You're looking at the entire crew. Not counting the doctor or the one locked in the escape trunk."

"That's it then? Three officers. And a doctor somewhere." She inhaled deeply. "Well, it'll be tough. The three of us can stay on the conn as much as possible. Use the automated systems when we can. We don't have much choice. Autopilot is driving us now, seems like that's working at least."

"Yes, ma'am," said Frank.

"And how are our systems?"

"Everything vital is running, with the exception of radio. Propulsion is good, all combat systems are good."

"Oxygen is low," interrupted Pete. They both looked at him.

"How low?" said Moody.

"Fourteen percent in the forward compartment."

"Christ, no wonder I was falling asleep up there. Can we increase the bleed?"

"One bank is empty," said Pete. "The other is less than twenty-five percent."

"And none of us can operate that oxygen generator," said Moody. "We'll just have to ventilate when we can."

"Yes, ma'am," said both Frank and Pete.

"One more thing," said Moody, looking at Frank. "After the degaussing range, take Ramirez to the torpedo room—let's shoot his body overboard as soon as possible. Before long he'll start to . . . smell. Bad for morale. And we've already made an unholy racket—one body shot overboard won't matter much at this point. Do you need help?"

Pete froze, filled with dread that he might have to help move the body of his dead friend, the friend he killed.

"No," said Frank as he smirked and involuntarily flexed his arms. "I can get him down there."

"That's not what I meant," said Moody, rolling her eyes. "Can you operate the torpedo tubes? Shoot him overboard?"

Frank bristled. "Of course," he said. "I've operated those tubes a dozen times."

"OK," said Moody, doubt in her voice. "Just checking. Get help if you need it, just get it done. The sooner the better."

"Do we want to do the whole burial-at-sea ceremony?" he asked.

"Absolutely not," said Moody. "We won't ring any bells for a traitor."

Frank stood and snapped to. "Aye aye, Captain. I'll do it right after we finish at the range." He started to turn.

"Wait," she said. "Grab a bowl." She tossed a small box of cereal at him. "Let's eat dinner first."

———

After a silent, quick dinner of slightly stale cereal and thin artificial milk, the three of them headed to the control room together.

Pete stepped up to the command console and took it in.

Their own ship was represented right in the middle of the screen by a small green silhouette of a submarine. Behind them, about two miles aft, an upside-down V represented their mysterious shadow submarine. And directly ahead of them were two bold, parallel lines. From the scale on the screen, Pete could see they were about five miles away.

"The degaussing range," said Moody. "I was privy to this part of your orders. I'm assuming for the drones . . ."

"Yes," said Hamlin. "To reduce our magnetic signature."

It came back to him with a powerful clarity. Not only the mechanics of the degaussing run, but the entire control room as well. It came, he realized, from a different layer of memory than the one that had been somehow erased. It came from a thousand hours of practice in this very room, etched on his brain like acid on glass. For the first time since he'd awoken on his stateroom floor, he knew what was going on, what he was doing. The feeling was intoxicating.

He stood on a small raised platform in the middle of the control room: the conn. On each side of him were the polished steel cylinders of the two periscopes, both lowered into a forty-foot well beneath his feet. In front of him, Frank climbed into a large pilot's chair. At Frank's knees was a control yoke that would actually drive the ship. To the left of the yoke was an old-fashioned brass engine order telegraph he would use to control the ship's speed. Despite the gesture toward nostalgia with the brass control, Pete knew that it was an entirely automated system, channeling his orders for ship's speed directly to the engine room. And while Pete would give the rudder and depth orders from the position of command on the conn, Frank would actually be driving the ship from his seat, his hands on the controls.

Directly in front of Pete was a console with several selectable displays. Currently it showed the sonar display: the two bright parallel lines that marked the walls of the degaussing range, and the shadow submarine behind them. He could turn a switch, and the same screen could display the status of the drone cloud, sensed via a floating wire that trailed behind and above them, registering each drone as it passed. If he turned the switch yet again, he could read reports on all the ship's vital systems.

Where Frank could see them from the dive chair were the controls and indicators for the ship's non-tactical systems: the hundreds of pipes and valves that kept the ship and crew alive. The panel was speckled with yellow warning lights and a few red alarms. Pete couldn't read them from his perch on the conn, but he knew most of the alarms represented damage done by the mutiny. Of all the valves and controls, the most imposing were the two large yellow levers directly over Frank's head: the "chicken switches" that activated the ship's emergency blow system. They controlled a direct mechanical linkage that would fill the main ballast tanks with air and shoot them to the surface in the event of a severe emergency. It was the last-ditch safety measure they possessed, something they could use only once and only when nothing else would do, the submarine's equivalent of a fighter pilot's ejection seat. Both were designed to get vessel operators safely to the surface of the earth, albeit from different directions.

Pete flipped the switch back to the drone display. Hana looked over his shoulder.

"Medium density, undirected," she said. "That's expected

given our proximity to the island. A flyover every ten minutes or so; doesn't look like they're actively seeking us or dancing each other in."

"Very well," he said. "Prepare to go to periscope depth."

Moody looked at him, and Frank guffawed.

"PD?"

"I want to see the action of the drones myself, before and after. It's the only way we can assess if the degaussing has been successful."

"And?"

"And it'll help us get away from our friend out there."

"How's that?"

"She won't be able to do what I'm about to do."

"That's my boy," said Moody, an intense smile on her face. Frank grimaced in disgust, and turned back to the controls in front of the dive chair. Hamlin hesitated for just a moment before giving the order. He thought about McCallister locked in the escape trunk, and Hana here in control. Who exactly was he working for now? He wondered if Moody and McCallister were wondering the same thing.

"Dive, make your depth eight-five feet."

"Make my depth eight-five feet, aye, sir," Holmes responded. He pulled slowly on the yoke in front of him. Pete felt the angle in his feet as the big ship began to drive upward.

"Ahead one-third," he said.

"Ahead one-third, aye, sir," repeated Frank. He reached down to the engine order telegraph to order the slower bell, and the automated system immediately answered with a ding. Pete and Hana watched the speed of the ship drop on a red digital indicator until it fell below ten knots. Any faster than that, and the scope could be damaged.

"Raising number one scope," said Pete. He turned the orange ring over his head. He put his eye to the scope as it rose, and he began turning slowly around, looking through the optics underwater. Even though he knew their shadow sub was too far behind them to see, and too deep, he found himself pausing briefly on that bearing directly behind them, looking into the murky ocean for their invisible pursuer.

The darkness in the scope turned steadily lighter as they came shallow, from black to gray to green. Suddenly, the scope broke through.

"Scope is clear," said Hamlin, exhilarated both by his sudden proficiency and clarity of mind, and by the view of the sky—for as far as he could see, glorious sunny blue sky. He didn't realize how imprisoned he'd felt by the steel walls of the *Polaris,* and the gloom that pervaded her, but in an instant, through the pristine optics of her periscope, he could see for miles. "No close contacts."

He twisted the right grip on the scope toward him, tilting the optics as far up as he could, looking into the sky.

"No visible drones," he said.

He heard Moody from the console. "ESM shows the nearest drone about two miles away on a relative bearing of zero-nine-zero, heading this way."

"Seeking?" he asked.

Moody turned some knobs on the command console. "Negative, not seeking, standard random search pattern but on our vector. Should be visible in five minutes."

She stepped up to the conn. "And it'll see us right after we see him." She was concerned, but willing to let Pete execute his plan.

"Understood."

Hamlin swung the scope around to the starboard beam and looked, and waited.

He saw it three minutes later, a tiny black dot on the horizon, barely visible even with the scope in high power. It looked almost like a big seabird, a cormorant, but Pete knew they were too far from land for it to be anything natural. And soon enough, he saw the sun glint on its metallic head. "I have a visual on contact Delta-One," he said, pushing the red button on the scope to register the bearing in their fire-control systems.

The drone was flying near the surface, in a leisurely serpentine pattern that betrayed no urgency. It was hunting, Hamlin somehow knew, but it hadn't seen them yet, as it swooped gracefully back and forth. While it was hunting, it was also conserving energy, flying slowly, its wings turned efficiently upward to soak up energy in its solar cells, its computer steering it to take advantage of the winds, gliding when it could. In good weather, it could stay airborne for weeks.

He also knew that the drone wouldn't see their periscope visually—its cross section, about three inches, would be invisible among even the light waves at this distance. The only effective sensor the drone had for shallow submarines was its magnetic anomaly detection, or MAD.

As long as men had made ships out of metal, people had attempted to use magnets to detect and kill them. Everything made out of steel distorts the earth's magnetic field as it passes through, and relatively simple sensors take advantage of this. It was a time-tested method—the Germans developed very effective magnetic mines in World War II. In short order, navies began using those same magnetic effects to detect submarines. A submarine could become invisible to radar by submerging, and invisible to sonar by silencing, but the way its steel distorted the earth's magnetic field was a physical constant, seemingly impossible to mask. MAD was a big enough threat to submarines that the Soviet Union, during the cold war, had built an entire fleet of subs out of nonferrous metals, materials that were scarce and difficult to use but produced no magnetic signature.

MAD was also a very effective method for the drones—it worked well because the drones could sweep large areas of ocean as they flew, and with large numbers of drones they could cover vast swaths of the world. Submarines could avoid detection by staying deep, but this was tactically fine with the drone strategy—a submarine forced deep was a compromised asset, limited in what it could do.

To counter this, the *Polaris* would try to erase her own magnetic signature, or "degauss." This was named for the "gaus," a scientific unit of magnetism, and was accomplished by steering the ship between two giant electromagnets. The electromagnetics would temporarily erase the field of the *Polaris,* making her, for a time, invisible to MAD detection. This was the first step of Hamlin's mission, getting the *Polaris* through the range. But first he had to see the drones.

Looking through the scope, Hamlin could tell the instant the drone had sniffed them out. It was close enough by then that Hamlin could see the glint of the sun on its solar cells, its power-giving wings. Suddenly its graceful, lazy swooping changed. Its wings tightened up from the ninety-degree angle to its body into an attack posture, pointed and fast. It dived until it was just above the surface of the water, corrected its course slightly, and flew directly overhead. He swung the scope to watch it pass by as ESM alarms shrieked in the control room.

"Flyby!" Hana shouted, cutting out the alarms.

"Confirmed," said Pete calmly.

"Want me to go deep?!" said Holmes.

"Not yet," said Hamlin.

"Why didn't it bomb us?"

"A sub at periscope depth, with just a single drone in the area—it doesn't like its odds. Every algorithm is designed to optimize its chances for a kill, and a single shot at a periscope isn't good odds. They're designed to work best in swarms."

"So now it's going to get its friends?"

"Exactly," he said. But still he waited, and watched.

The drone flew high into the sky, almost straight up, twisting as it soared, a motion designed to attract its comrades. An upward-looking sensor on the head of the drones was designed to look for exactly this behavior. Pete found himself curiously pleased at how well the system functioned.

"Drones approaching from all bearings," said Hana.

Pete had no intention of allowing a swarm to get on top of the *Polaris* in attack formation, but at the same time he couldn't help but stare at their deadly, beautiful efficiency. The lead drone, the one that had spotted them, banked sharply away from them, and came down to just a few feet above ocean level. The others soon aligned behind it, in a delta formation, pointed right at the *Polaris*. It had all taken just minutes.

"Emergency deep!" he ordered.

Ready for the order, Frank immediately pushed forward on his control yoke, and the ship took a steep downward angle. Pete lowered the scope and braced himself against the angle as they dived. Within seconds, they were at two hundred feet.

"Make your depth six hundred thirty-two feet," he said.

Frank acknowledged the order and drove them deeper, to a point just a few feet above the ocean floor.

"Will they drop their bombs?" asked Moody.

"No," said Pete. "We're too deep and they know it. They won't waste their bombs, won't drop unless they register a ninety percent chance or better of a hit. Like bees with stingers: they only get one shot, and they want to make it count."

"So what's the point?"

Pete shrugged. "They know we're here, that's now stored in their memory; they'll increase their concentration around us, in this whole sector, ready to pounce if we surface again. They'll shift the priority of this area, intensify the search patterns. There are thousands of them, and only one of us. They know that time is on their side if we show our heads."

"Which we won't," said Moody.

"We will," said Pete. "In just a few minutes. But if everything goes according to plan, we'll be invisible."

He sat back down at the command console, switching it back from ESM to sonar. Just as planned, they were pointing right at the two bright, parallel lines of the degaussing range. "Right five degrees rudder," he said.

Frank repeated the order and eased the ship right.

"Steady as she goes," said Hamlin, reaching down to change the scale of the display as they approached.

While the sonar display just showed two bright green lines, vivid visual images of what lay in front of them came to Pete. First, he saw the degaussing range like an engineering diagram, the spirals of electrical coil, the parallel lines of switches, the banked symbols of the massive batteries that powered it. A remotely activated magnetic switch and a sensor at the entrance, the ship's magnetic signature activating the range even as the range would soon erase it. This textbook diagram in his mind then gave way to a photographic image, a memory of an underwater survey, stark white lights trained on coral-covered walls, the coils of wire protected by heavy conduit, impermeable to the sea but completely transparent to electricity and magnetism. In this mental movie, a recovered memory from somewhere in his training: a lonely crab skittered across a horizontal beam encrusted in coral.

"Approaching Point Alpha . . ." said Moody, jerking him from his reverie. "We're at the entry point." It was like trying to pull a car into a one-car garage blindfolded.

"All stop," said Hamlin.

"All stop, aye, sir," said Frank, immediately ordering the bell.

He and Moody stood over the display and watched as the giant ship slowly drifted between the two bars on the screen, perfectly centered. In a box on the right hand of the screen, Pete saw the ship's acceleration in all three dimensions, and watched carefully to see if he would need to add a small rudder angle to counteract a stray current.

"Nice driving," said Moody, looking at him with a smile.

"Thank you, ma'am," he said. The back of Frank's neck turned red.

There was a moment of concern as they drifted inside the range and nothing happened. Pete worried that it had been disabled, either by the relentless destructive power of the ocean and nature, or by an act of war. But then suddenly, the lights in the control room dimmed, and a dozen new alarms went off as the ship was engulfed by a powerful magnetic field.

"The range is active!" said Moody. "It's working!" Frank was leaning forward, cutting out the alarms that had sounded as a result. Pete could almost feel the effect upon them, stretching the magnetic field of the *Polaris* into line with brute, electric force, making them invisible in at least one, crucial way. Frank ably managed their depth as they continued to drift through, no easy feat as the ship's speed continued to decrease, making ship control difficult.

"We're clear of the range," said Moody as they passed beyond the two bright lines on the console. Their speed had dropped to under three knots. Pete confirmed on the screen in front of him that they had drifted completely through.

"Ahead one-third," said Hamlin. "Make your depth eight-five feet."

They repeated the process of going to periscope depth. As the scope broke through, Pete immediately turned the ship's single eye upward.

A dozen drones swooped around them in circles, their electronic brains excited by the recent sighting. They swooped, dived, and circled around, many of them virtually buzzing their periscope. But none of them attacked.

"Captain," said Hamlin, "the ship has been successfully degaussed."

"Very well," she said. "Take us deep and report to my state-room for debriefing."

Carlson and Banach watched the *Polaris* slow and go deep in front of them, immediately after her strange, short trip to peri-scope depth. They'd done nothing at PD, didn't shoot trash or broadcast a message. The only thing they seemed to accom-plish was attract a swarm of drones, which quickly developed attack formations, forcing the *Polaris* underwater just in time.

More precisely, they listened, as they heard the hull pop-ping of a ship descending and the slowing of the ship's main reduction gear.

"What are they up to?"

Carlson shook her head. "I have no idea. They are very deep. Almost to the bottom."

Banach took the two strides necessary to get to the other side of the control room, checked the chart. "Are they trying to lose us?"

"I don't think so," she said. "They seem to have other things on their mind."

"Can our friend onboard tell us anything?"

She shook her head, frustrated. "Haven't heard from him lately. That would make this entirely too easy."

She walked over to the cramped corner of the control room where Banach stood, where the chart was spread out. In the lower corner of the chart was Eris Island. They'd followed the *Polaris* up here, to the opposite corner, to a spot that was strangely featureless on the chart, devoid of geological marks or even soundings.

"Stay at this depth, and slow," she said. "Let's see what they are up to."

They drifted closer, staying about a mile away, waiting to see what happened. She tried to visualize what they were doing as they slowed almost to a standstill, drifting forward at a speed of just a few knots. She thought about their man on-board, wondered if he was still alive. Maybe he'd been discovered in the ruckus that they'd overheard, exposed, perhaps even executed. No, she thought again, the Alliance prized themselves on their civility too much for that.

Suddenly, a noise spiked on their sonar. She could hear it right through the hull: a dull *ka-chunk*.

Before she could say anything, a delicate alarm sounded next to the chart, a rarely heard alarm that took her a moment to recognize.

"Captain," Banach said, "the inertial navigation system is failing. . . ."

She looked up at the central panel in front of the dive chair, where a number of other alarms had sounded. Some of the smaller circuit breakers on the ship had opened, and the electrical system was busily resetting itself into a safe mode.

Meanwhile the *Polaris* continued drifting slowly forward.

"Is it some kind of weapon?" asked Banach. "An electric pulse? Are we under attack?"

"No," said Carlson. "I don't think so. But we are at the edge of some kind of electrical field . . . a powerful one."

They waited a few more minutes and then the *ka-chunk* sound repeated, and the alarm for their navigation system cleared. Breakers continued to reset around them, and she realized that the sound was similar to the one that had come to them on the bearing of the *Polaris*.

Once again the *Polaris* sped up and changed depth, ascending to periscope depth.

"Let's follow them up this time," she said, heading for the scope. Banach climbed into the dive chair and efficiently brought the ship shallow.

She raised the scope as they came up. Soon they were at periscope depth, and Carlson squinted at the bright equatorial light through the scope. The *Polaris* was a mile or so away, too far for them to see the scope.

But she could see the drones everywhere, attracted by their earlier trip to the surface. They were swooping overhead, many of them directly above where she thought the *Polaris* was sticking up her nose. They were no longer in the tight pattern of attack that she'd seen earlier. The drones were swooping and searching.

"Captain?"

"They've made themselves invisible to the drones," she said, the solution suddenly dawning on her. "At least at periscope depth."

"How?"

"Degaussing," she said. "They must have passed an underwater degaussing range." It made sense, in a way, this close to Eris Island, probably the outcome of another, earlier research product. She grudgingly respected the Alliance and its technology; it always seemed to work when they needed it. Her leaders, on the other hand, couldn't provide her ship a microwave oven that would work without bursting into flames.

"So the drones use MAD?"

"Apparently," she said, watching the drones fly obliviously over the *Polaris*. "At least for shallow boats."

"Well!" said Banach. "That is good news for us!"

She took her eye off the scope and smiled at him. "Yes, it is, Lieutenant. Very good news."

Her submarine, like their entire fleet, had been designed
with coastal warfare in mind, where mines might be concentrated at strategic chokepoints. And while her government
might not be able to make a decent microwave oven, they did
control 90 percent of the world's titanium supply. And if they
couldn't make a decent microprocessor or a clever movie or a
decent rock-and-roll record, they could, better than any government on earth, marshal the huge labor forces necessary to
mine titanium ore from its inevitably difficult locations, smelt
it, and refine the metal. Titanium was a complete pain in the
ass to work with. Every weld on her big boat had to be conducted in an inert atmosphere, a blanket of argon or helium to
prevent the introduction of oxygen. But that was exactly the
kind of laborious process at which her people excelled, and
her boat was entirely crafted out of that difficult, rare metal.
The *Polaris,* made out of strong American steel, had to subject
itself to an ancient and clever degaussing range to make itself
magnetically invisible. But her titanium boat had been born
that way.

CHAPTER SEVEN

The ship had limited exercise equipment, but Frank Holmes diligently used it all. He bench-pressed every free weight they had, 220 pounds total, and now he could do twenty-five reps at that weight. He would then curl 100 pounds at a time, five sets of ten, and finish by squatting the full 220 pounds. He felt he was capable of squatting maybe twice as much, but those were all the weights they had, so that was that.

On off days he did bodyweight exercises: push-ups, pull-ups, dips, and hundreds of crunches. He'd run on the ship's lone treadmill to chisel off the tiny amount of fat left on his body, and punch the heavy bag that he had diligently repaired over time until now it was virtually constructed of duct tape. Most guys got soft on submarines, he knew, but he'd put on fifteen pounds of pure muscle since deploying on the *Polaris* two years earlier. Two inches on his chest, an inch on his arms. He would be even bigger, he thought, if the ship had any decent food, but the animal protein his body craved was hard to come by. He'd hoarded some beef jerky, but the last of the real chicken and eggs had long since been consumed, and the next trip to

the tender could be months away. As often as he once dreamed
about sex with the soft, sweet girls he'd grown up with in Katy,
Texas, he now dreamed about protein. He was a proficient
masturbator after two years at sea, but there was no equivalent way to satisfy his primal need for meat. Visions of ribs,
cheeseburgers, and T-bone steaks filled his dreams. Still, he
was enormously strong.

So moving Ramirez's dead body was easy once he got past
a small, initial burst of squeamishness that came with the
sight of all the blood.

The torpedo room was directly below the staterooms, the
lower-most, forward-most compartment on the ship. Frank
dragged the corpse to the ladder and briefly tried to think of
a more dignified option before simply dropping him down the
hatch. The body landed with a thud on the steel deck below.
Frank climbed down after it, then dragged Ramirez to the
front of the torpedo room, past the racks of indexed Mark 50
torpedoes, and caught his breath before proceeding.

The torpedo room had always been one of his favorite
places on the boat. Filled with forest green torpedoes, it
seemed more military than any other place on *Polaris*, full of
manly, menacing firepower. There were four firing tubes in all,
two port and two starboard, with the control panel between
them. It smelled dank, both because of its low position on the
ship and because the torpedo tubes were often filled, drained,
and filled again with the sea that surrounded them. When he
had volunteered for submarine duty, Frank had a picture in
his mind of what a submarine would be like. The torpedo room
was one of the few places on the boat that somewhat looked
like that picture.

He had fond memories of the torpedo room as well: during his walk-through for his qualifications, the torpedo room
was where Captain McCallister had brought him his final task:

to line up the system and shoot a water slug—basically a tube full of water, although the actions would be nearly the same if firing an actual torpedo. Captain McCallister had been patient as he plodded through the procedure, and had given him a few key hints along the way when he was stuck. But he had succeeded, finally pushing that red button and ejecting a thousand pounds of seawater back into the sea with a satisfying *whoosh*. He still recalled the subsequent ratcheting and hissing of valves that returned to a firing position, the popping of the ears as the pressure changed with the expulsion of the compressed firing air. Later that night, after dinner, Captain McCallister had pinned gold dolphins on his chest, Frank's proudest moment aboard. So he fancied himself as something of an expert.

The memory gave him a brief stab of guilt about the captain. The man had always been good to him, and he obviously knew the submarine better than any man aboard. Hell, he had designed the thing. But Moody said that he was a traitor, and he'd seen it himself. Somebody was giving them away, and with an enemy boat behind them, this wasn't a time to screw around. He was taking his orders from Moody now, and he was comfortable with that.

He reached for the bound yellow book of torpedo room procedures, thumbed through it until he found the correct one, and reviewed it carefully, a thick index finger pointing to each step as he slowly read it. He remembered the way Moody had raised an eyebrow at him in the wardroom, the doubt in her voice: he was determined not to screw this up.

Three of the four tubes had small signs hanging from their breech doors: WARSHOT LOADED. The lower port tube was empty; that would be the one he would use. Everything on the submarine, Frank knew, was controlled by switches and valves. Therefore switches and valves were everywhere, and,

amazingly to Frank, every one of them had a specific purpose, a reason for being. He went through the initial lineup
in the procedure, verifying the positions of valves and pushing buttons until he thought he was ready. But when he tried
to open the big breech door of the lower, port tube, it wouldn't
move. He knew from his practice down there that when
things were properly aligned, everything moved with a liquid, well-engineered ease. But when something was amiss,
the strongest guy in the world couldn't make it budge. He
studied the panel, trying to figure out what was blocking his
progress. An interlock prevented it, he saw, because the muzzle
door was open; the ship's designers logically made it impossible
to open both the muzzle and the breech simultaneously. Somehow he'd skipped that step in the procedure, so he backtracked, pushed a button to close the muzzle door, and tried
again. Still the breech wouldn't open.

He sat down and reread the procedure again, starting to
get nervous. He was stuck in the middle of it, and if he had
screwed something up, he didn't know how to recover, how to
back out, how to start over. He remembered Captain Mc-
Callister talking to him two years earlier as he nervously attempted the procedure. "You can't sink the ship from here,
Holmes," he said. "Don't worry. Torpedo tubes have been around
for over a hundred years, and they've pretty much idiot-proofed
them."

But Frank wasn't worried about the quality of the ship's
idiot-proofing. Rather, he was worried about the ship proving
that he was an idiot. He imagined telling Moody that Ramirez's
body was still cooling away on the torpedo room deck. Or stuck
in the breech door. Or jammed in a tube. No, he couldn't face
her with that kind of news.

Reading the procedure for the third time, he noticed a
warning on the bottom of a page that cautioned not to open

the breech door until the tube was fully drained. In fact, yet another interlock prevented it, so that a thousand gallons of seawater wouldn't gush from the tube onto the deck of the torpedo room. He eagerly found the drain valve for the port tubes and opened it. At first he was alarmed to hear so much water draining from the tube. Submariners were conditioned to worry at the sound of gushing water. But the noise soon diminished as the tube emptied, a yellow warning light went off on the console, and he approached the breech door once again.

As if he had spoken a magic spell, the locking ring turned smoothly, and the door swung open with barely a tug. He bent down and looked inside, peering into the tube with the small flashlight he kept on his belt. It was polished smooth, still damp, and smelled of the sea. He rejoiced for a moment, the battle seeming half won. Now he just needed to get Ramirez inside.

The tube was, he remembered randomly from his qualifications, twenty-one inches in diameter. Seemed like a lot, and Ramirez wasn't a big guy, but as Frank lifted him up and tried to shove him inside, he saw that it would be difficult. He decided put him in headfirst, because it seemed like the right thing to do. He grabbed him from behind, around his waist, and tried to flop him inside. Frank winced as he heard Ramirez's teeth crack on the edge of the tube. One of them broke off and fell to the deck. He continued pushing, got Ramirez in up to his hips, where he became stuck. *Of course*, thought Frank, *he probably has a thirty-two-inch waist, and this is a twenty-one-inch tube. But wait—that would be the diameter, whereas the thirty-two-inch waist was a circumference.* . . . He was certain there was a formula he could use to convert one to the other, but even if he remembered it, he wouldn't be able to do the math in his head. Rather, he just kept shoving, with all his considerable strength, until he could move

Ramirez no more. His lower legs stuck out of the tube, the thick soles of his heavily worked engineer's boots dangling in the air.

So close, thought Frank. He saw the tooth he'd knocked out of Ramirez's head, kicked it across the deck and into the bilge in frustration. He'd be all the way in the tube if he were just five pounds skinnier. Or one inch.

And then he realized what he needed to do: he would have to undress him.

He sat down on the floor and braced his feet against each side of the tube, grabbed one of Ramirez's feet with each hand, and pulled. It took all his strength to reverse the work he'd already done, but at last he got him out of the tube.

He untied the boots and pulled his pants off. Then he unbuttoned his shirt, threw it on a pile with the pants and the boots. Ramirez was down to his undershirt and his Jockeys, and Frank prayed that he had reduced the man's diameter enough; he couldn't bear the thought of stripping him naked. It already felt increasingly like he was doing something wrong, something close to desecrating the dead, with possible legal and moral consequences. For all of Ramirez's sins, Frank didn't want to shove his naked body into a torpedo tube.

He lifted Ramirez again, and shoved him inside headfirst. Undressing him had worked, and this time, he went in all the way, until the toes of his feet touched the inside of the tube. It was tight, which made Frank worry, but he remembered how completely those green torpedoes filled the tubes, each weighing many times what Ramirez weighed, and the system hurled them effortlessly into the sea. He closed the breech door, deeply grateful to be no longer looking at the feet of his dead engineer.

Now he found himself in the procedure again, determined for things to proceed smoothly from that point on. *Flood the tube.* He pushed the button and heard the valve open, heard the movement of water from the tank into the tube. He tried not to picture Ramirez's dead body in there, now surrounded by seawater inside the brass tube. *Pressurize the tube.* He opened the pressure valve, allowing the pressure of the tube to equalize with the sea, so the muzzle door could open. He opened the muzzle door, and the light on the console turned from an amber line to a green O, indicating success.

Now nothing remained but to shoot him out. The tube was a loaded gun, and Ramirez was the bullet. Frank paused for a moment. The Navy had a ceremony for burials at sea, he knew—rituals that had been handed down for hundreds of years, rituals older than the republic. They'd done one when he first got to the boat, fulfilling the request of an old retired submariner, and he still remembered the somber announcement Captain McCallister had made on the 1MC, *"All hands bury the dead."* But they didn't have a procedure for this, disposing of a traitor. Frank sighed, just wanting it to be over.

He pushed the FIRE button, and a pressurized air bank forced a slug of water into the tube, instantly ejecting its contents. The machinery reset itself in a way that Frank remembered, the sliding of hydraulics, the hissing of compressed air, the popping in his ears.

Frank shut the muzzle door and reversed the process he had just done until he could once again open the breech door.

Slowly, he opened it. He sighed with relief to see that the tube was completely empty again. Ramirez was gone.

He shut the door and locked it, noticed the pile of Ramirez's clothes at his feet. He was excited again now, eager to report his success to Moody, and the clothes gave him an idea. He searched the pockets, hoping to find evidence of some kind, notes about the conspiracy, maps, codes, who knows? In the back pocket, he found a standard-issue green notebook.

He flipped through the pages until he found the most recent entry. It was a neatly kept table of handwritten data, in two rows, with "PH" at the top. He got excited—Pete Hamlin? Was this some record of their communications? A table of codes that they used?

He looked at it further until he realized that it wasn't "PH," it was "pH": a measure of the water chemistry of the primary plant, one measurement for each day of the last two weeks. The numbers meant nothing to Frank—he could see that they were drifting downward, but he didn't know if that was bad or good.

Frank was disappointed at that, and all the rest of the routine engineering data that filled Ramirez's notebook. It wasn't very compelling evidence of a conspiracy. In fact, it was downright boring.

He gathered Ramirez's clothes and threw them into a trash can in the back of the torpedo room. There was a shredder back there, too, so Frank dropped the notebook in it as he passed.

There, Ramirez, he thought with a smirk as the shredder whirred to life. *I deleted it.*

After the degaussing, Pete followed Moody down to her stateroom, which was immediately adjacent to the captain's. In a passing glance, he saw pictures of Captain McCallister's family, a wife and two kids, smiling from the wall. They looked familiar to him, he thought, like maybe he had met them, or maybe they just looked familiar in the way that all happy families do, like Tolstoy said. The bed was made with military precision, but at the foot of it was a comfortable-looking striped blanket.

Moody's walls, in contrast, were bare of personal effects. A few professional decorations, pictures of herself from her training class, a citation from the Alliance. Files and binders neatly arranged, Navy procedures sharing a shelf with binders of Alliance doctrine. It looked so much like an office that the neatly made bed seemed out of place.

"Nicely done up there," she said as they entered. She reached behind him to shut the door, close enough in the small room that Pete could smell her shampoo. "I guess you're starting to feel like yourself again."

"I guess," he said.

"So now that we're degaussed, we're ready to begin the high-speed run?"

"You're asking me?" he said. "I thought you were in charge."

"I am now," she said. "And keep in mind that your friend up there—" She pointed upward, in the direction of the escape trunk where Finn was locked. "—he tried to destroy it all."

Destroy what? he thought, but kept his mouth shut.

"You know that in a very real way, the fate of the world is in our hands," she said. "In *your* hands."

"That's what they keep telling me," he said.

"Things have gotten worse out there. We rarely get any radio transmissions from land anymore . . . haven't heard from command in weeks. We used to hear surface ships up there, occasionally. They're all gone, driven away. Before long, we're going to need a tender, and I'm not sure there is one out there anymore. Without our radio room, we can't even ask."

"So what do we do?"

"We complete the mission at hand. That's all we *can* do."

Pete cleared his throat and waited for her to indicate what was next. "So what is our mission?"

She raised an eyebrow. "Don't be a smart-ass. McCallister

never saw fit to share it with me, as you well know. But I have my guesses. I think it's something to do with the illness. The epidemic, whatever you want to call it. I think that's why you're here."

"The illness?"

"Here," she said. "Take a look at this." She pulled a book off her shelf and opened it to a page that she had bookmarked. It was an aerial photo, stamped SECRET, of what looked like a massive refugee camp.

"This is outside Los Angeles," she said. "The disease was killing a hundred people a day, everybody was streaming out of the city—the government built this place for a thousand people out in the desert. Currently it's holding five thousand, and there's a tent city being built outside the fence, a shanty-town, people waiting to get in. Cities like this are going up on both coasts."

"Just the coasts?"

"They seem to be hardest hit," she said. "Which is contrib-uting to the rumors that this whole thing is some kind of bio-logical weapon planted by Typhon. Some of the rumors say the virus is delivered by submarines."

"Jesus," said Pete. The photograph was startling, Ameri-cans looking up at the sky with real dejection in their eyes. The camp was a jumble of unfinished wood and barbed wire. But he noticed, curiously, that about every fifth building had been constructed from thick concrete and had what appeared to be a heavy plate of metal for a roof. A strange defense against a disease.

"That's what we're fighting for, Pete," she said, taking the book away. "The people back home."

"And what can we do about it?" said Pete.

"I'm assuming you're about to tell me," she said.

"I am?"

She fought to hide her annoyance. "I understand your hesitation," she said. "Your orders were highly secret, and the captain shared them with whom he saw fit. Whatever. But *I* am in command of this ship now, and you need to share them with me."

"What if I can't?"

"Then you might be sharing that escape trunk with McCallister, Pete."

She reached into her desk—Pete thought momentarily that she was reaching for her Taser. But instead she pulled out a large brown envelope and handed it to him.

It was sealed with a small electronic keypad.

"I took these from McCallister's office. I would have opened them earlier myself—no offense. The situation called for it. But I think they would auto-destruct with one false entry. So I'd like to ask you, as your commanding officer, to share them with me."

Pete hefted the envelope in his hand and could feel that a small tablet computer was inside. Perhaps a tablet with all the answers he needed.

"Open it, Pete," she said.

He hesitated, but in fact, the curiosity was more than he could bear. Pete wiped his thumb across the locking device. A light turned green, and he opened the envelope and pulled out a small tablet computer. When he touched it, the screen came to life, and three icons appeared. One icon said BACKGROUND, another said SERVICE JACKET: HAMLIN, PETER, and the third said PATROL ORDERS.

He reached for the background icon.

"Haven't you already reviewed these?" she said. "Let's look at the patrol order."

"I thought you wanted to see everything?"

She sighed impatiently, but let him touch the icon.

A computer animation launched, showing the earth's oceans

rising several years in the past. Low-lying cities and islands were wiped out.

In the second part of the video, the more recent past, populations became more concentrated as people moved inland. Food supplies, shown in yellow, began to dwindle. Regional conflicts broke out, and soon global war did as well. Typhon formed, and the Alliance followed in short order. Looking at the timeline on the bottom of the screen, Pete saw that this brought them to the present day.

A new wave of color began to spread across the global map, the time now projecting into the future. Pete understood it to represent the spread of an epidemic of some kind, brought on by the war, the rising waters, and the concentration of the population. According to the video, the epidemic would soon decimate the world's population.

It ended five years in the future, as the formerly bright-red population centers dimmed and turned black.

"Jesus," said Hamlin.

"I can see why these projections are so classified," she said. "It would cause a panic. People might turn against the war effort."

Hamlin turned to her. "Maybe they should."

She smirked at that. "You're still an engineer at heart, Hamlin. Which is why I'll let that go. But the good guys are going to win this one, and *you* are one of the good guys. Now, let's see what's in your orders that I don't already know about." She reached over his shoulder and touched the PATROL ORDERS icon, but it didn't work: the tablet was keyed to Pete's fingerprints alone. Frustrated, she tapped the screen with her fingernail and handed it back to Pete.

Reluctantly, he tapped the screen, and a document came to life. It was all text, with a number of embedded coordinates on it and a few interactive colored charts. In the first section of the orders was a chart that Pete instantly recognized as the degaussing range. He scanned it quickly as Moody read over his shoulder.

"Complete, right?" she said.

Pete read that section and saw that she was right—they had orders to degauss, which he had done completely. He scrolled down and saw a block where he was to verify completion with a swipe of his finger.

As he did so, a new section of orders immediately came to life. Hana inhaled eagerly as the screen changed. She looked over his shoulder, staring at the chart that came up first.

"There!" said Moody, pointing, excited. "I knew it!"

Pete scanned the text section. *Top secret . . . vaccine at hand. Locate and deliver to global medical command . . . critical importance to war effort . . . Engineering Research and Implementation Station.*

Moody, on her feet now with the excitement, put a hand on his back. "It makes perfect sense! I told Frank this is where we were going. All those eggheads out there—and I knew you'd been stationed out there! Plus, I'd heard what happened to your wife. . . ." Pete looked up at her quickly, a stab of heartbreak going through him at the mention of a wife he didn't even remember.

Moody quickly changed the subject. "At ahead flank—" She looked at her watch and did a quick mental calculation. "—we can be there in two days."

Pete swiped the screen with his finger, expanding the small chart of their destination. A tiny spot of land became visible. Several bands of dotted lines surrounded it with the words RESTRICTED ZONE. It was the research station, he could see. And on the chart its name had been abbreviated.

ERIS.

Pete touched the map, and the image of the island expanded.

It was a navigation chart that looked deeply familiar to Pete, in the same way the control room felt familiar, something borne of thousands of hours of studying. A TOP SECRET label adorned it on top and bottom.

He tapped a button on the screen, changing it from a map view to a satellite image. The island was roughly kidney shaped. At the north end of the island, right up against the shore, was a tower. At the far other end of the island were two small buildings, also facing the sea. The roofs were darker in color, worn, conveying a greater age, and seemed disconnected from the work on the other side of the island. The center of Eris was taken up almost entirely by an airfield, with a few scattered maintenance buildings in between.

Pete used two fingers to change the scale of the chart, zooming out, and changing it back from a satellite photo to a nautical chart. Two concentric rings circled the island, both colored in red to convey danger. The innermost ring was a perfect circle with the tower at its exact center, a five-mile radius. It was labeled EXCLUSION ZONE. Pete noticed hash marks on the outside of the circle . . . it seemed to indicate that safety lay inside.

Farther out was a more irregular dashed red line, about seven miles from the island. This line was jagged and imperfect, unlike the inner circle, and seemed to be a product of nature. Pete could see the italicized soundings indicating the depth of water around it: it was shoal water. Serious shoal water, as shallow as ten feet in some spots, a superb natural barrier to the island. And it had been there eons, Pete could tell. All around the perimeter were the dotted-line profiles of wrecked ships, the chart symbol for the vessels that had wrecked themselves upon the shoals over hundreds of years.

There were a few shallow breaks around the shoals where a careful surface ship might approach, but no submerged submarine ever could. And that meant a two-mile stretch between the two circles, some kind of no-man's-land . . . Pete traced the circle with his fingers until he found one tiny spot in the shoal line where the water was 120 feet deep. If the tower was the center of a clock, the break in the shoal water was at about seven o'clock.

"There," he said, tapping the break. "We could get through right there at periscope depth."

Moody suddenly pulled him to his feet, turned him around, and kissed him hard upon the lips.

He jerked backward, almost falling over his chair, and dropped the tablet with his orders to the deck.

"What?" said Moody, clearly annoyed. "What's wrong?"

"It's . . . my head," he said. "It still hurts."

She looked him up and down. "You haven't been the same since the mutiny," she said.

"Tell me about it."

"Go get some rest," she said. "That's an order. But the next time I see you, be ready to work."

"Aye, aye," he said, grabbing the tablet and backing out of her stateroom.

WELCOME ABOARD THE USS *POLARIS*

A Legacy of Freedom

THE *POLARIS*-CLASS SUBMARINE

The *Polaris*-class submarine is the latest advancement in submarine technology. It is well equipped to accomplish its assigned mission, providing significant advances over previous classes of submarines. Specifically:

- Each *Polaris*-class submarine carries 50 percent more missiles than its predecessors (36 compared to 24).
- Ease of maintenance has been designed into the class, minimizing maintenance requirements and extending the period between lengthy shipyard overhauls. *Polaris*-class submarines are able to stay on patrols for longer periods with shorter time between patrols.
- The increased range of the C-6 missiles enables the *Polaris* to operate in ten times more ocean area than previous submarines.
- The central command and control system of the *Polaris* allows significant automation and reduction of crew size. For example, Trident submarines, the workhorse missile submarine of the Cold War, carried a crew of

over 150 men. The *Polaris* will go to sea with just 18, and can operate with as few as 6.

- The total system was designed to ensure that the United States and her strategic allies have a modern, survivable deterrent system in the 2020s and beyond.
- The *Polaris* is vital to the Alliance submarine force. Her mission is to maintain world peace.

CHAPTER EIGHT

Instead of heading to his rack, Pete turned toward the escape trunk where Finn McCallister was being held prisoner.

He saw the bottoms of McCallister's feet against the grate, motionless. It looked like he was sleeping, his head hanging, his mouth open. His face was somewhat hidden in the shadows inside the trunk, but Pete could see that he looked haggard, exhausted. His uniform had been ripped, like Pete's. The captain awoke with a start.

"Pete!" he said, overjoyed to see him. He jumped down on his hands and knees so his face was against the grate. "Are you alone?"

"I am," he said.

"I knew you'd be back," he said. "You've got to get me out of here."

"I'm trying . . . to figure out what's going on."

"Do that," he said. "Keep your head up. You can't trust anyone right now."

"Can I trust you?"

Finn looked stricken. "Of course," he said.

"How much do you know about my orders?"

The captain looked confused. "Everything that I could read," he said. "And what you told me after I read them, when you came on board. You said the Alliance had identified this epidemic as a massive threat, not just to the war effort, but to humanity. I also saw in your service jacket that you're an engineer, not a doctor; that's why I brought Haggerty in the loop. We're the only ones aboard who know the full patrol order."

"How much do you know about the epidemic?"

He shook his head. "Not much. We've been at sea so long . . . but I know everything has changed up there since we left. You showed me the projections, though, showed me what it was doing to the civilian population. And . . ." He hesitated.

"What else?"

"Your wife," he said. "You told me your wife was killed by the disease."

Pete was rocked by a real sadness, a profound sense of loss. A memory of her flashed in his mind, blond hair, blue eyes. The death of his wife, he knew, was what had put him on the boat somehow, the event that set him on a path that ended onboard a nuclear submarine. And while it made him tremendously sad, he was grateful to Finn for sharing this information with him, to give him a real memory that he could build upon. He decided at that moment to trust McCallister.

"There's a lot I don't remember," said Pete.

"About?"

"The mutiny."

McCallister shook his head, still angry with the memory.

"Moody has gone completely crazy," he said. "It all really started when that shadow boat showed up. With your orders, and that boat tailing us, she just started getting increasingly paranoid. Frank—that idiot—convinced her that someone had been giving our position away somehow. We had a huge fight in the control room; none of us had slept for days. She wanted to shoot the shadow boat, I ordered her to stand down, and then Ramirez ran out of the room. Alarms started going off, fires broke out—it looked like someone was trying to sabotage us."

"Ramirez?"

"That's sure what they thought. And they assumed we were in on it together—the two Navy guys aligned against the two Alliance officers. So she snapped, and here I am."

Pete hesitated for a moment. "I think I killed Ramirez," he said.

"Jesus, Pete, really?"

"I woke up with a gun in my hand, and he was dead." He looked at his feet, unable to face the captain. "I guess that means that one of us, me or Ramirez, was a traitor."

McCallister shook his head again. "I don't know what happened, Pete. But I do know this: those two maniacs are the only traitors. And god help us with them in charge."

Pete looked into Finn's eyes, and believed him. "I'll get you out of there," he said.

"Please do," said McCallister. "But don't let it get in the way of the mission."

"The mission?"

"We have to get that cure," he said. "Whoever finds it first will control everything. We have to make sure we get to it before anyone else does. I have no idea what's going on up there," he said, pointing upward. "Eris Island may be the last piece of land the Alliance holds. It should be—it's a goddamn fortress surrounded by ten thousand drones. But if we can get the cure, and secure it for the Alliance, then we win."

"I'll get you out of there," Pete said again. He started looking around for whatever implement had been used to bolt the grid in place at McCallister's feet.

"It's in that locker . . ." said McAllister, sticking a finger through the grate and pointing.

Pete opened it and saw a large wrench. He started to get it out.

There was a sudden *whoosh* below their feet.

"Are they shooting torpedoes?" asked the captain, recognizing the sound, alarm in his eyes. "What are they shooting at?"

"No," said Pete after a moment, realization setting in. "Getting rid of Ramirez's body."

Their ears popped as pressure changed in the boat as a result of the shot. Then they heard footsteps on the forward ladder, and locked eyes.

"I can wait," said McCallister.

"I'll be back," whispered Pete, returning the wrench to the locker.

"Hold on," said Finn. "Before you go," he pulled a key from around his neck, "take this. It'll give you access to everything in memory on the central computer. There's a key slot in the deck right by the main console in control. No one even knows it exists, it's unique to *Polaris* submarines. I designed it myself."

Pete took the key and looked at it. It was a simple, flat steel key with no identifying markings. "Old-fashioned," he said.

"Yeah, old-fashioned. Like me," he said. "Now, get out of here before anyone sees you talking to your traitorous captain."

Pete walked away quickly and hung the key around his neck. As he did, he was surprised to find another key already hanging there, this one painted red.

CHAPTER NINE

Pete walked forward, distracted by all the new information, and found himself at the door to his stateroom.

Ramirez's body was gone. A large red stain streaked against the bulkhead and trailed out the door. Pete had walked through it, he saw to his revulsion, and the soles of his shoes were now stained by his friend's blood. Holmes had dragged the body out of the room, pulling him across the floor like a hyena dragging a carcass across the plain.

Trying to avoid the blood, Pete sat down on the small chair at the stateroom's desk and pulled out the tablet computer that he'd gotten from Moody. He turned it on, hesitated, and then opened the file that contained his service jacket.

Doctorate in engineering. Cum laude from Georgia Tech. A list of military commendations. Marital status: widower. No children.

He scanned backward in time, flipping through the years with the tip of his finger, going further back into his own, unknown history. He saw that he had been an overachiever, but not one without a blemish. He'd been reprimanded lightly for a bar fight in Tokyo. Worse: he'd been demoted for a time for another altercation, this one with a superior at Eris Island. Clearly, his talents had been desperately needed by the Alliance, or they never would have tolerated him.

At the thought of Eris Island, he skipped ahead to that tour of duty, which had lasted for almost a year. When he got to that part of his biography, though, he reached an electronic dead end. The tablet read CLASSIFIED and wouldn't let him proceed any further.

He sighed and looked around his stateroom for additional clues about who he was. He identified the desk that was his— it was mostly filled with military documents, but there were a few personal items. A worn novel by Stephen King. He flipped it open and saw an opening passage that had been highlighted:

Sometimes human places create inhuman monsters.

He picked up a digital music player, but the battery was dead; even his own taste in music remained a mystery to him. Above his desk there was a coconut that had been carved into a woman with obscenely large breasts. On the bottom of the coconut-woman were etched the words BEAUTIFUL HAWAII. Someone had drawn onto its chest with a black marker, like a nametag on a uniform: *POLARIS*.

He inventoried the information he had assembled about himself: it wasn't much. He searched his mind for more than what the paltry artifacts in his stateroom and the scant information in his service jacket gave him. The effort soon exhausted him.

He stood and climbed up into his rack, needing to lie down even if he couldn't sleep. There he found something that contained more information about his life than everything he'd seen since regaining consciousness.

Taped directly above him in the short distance between his mattress and the overhead was a photo of a woman: he knew instantly she was his wife. Her name came back to him suddenly with a power that took his breath away. Pamela.

She was blond and athletic, with a smile that electrified him. In the picture, she was dressed in hiking clothes, laughing at the camera, her hair tied back in a ponytail. A green tropical forest closed in behind her, not another person in sight. She was standing by a sign at a trailhead that read: KEALIA TRAIL. Pete knew he had taken the picture; he could remember the moment. He could smell the sweetness of the flowers, the tang of the rotting mangoes, the cleansing sea air. He felt an incalculable sense of loss.

Soon he couldn't look at it anymore, the pain was too great. He turned over and fell into deep sleep.

He had a vivid nightmare about the mutiny. He was fighting in the stateroom, and he knew he was fighting for his life. It was dark, and the quarters were so close that he could barely see whom he was fighting as they struggled. His opponent was strong and fast, but Pete soon had the edge and began to wear him down. Finally he got behind his adversary and put him in a choke hold, just as he had done to the doctor. But this time he didn't let up. He held his grip until the body beneath him slackened and died.

He rolled the dead man over, and looked into his own face.

He awoke with a start. A piece of paper, folded in half, had been placed on his chest while he slept. He opened it.

MEET ME IN SHAFT ALLEY—0600

He looked at his watch: he had ten minutes. He didn't know whom the message was from, or what it meant, but the rendezvous might provide more answers. He took a final glance at the photo of his wife, and slid out of bed. He tried not to walk in blood as he exited, but there was too much to avoid.

WELCOME ABOARD THE USS *POLARIS*

A Legacy of Freedom

THE NUCLEAR PROPULSION PLANT

The propulsion plant of a nuclear-powered ship is based upon the use of a nuclear reactor to provide heat. The heat comes from the fissioning of nuclear fuel contained within the reactor. Since the fissioning process also produces radiation, shields are placed around the reactor so that the crew is protected.

The nuclear-propulsion plant uses a pressurized water reactor design that has two basic systems: the primary system and the secondary system. The primary system circulates ordinary water and consists of the reactor, piping loops, pumps, and steam generators. The heat produced in the reactor is transferred to the water under high pressure so it does not boil. This water is pumped through the steam generators and back into the reactor for reheating.

In the steam generators, the heat from the water in the primary system is transferred to the water in the secondary system to create steam. The secondary system is isolated from the primary system so that the water in the two systems does not intermix.

In the secondary system, steam flows from the steam generators to drive the turbine generators, which supply electricity to the ship and to the main propulsion turbines, which in turn drive the propeller through a reduction gear. After passing through the turbines, the steam is condensed into water, which is fed back to the steam generators by the feed pumps. Thus, both the primary and secondary systems are closed systems where water is recirculated and reused.

There is no step in the generation of this power that requires the presence of air or oxygen. This allows the ship to operate completely independent of the earth's atmosphere for extended periods of time.

CHAPTER TEN

Pete walked aft, guided by that interior autopilot that seemed to know the layout of *Polaris*. Darkness and silence were everywhere.

He passed through a watertight door into the missile compartment once again and found himself wandering in a forest of missile tubes, two rows of eighteen missiles each. Numbers were etched on each tube, and he saw the numbers decreasing as he continued aft: even numbers to port, odd numbers to starboard.

The noise level increased as he walked, which he found somewhat comforting, a sign of life in the otherwise ghostly ship. He arrived at the watertight hatch to the engine room, and opened it.

He stepped into a warm, white tunnel that was, he knew, a heavily shielded passage through the reactor compartment. Once on the other side, he was in the engine room, surrounded by the machinery that made the voyage of the *Polaris* possible. He felt the power of the place, the rumble of the deck plates starting a vibration that coursed through his whole body.

He was in the middle of a symphony of machinery, an orchestra of turbines, valves, and pumps that had been exquisitely engineered to make a ship move and a crew survive: *"the lights burning and the screw turning,"* as Moody had said. It thrilled him.

He remembered some of the specifics, at a rudimentary level. He sensed that while he was comfortable with machinery in general—Hana had called him an engineer—he had never been an expert on the inner workings of the submarine. He walked past the giant evaporator, the machine that turned salt water into pure water that both they and their thirsty propulsion plant could drink, water that was now a thousand times more pure than anything available on the surface. But like the oxygen generators, this life-giving machine wasn't running. Just as with their oxygen, they were drawing their water from their reserves. Reserve feed tank number one, Pete saw, was empty. Reserve feed tank number two was down to 15 percent. As he stared at the indicator and breathed in the engine room's humid air, it dropped to 14 percent. The ship was slowly suffocating, and also dying of thirst.

He continued into the turbine room, where steam turned the giant machines that made their electricity. Their twins turned the main engines, which in turn made the screw move, and powered them through the water. He was close to his destination now.

Down a ladder, where it got darker, quieter, and cooler, away from the throbbing power of the turbines, he saw where the main engines connected to a giant set of gears, which in turn connected to the screw. Suddenly, it was there, the enormous shaft that penetrated the back of the submarine. It turned slowly, steadily, and silently, the most primal expression of the engine room's immense power. He was as far as he could go from his watchers in control. He realized that's why this location had been selected.

No one was there.

He looked around, increasingly apprehensive. He felt the gun in his pocket and felt some comfort in that. He looked at his watch: 0610. He wondered how long he should wait around.

While it was quieter in shaft alley than it was near the turbines, it still took Pete a while to recognize the electric crackling that was periodically sounding near his head. It was regular and rhythmic, as if a signal. It was also a contrast to the mechanical noises of the engine room. He followed the noise to an alcove along the bulkhead, and reached in. He pulled out a small handheld radio.

A red light was blinking on it. He pushed the button and spoke. "Hello?"

"Pete! Jesus! Where have you been?" It was a female voice, unfamiliar to him, with a slight accent he could not place. The voice was electronically scrambled and delayed in reaching him. He had an inkling that it was being sent from outside the boat.

"Who is this?" he said.

"Carlson," she said. "Commander Jennifer Carlson."

"Where are you?"

Even through the electronic noise of the radio, he could make out an exasperated sigh.

"I'm about two miles directly behind you," she said.

Pete almost dropped the radio as he realized what she meant. She was communicating with him from the shadow submarine.

"Report," said the radio.

"Who are you?"

There was a pause. "What do you mean?"

"Are you with the Alliance? Or are you the enemy?"

"We're not your enemy," she said. "Now, make your report. What's going on in there?"

"I'm not telling you anything," he said angrily.

"What's wrong with you?" she said. "We've only got about five minutes on this link, and you need to tell me what's going on. We heard the noise, heard the torpedo tube cycling a few hours ago. We almost fired at you then until we realized there wasn't a weapon in the water. Who is in control of the ship?"

"I am an officer on an Alliance submarine," said Pete, his face getting hot. "I'm not telling you a thing. I *will* help them blow you out of the water."

"Pete, I don't know what's gotten into you. But you need to get your head on straight. We're running out of time. You were supposed to disable the boat completely after the degaussing. We kept waiting for your signal, but then you disappeared."

"Why would I help you?" said Pete.

"Why?" She was getting angry. "Because it's your sworn duty. Because it's the plan we worked on together for months."

"Bullshit . . ."

"Because of Pamela," she said, stopping him cold. "To avenge Pamela."

"Avenge her?" he said. "I thought she died in the epidemic. . . ."

"Bullshit," said Carlson. "The disease killed her because the Alliance won't release the cure. They're saving it for military purposes, sacrificing millions of lives in the process, including your wife's."

"I don't . . ."

"It's bad out there," she said. Despite the distortion of the radio, Pete could hear real fear in her voice. "Every day we get new reports of whole cities that are quarantined. Whole boats have been wiped out after one person gets infected—no one has been off my boat in over a year. If one person gets sick—"

The radio made a beeping sound, and the red light began to blink rapidly.

"We're almost out of time. Do your duty, Pete. Do what you know is right. We'll be waiting for you, we'll know when you've disabled *Polaris*. But don't wait much longer or it will be too late. We can, and will, proceed without you."

The radio clicked off, and the light turned dim. Pete glanced around, and then placed the radio back in the alcove where he'd found it.

CHAPTER ELEVEN

McCallister awoke from a quick, shallow sleep, never deep enough to escape his small prison even in a dream.

He looked over the small egg-shaped cell in which he found himself, and once again saw no possibility of escape. Ironic, inside a system that had been expressly designed to give the crew a chance to escape a doomed submarine.

The escape trunk consisted of three hatches. One below his feet, which was now covered by a steel grate and represented his only window into the ship he once commanded. The second was directly over his head, and was designed to mate up with a rescue vehicle. The third was at his knees, and represented the "swim out" hatch that would be used to escape the submarine with no rescue vehicle present. For either of the escape hatches to work, the trunk had to be flooded with seawater, until the pressure inside the cylinder was equal to the surrounding sea pressure. At that point, the outer hatches could swing open easily and allow egress. That's why the trunk made such an ideal prison—if it could withstand thousands of pounds of sea pressure, it could withstand the worst that a recalcitrant prisoner could throw at it.

Even with sea pressure equalized, escape from a crippled submarine was fraught. In a locker below the trunk, in the same locker that held the wrench that had bolted him in, were exposure suits and hoods that filled with air and helped pull submariners to the top. As they ascended, the air in their lungs would expand with the decrease in pressure, requiring that they exhale forcefully the entire way. Generations of submariners had learned to shout *HO! HO! HO!* on the way up. In an earlier era, the skyline of every submarine base was dominated by a cylindrical dive tower in which submarine crews practiced the procedure to escape a submarine, which was usually the capstone of training, a rite of passage, the ultimate skill of a submariner. Doctrine stated that the procedure could work at depths up to six hundred feet. In the nuclear age, new submariners were often shocked to learn that they nearly always operated in water much, much deeper than that.

McCallister stared at the flood valve and contemplated opening it. Water would pour into the trunk, then into the ship through the grate at his feet. He'd be discovered immediately, of course, the roar of flooding at this depth would sound like a freight train. And sinking or crippling the ship wasn't his goal anyway. He'd been accused of being a saboteur; he wasn't about to become one. He assumed that's why Frank had left the valve unlocked when he put him in there: he knew it wouldn't do McCallister much good to open it up. Or, more likely, he just didn't understand the ship well enough to worry about it. When McCallister had qualified on the *Alabama*, all those years ago, he had to draw every system on the ship from memory, know the location of every valve, breaker, and fire hose. Every man with dolphins on his chest, from the captain down to the cooks in the galley, was an expert on his boat. Gradually, as the technology on submarines became more complex, they required less and less of that, block diagrams and black boxes becoming acceptable substitutes for real physical knowledge. The introduction of nuclear missiles sealed it. The goal was to launch missiles, not to repair them. If a part was broken, swap it out. No one considered it possible, or desirable, for a sailor to know how to build or repair a nuclear weapon.

His first boat had a crew of 125 men. The Navy, understandably, had staffed submarines like ships, making them self-sufficient cities that could make their own air, water, and repairs to every system, keeping them at sea for as long as the food and spare parts held out. It was the dream of nuclear power: a "true" submarine that never needed to rise to the surface to take a breath. Steadily, however, automation took over, and crews got smaller. The Navy, in its wisdom, made them more like the crew of an airplane now than the crew of a battleship, a few specially trained men and women riding on a mass of high-priced technology. The *Polaris* required a crew of thirty men in the initial design phase, a crew that seemed revolutionarily small at the time for the United States, although the Soviets had for decades been sending out similarly sized crews in their small, rickety submarines. They pared this down to eighteen, which was what he first went to sea with. With attrition, however, and the losses the Alliance was taking, the number kept getting smaller and smaller. There was a joke in the fleet, before things got so serious, that the Navy was using the *Polaris* as part of an experiment to see how small a submarine crew could get before things fell apart. They seemed to have found the limit.

He sighed and looked at the green bucket sitting on the small bench across from him; Frank had thrown it in there with him when he locked him up, it was his toilet. He'd actually watched the asshole check it off the procedure that he held in his hands and studied with furrowed brow. There was a thin layer of urine in the bottom, which did nothing to improve the smell in the escape trunk. But there was more, too. McCallister had been on submarines a long time, long enough to recognize when the air was going bad. Almost all the things that could poison a sub's atmosphere were odorless and tasteless: hydrogen from the battery, carbon monoxide from combustion, carbon dioxide from their own lungs. But while odorless, the combination of those things, along with the depletion of oxygen, created a palpable staleness that McCallister was familiar with, a burning in the throat, a headache right behind the eyes, an overpowering sense of fatigue.

"Wake up, McCallister."

Moody had appeared beneath his feet.

"Moody," he said, his throat dry. "What do you want?"

"Wanted to take a look at you. Make sure you're OK. See if you're ready to cooperate."

"Ready to cooperate?" He laughed. "It seems you and Frank have already taken over the ship. What do you need me for?"

"Not just me and Frank," she said. "Hamlin, too."

"Bullshit," he said. "I don't believe you."

"He killed Ramirez."

McCallister hesitated at that, wincing at the dead man's name. "I'm sure he had his reasons."

She snorted. "And you believe that? I saw him. He was standing over his dead body, the smoking gun in his hand. The only difference between Hamlin and me is that he doesn't have the balls to tell you where he stands. He wants me in charge, but he still wants you to think he's a swell guy."

"I don't know what happened. Maybe Ramirez attacked him, maybe Pete got scared. That doesn't make him one of your conspirators," he said. But Hana could hear the doubt creeping into his voice.

"Then consider this: we were just in my stateroom, reviewing his orders. He showed me everything. Unlocked the patrol order and read it in front of me."

"No," he said, shock in his voice. "I don't believe it. Pete's a good man. He would never cooperate with you."

"Oh really? Let me review the patrol order with you: we're going to Eris Island. Now that we've degaussed, we can approach the island at periscope depth and go ashore. Our mission is to collect the cure and return it to the Alliance. Pete showed me the projections of the epidemic, everything."

McCallister slumped against the side of the trunk.

"Everything you wouldn't."

McCallister looked down at her. "Jesus, is that what this is about, Hana? That Alliance chip on your shoulder? You took over the ship because you felt slighted?"

"I *was* slighted!" she yelled. "You shared those orders with the ship's doctor, for Christ's sake, but not with me, your XO!"

"Exactly," he said. "I made you my XO. I trusted you."

"The Alliance made me XO," she said. "But I made myself the captain. So now the Alliance is really running this ship, the way it should have been from the beginning. Guys like you and Ramirez—you're *mechanics*. Drivers."

"Based on the atmosphere on this boat," he said, sniffing the air, "you're going to need a good mechanic soon. How's the oxygen level, Moody? And by my calculations, we're about out of water, too, right?"

"You have no loyalty to the Alliance—"

"And your life depends on machinery that you don't understand."

"You have no sense of mission—"

"No sense of mission?" He laughed loudly at that, the sound amplified and sharpened by the steel walls that surrounded him. "Moody, in my career I have targeted Trident missiles at

Russian cities. I have *launched* cruise missiles at Tripoli and Tallil. On my first patrol, I had to fight a scram in maneuvering when the only light I had to read the procedure by came from a fire that burned in a main seawater pump breaker behind me. You think you're the expert on the mission of this submarine? I've got more time eating ice cream at test depth than you've got under way."

He stopped, out of breath from his rant. Moody reached in her pocket and McCallister flinched, certain she was reaching for her Taser. Instead, she handed him two granola bars through the grate.

"Here," she said. "I'm sure you're hungry."

"You brought me food?" he said.

"Of course," she said. "We're not barbarians."

CHAPTER TWELVE

Pete walked briskly out of the engine room, through the tunnel, and into the missile compartment. He was greeted immediately by Haggerty.

"Pete! I've been looking all over for you."

"I was . . . walking . . . touring."

Haggerty gave him a quizzical look. "Clearing your head, too, I'm sure. Completely understandable. The engine room is one of the few places you can find some peace around here. Nobody goes back there unless they have to." He looked around. "Are you starting to remember anything?"

Pete shook his head. "Bits and pieces," he said. "Not really."

"What else do you want to know?" said Haggerty. "Maybe I can help."

Pete looked him in the eye. He had a million questions, wanted to know more about his mission, what was happening onboard *Polaris* before the mutiny. But one question overwhelmed him more than all that.

"I'd like to know more about my wife."

The doctor shook his head sadly. "Come on," he said. "Let's do this in my stateroom."

The doctor had done what he could to make his stateroom comfortable. There was an antique medical diagram of a skeleton on the wall, next to a calendar with nature scenes. The calendar, Pete noticed, was three years out of date. A stethoscope hung on a hook, next to an old-fashioned black doctor's bag. He had a quilt covering his rack, and a shelf of well-worn novels.

An object on the second shelf caught his eye: a Lucite block with bees trapped inside.

"Honeybees," said Haggerty, watching Pete closely as he picked it up. "At each stage of its life cycle."

It was fascinating to look at: some tiny relic of the natural world entombed in perfectly clear plastic, each stage numbered, one through ten. Tiny white eggs, almost too small to see. A slightly larger larva, then the pupa, which was starting to look like a bee, with tiny legs and wings. A mature worker bee, and a queen. A perfect cube of honeycomb. The queen's cell, worker foundation, and finally a tiny vial of honey that poured back and forth as Pete tilted the block. He could have stared at it for hours.

"Something we studied in Biology, back when I was an undergrad," said the doctor. "Fascinating, don't you think?"

"It's beautiful," said Pete.

"Here," said Haggerty. He'd poured two small glasses of scotch from a bottle he had hidden beneath socks in a drawer. They clinked the shot glasses together cheerlessly and drank them down.

"I never met Pamela," said the doctor. "Your wife. But you talked about her all the time."

"What did I say about her?"

"You met on the mainland. You had a whirlwind romance. You left her behind for your tour on Eris Island. You'd see her on leave, but honestly, Pete . . ."

"Yes?"

"You were plagued by guilt about it. Devastated, actually. We got your fitness reports before you transferred here, Finn shared them with me before you arrived—I'm the closest thing to a psychologist onboard and I guess he wanted my opinion. They all said the same thing—you were brilliant, had made vast contributions to the Alliance, but that after her death you were . . . a changed man. Said you'd been overheard blaming the Alliance for her death. Frankly, reading between the lines . . . it seemed like some of them were even beginning to doubt your loyalty."

The word hung in the air, and the doctor and Pete looked at each other.

"What about you, Doc? Do you doubt my loyalty?"

The doctor shook his head. "I think, after all these years, after all the loss . . . any thinking man would begin to have doubts. About everything. Thank god we're not all like Frank and Hana. Or McCallister, for that matter, all blindly giving ourselves to the cause without ever thinking about right or wrong."

Pete thought about his radio conversation in shaft alley. "I'm thinking about right and wrong," he said. "I'm thinking about it all the time."

The doctor leaned in and put his hand on Pete's shoulder. "Think about your mission now—you're going to Eris Island to get the cure for this terrible disease. The disease that killed your wife. It's a goddamn humanitarian mission if there ever was one. How could finding that cure be anything but good? I don't care who is doing it."

Pete shook his head—the doctor's words certainty felt good. "That's true," he said.

"That's why I want to help you," said the doctor. "Let's have another drink."

As the doctor poured his shot, Pete's eyes drifted back to the honeybees in the clear plastic block. Trapped, dead. So light, you couldn't feel their weight. And yet those tiny insects were part of a hive—a society, really—that was incredibly complex and captivating.

"Still looking at my little friends?" said the doctor. "Those guys have kept me company awhile now."

"They're all female," said Pete, surprised with the suddenness of that knowledge.

"What?"

"All the worker bees in a hive are female. The males, the drones, they keep them alive only long enough to impregnate the queen. Then the workers let them starve. The bees in that block: all female."

The doctor shifted in his seat, uncomfortable with Pete's hard stare. "Of course," he said. "You know something about bees?"

"I do," said Pete.

And he knew, suddenly, that the bees in that block belonged to him. The doctor was lying to him.

"Thanks," said Pete, putting down the honeybees and taking a second shot from the doctor. But this time Pete drank a silent toast to himself: *Here's to finding out the truth.*

CHAPTER THIRTEEN

The alcohol had the desired effect of clearing his head. Pete excused himself from the doctor's stateroom after the second shot, pretended to head for his own stateroom, and then turned and walked into control, where Frank was standing watch.

He looked up at Hamlin, surprised. "Here to relieve me?" he asked.

"If you ask nice," said Pete.

"OK: fuck you," he said.

Pete walked around control and stood in front of Frank. He extended his hand. "It's been a rough day," he said. "I'm sorry if I stepped on your toes. I got whacked on the head down there pretty good—let me use that as my excuse."

Frank looked at him warily but then took his hand. "Fine," he said. "I appreciate that." His grip was like a vise.

"And I am ready to relieve you," said Pete. "Go grab some sleep, or get something to eat. Better yet, go to Haggerty's stateroom: he's handing out shots from his secret stash of scotch."

"Now you're really starting to get on my winning side," said

Frank. He pointed at the monitor in front of them. "We're on course two-six-zero, heading for Eris Island at ahead flank."

"Our shadow?"

"Right behind us, as always. She crept a little closer at about 0600, we caught a whisper of some kind of active transmission. But it was directly behind us and the recording sucks."

"Interesting," said Pete. It was his conversation from shaft alley.

"But now: status quo. Looks like she's following us all the way to Eris Island. I wish Moody would let us shoot a torpedo right down her throat."

"I'm sure she has her reasons."

"Whatever," said Frank. "I'm ready to be relieved."

"I relieve you."

"I stand relieved."

"This is Lieutenant Pete Hamlin," he said into a microphone over his head, recording the procedure for the ship's digital deck log. "I have the deck and the conn."

Frank stomped out of control without another word.

Control was quiet. Several alarms were still cut out, their lights a steady red on the main status board, the residual effects of the fire and the destruction in radio. Occasionally he felt a vibration and heard a slight whir, the sound of a hydraulic pump cycling to maintain pressure, or a fan cooling one of the ship's many computers, some of which chirped quietly as their screens updated. But other than that, the big ship was silent. Pete waited a few minutes, to make sure he remained alone, and then he sat down in front of the main computer.

He scanned the deck near his feet, looking for the key slot McCallister had told him about. The deck was covered in smooth plastic tiles. He began pulling at the corners of them until one of them came up. Beneath it, as innocuous as the captain's key itself, he found the keyhole. He inserted the key and turned it. As he sat up, the console in front of him was resetting, the normal sonar display disappearing. He put the key back around his neck and the tile back in place as the new display generated.

CAPTAIN'S MASTER TACTICAL ACCESS

Below that was an extensive menu of options. There were maintenance records, personnel files of everyone who'd ever been onboard, and access to the deck logs. It appeared to be the entire digital history of the command. Additionally he could access secret Navy and Alliance documents, detailed descriptions of the actual capabilities of the ship's systems—capabilities far beyond the conservative constraints they operated by, like test depth and maximum speed. Pete clicked on the heading PATROL ORDERS and suddenly accessed a library of the ship's entire tactical history, starting when Finn took command years before. He scanned all the way down to the present, to see the orders he'd brought with him. The parts they'd accomplished, like the degaussing run, were available. Subsequent sections were not.

Curiously, a single more recent order was highlighted as ACTIVE on the bottom of the list. Pete clicked on it. The order was in the form of a message written from Hana to the Alliance. She reported that she had captured two traitors, taken command, and that she was proceeding to Eris Island as ordered. Once there, she continued, she intended to seize the cure, by force if necessary, to keep it out of enemy hands.

If it looked at any point like the cure would be lost to the enemy, she wrote, she would destroy it. And the *Polaris,* too, if required.

The Alliance hadn't responded.

Pete switched back to the main menu and searched for more

message traffic. It looked like they hadn't received any messages from the Alliance in weeks—and all their outgoing messages had gone unanswered. Hana's message hadn't even been transmitted—the radio room having been destroyed during the mutiny. Apparently Moody had created it just for the record, to demonstrate that what she had done was legal and justified.

A total lack of communication. What did it mean? He sat back and contemplated it. Were they the Alliance's last hope? Or was the war over and they were just a fighting remnant, like one of those Japanese soldiers in the jungle fighting long after the emperor had told them to go home?

Pete began scrolling through the rest of the computer menus, looking for clues. There were highly classified reports of Alliance losses at sea, and on land. The drones had turned the ocean into a vast no-man's-land, bringing commerce and trade to a complete halt. Pete tried to decipher who was winning the war, but it was impossible to tell in terms of victories and defeats. In dry, military language he could only tell that massive suffering had been unleashed on both sides.

He clicked on a digital map labeled TOP SECRET, and at first he thought it was a different rendering of the flu projections he'd seen in his own orders: there were bright splotches of color highlighted on both coasts of the United States. But when he looked closer, he could see it actually represented drone attacks. The drone attacks on land that were supposed to be impossible.

"I knew it!" a voice yelled.

Pete jumped out of the way just in time, as Frank swung a roundhouse punch at his head. "You hacked the main computer!"

Even though the blow just grazed him, it knocked Pete to the ground. He rolled as Frank stood over him. Pete noticed for the first time that there was dark, dried blood around the cuffs of Frank's pants. It was the blood of his friend Ramirez. "I told Moody we couldn't trust you!"

Pete kicked him in the balls.

Frank buckled over in pain. Pete rolled out from under him and got to his feet. He swung hard and connected with Frank's jaw. Frank fell against the starboard periscope with a grunt. Pete's hand felt like he'd hit a brick wall.

Pete readied himself to punch Frank again, this time with his left hand. He saw too late that Frank was reaching in his pocket. He saw a quick blue flash, and then felt blinding, electric pain as the Taser made contact with his chest.

Every muscle in his body contracted, incapacitating him. He fell over, unable even to brace his fall. His entire body was cramping, making it impossible even to yell in pain. When the agony stopped, Frank was standing over him again, the Taser pointed right at his head.

"It's supposed to be a 'nonlethal' weapon," he said. "But I've heard this thing can kill you if you get it right in the head enough times."

Pete tried to respond, but his mouth wouldn't move.

"We don't really know anything about you, do we?" There was a deranged smile on Frank's face. "I think we should tie you to a chair, zap you with this thing in the nuts a few times until you tell us who you are, where you really come from."

"I wish I knew," Pete rasped.

"Smart-ass," said Frank, training the Taser on him. "Hana was blind to it, she liked you for some reason, trusted you. Maybe she was just sick of looking at all of us after all these years, happy to have a new man onboard. But now I've got you. And I'm going to get some answers." He pointed to the screen. "How did you access this?"

"Fuck off."

Frank smiled and pulled the trigger of the Taser.

Pete's entire body went rigid again with pain. He blacked out momentarily, waking with the taste of blood in his mouth. Frank was looking down at him with a broad smile, the Taser still trained on him.

"I missed your balls," he said. "Hit you in the belly. But I think I know how to aim this thing now."

"OK, OK," said Pete, raising his hands. He was having a hard time forming words. "I'll tell you everything."

Frank snorted. "What a pussy. I thought you would at least take one more shot."

"What do you want to know?"

"This, dumbass!" he said, rapidly tapping the computer screen with a thick finger. "How did you access all this? It looks like everything in the entire main computer. And more! I've never seen any of this."

"McCallister showed me how," said Pete. "He gave me a key."

"A key? Like a code word?"

"No. An actual key. A backdoor into the computer system only he knew about. He gave me the key and told me how to access it. He designed it himself."

"Bullshit," Frank said, raising the Taser.

"See for yourself," said Pete, gesturing toward the deck. "There's a keyhole there, under that tile, it gives you access. Right where your left foot would be when you're sitting at the console."

Frank looked skeptical. "You show me. Open it."

Pete dragged himself over, and reached for the tile with one hand. He lifted it up so the keyhole was visible. The effort exhausted him.

"Shit," said Frank. "You weren't lying. Give me that key."

"I can't do that," said Pete.

"Now," said Frank. "I'm not fucking around." He slowly raised the Taser.

"OK," said Pete, surrender in his voice. "Whatever you say. Just don't shoot me again."

Reaching into his pocket as Frank smirked, Pete put his hand on the gun that had killed Ramirez. Aiming as best he could through his pocket, he pointed it, and shot Frank through the stomach.

A look of utter shock on his face, Frank fell on top of him.

Pete pushed Frank's body aside and stood up. Frank still clung to life, but wouldn't live for long, as his blood poured onto the deck. He clutched the bullet wound with both hands. The shot had been deafeningly loud; Pete knew he wouldn't be alone much longer. When Hana discovered that he'd killed Frank, there would be no doubt in her mind anymore that Pete was either a traitor to the Alliance or a dangerous psychopath.

Pete quickly closed out the main menu on the console and returned it to the normal sonar display. To his shock, he saw immediately that the tactical situation had changed—the shadow submarine had maneuvered closer to them. Much closer. He heard hard footsteps in the passageway outside control, footsteps that he now recognized as Moody's, running to investigate the gunshot in control.

Suddenly a bright red light came on above the console, and a recorded alarm sounded: *"Torpedo in the water!"* Red lights flared and sirens screamed.

Even more ominously, Hamlin could hear the sonar of the weapon itself through the hull, pinging rapidly as it homed in on them.

He grabbed a microphone and shouted, "Battle stations! Torpedo in the water!"

He was thrown to the ground as the ship was rocked by an explosion.

CHAPTER FOURTEEN

The ship took a huge upward angle, and Pete slid aft, against the conn. Frank's dead body did as well, leaving a red smear of blood along the deck, all the way to the dive chair.

Somehow Moody had fought her way to control. "What the hell is going on?"

"Torpedo!" said Pete. "They're trying to stop us before we get to Eris!"

She stepped over Frank's body, barely giving him a look. "What happened to him?"

"He was getting in the dive chair as the torpedo hit. He fell—"

"How far are we from the shoals?" she interrupted. "From the island?" Pete needn't have worried about providing a detailed explanation about Frank. For the moment, Moody was laser-focused on saving the ship and fighting the enemy.

Pete pictured the chart in his memory. "We're right on top of the shoals . . . maybe two miles away . . . nine miles from the island. Four miles until we're inside the safety radius . . ."

"Safety radius?" She looked at Pete quizzically.

"Just trust me," he said. "That's where we'll be safe from the drones."

"Four miles at twenty knots . . ."

"Twelve minutes."

"Good enough," she said. She lunged for two red levers over the dive chair and pulled them forward: the emergency blow system.

An enormous *whoosh* of air filled the control room as the actuating valves opened. All around them, huge banks of compressed air shot into the main ballast tanks of the *Polaris*, pushing out thousands of tons of seawater, making them instantly buoyant. The submarine shot to the surface.

"Ahead flank!" she yelled, and the automated system acknowledged the order with a ring of its bell.

The computer counted down their depth as they raced upward. *Ninety feet . . . eighty . . . seventy . . .*

Finally they broke through the surface, the ship actually rising fifteen feet into the air. It crashed back into the ocean with a splash, and soon reached equilibrium.

"We're still at an angle," said Pete.

"Because of the torpedo hit," said Moody. "We've taken on a lot of water aft, weighing it down . . . maybe we're still taking it on. Automatic flood control should limit the damage. On the surface, like this, can we make it over those shoals?"

Pete raised the scope after briefly glancing at their speed. Even at ahead flank they were moving at only seventeen knots, perhaps limited by the flooding and the angle of the ship. Moody scrambled forward and operated the trim system to limit the damage, frantically cutting out alarms to limit the noise in control.

The scope came up and Pete put his eye to it, quickly trained it toward the island. Directly in front of him, he could see the discoloration in the water that marked the shoals that surrounded Eris. Farther ahead, he could see the low brown shimmer that was the island. Above it flew a swarm of drones.

"We're right on top of the shoals . . ." said Pete. Just then, they heard the hull scraping bottom. The whole ship shook as they slid over the top.

Just as soon, it was over. Pete kept his eyes on the scope. A drone, a scout, was directly over them, soaring into the sky, signaling their presence.

"It doesn't sound like that worsened the flooding," Moody said when the scraping stopped. "Flood control has completely sealed off the engine room."

Pete took his eye off the scope to check speed; it was dropping. When he looked back outside, three drones were low to the water, flying directly toward them.

"Drones!" he said. They disappeared from view as they flew directly overhead.

The first bomb hit the missile deck directly behind them and exploded. The noise inside the ship was deafening. That part of the deck, however, was superstructure, and acted as armor for them, absorbing the explosion without further damaging the pressure hull. Through the scope, Pete saw a hole ripped in the steel, a jagged gash, but the pressure hull below was still watertight.

"How many drones?!" shouted Moody.

"Three so far," said Pete, just as the second bomb hit.

It landed right next to the sail. The scope jerked so hard from the force that Pete felt like he'd been punched in the face. The scope started to drift downward, but Pete fought to hold it up so he could keep looking.

"External hydraulics is damaged," said Moody, cutting out an alarm. "Pressure dropping fast." Pete watched as the third drone swerved to avoid its comrade. As a result, it dropped its bomb slightly off target, and it landed harmlessly in the ocean off their port side.

He barely had time to feel any relief before he looked up and saw at least a dozen drones heading directly toward them from the island.

"More on the way," he said.

"How many?"

"Too many."

They both looked at speed.

"How far do we need to go?" she said. "How far to this safety radius?"

"Maybe a mile left," he said. Speed had dropped to fifteen knots. Pete did the math: four minutes until they reached safety.

The *Polaris* kept churning through the water. Pete knew they couldn't survive a coordinated attack by that many drones, especially in their already damaged condition. One more hit might rip open the hull, ignite a fire in the missile compartment, and spread radioactive debris from the warheads. They were pointed directly at each other, the *Polaris* and the incoming swarm of drones. The island was clearly in sight now; he could see the control tower on the north side. More drones were taking off, sweeping up into the sky, ready to finish them off. The ESM alarms throughout the control room screeched.

Moody fought her way to the command console. "We're five and a half miles from the island!"

Pete kept his eye on the scope. "We have to make that five-mile line." The drones were screaming toward them.

"Four hundred yards," she said. "Three hundred . . . two hundred . . . one hundred."

"Brace yourself!" said Pete as the drones reached directly overhead. The lead drone dropped its bomb, which landed on the aftmost exposed part of the deck, tearing a new hole in it.

But then the rest of the drones pulled up, and circled them. They had made it, slipped across the five-mile line.

"Yes!" shouted Pete.

"All back full!" said Moody. It took Pete a second to realize what she was doing. While they were now safe from the drones, they were speeding at fifteen knots toward the jagged coral shore of the island. The big ship reluctantly slowed, then stopped.

The big engines changed directions, and the ship started to slow. Pete watched as the island loomed in front of them, the magnification of the scope making it seem like collision was inevitable. But the ship slowly ground to a halt, the speed dropping to zero.

"Are we good?" she said.

"Yes," he said. Through the scope, he felt like he could almost reach out and touch land. "Somehow."

Pete rotated and searched behind them—no sign of the Typhon boat. He knew now precisely where the five-mile line was, having seen the drones relent. But Carlson was out there somewhere. He had an idea.

"Keep backing up," he said.

"Why?" said Moody.

"We want to get close to that five-mile line," he said. "As close as possible."

"Without going over."

"Exactly," he said.

"All back one-third," she said.

He watched through the scope, trying to fix in memory the exact point where the drones had relented. "Here!" he said as they approached.

"All stop!"

The ship slowly drifted to a halt, dead in the water. Only the nose of the ship, and the tower, was above the surface, the aft end of *Polaris* weighed down by the flooding. Pete knew they were inside the five-mile radius—because the curious drones swooping above them weren't dropping their bombs. But he hoped they were very close to that line.

"They're out there somewhere," said Pete. "Watching us. They could kill us now if they wanted."

Moody shook her head grimly. "Those shoals might protect us—not sure how well their torpedoes would navigate over them. And they may not want to shoot us now. They could have done it long before. They may want to board us—seize us. Save their man McCallister. Find out what we know. Dissect every piece of technology onboard. There's no way I'm going to let that happen."

"We'll fight?"

"Not in this condition," she said. "But I'll scuttle the ship before I let those bastards have us." She started heading aft, and Pete yelled after her.

"We might not have to. We're safe here. But they're not safe where they are."

"Are you sure?"

"We're right on the line. Maybe we can lure them to the surface, let the drones attack them."

"Well," Moody said as a new flooding alarm shrieked and the *Polaris* continued to take on water. "I don't have any better ideas."

They hurried to the forward hatch, walking up a steep angle to get to it. As they left the control room, they could hear the rushing of water behind them as it flooded into the ship. They didn't have much time. Moody spun open the hatch, and together they muscled it open and climbed topside.

The sun blinded Hamlin at first; he hadn't realized how

dark it was inside the ship. The equatorial heat, as well—the humidity, the sea breeze—it was almost too much to bear. He found himself gasping, his body starved for good air. As he breathed it in, he could feel himself getting stronger. Seagulls swooped overhead, their shadows crisscrossing the battered deck of the submarine.

But they weren't gulls; they were the drones. Agitated, like bees, and the *Polaris* had approached too close to the hive. They swooped overhead, buzzing Pete and Moody so closely that they ducked. Each one clutched a bomb in its talons, but obedient to their coding, they didn't drop them. Hamlin noticed that they looked old, their wings battered in some cases and frayed, their bodies no longer shiny. But they still flew with deadly, precise alacrity.

"Out there," said Pete, pointing. "The Typhon boat is out there somewhere."

"They won't surface. They know better, with all these drones out."

"When they see the drones are avoiding us . . . maybe they'll think they're safe. Maybe they'll think the shoal line is the safety barrier. If we're right on the line and they surface out there—"

"The drones will get them."

"That's my plan," said Pete.

"So what are they waiting for?"

"Our surrender," said Pete. He quickly stripped off his uniform shirt, and then his white T-shirt. He waved it in the air. He did it for five minutes, hoping someone on the Typhon boat was observing him through their periscope. The sun pounded on his shoulders, and soon he was sweaty with exertion.

"There!" said Moody, pointing. Pete stopped waving his shirt momentarily, and looked in the direction Moody was pointing.

It was a periscope.

But instead of driving straight at them, the submarine adjusted course, and drove to the south.

"What are they doing?" said Moody.

"Not sure," said Pete. He could see them driving south a few hundred yards before turning back toward them.

"Which way is north?" Pete asked Moody, the realization dawning on him. She pointed forward.

If the direction north was twelve o'clock, the Typhon boat had driven itself to seven o'clock. Precisely the location of the break in the shoals.

"That's the break in the shoals," said Pete. "The one place they can pass at periscope depth. Somehow they knew."

Moody nodded grimly, her thoughts confirmed once again: they'd been betrayed.

The enemy submarine glided easily through the break in the shoals. It crept closer and closer to them; he could just barely make out the small V of water it left in the periscope's wake. Pete imagined Jennifer Carlson looking at him through the scope, magnified, with the crosshairs of the reticule on his chest. Soon it looked so close that Pete could see the glass of the scope lens. He was worried the two ships might collide.

Then suddenly, the giant submarine rose from the water.

The enemy boat rose faster than the water could fall from it, so the sea poured off it in sheets as it surfaced. Just as Carlson had told him in shaft alley, the ship had been at sea for years; its paint was chipped, and starfish adhered to the hull. It looked like an ancient ghost ship that the sea was relinquishing to them.

Instantly the drones adjusted their flights, a contingent of them peeling off the *Polaris* and swarming over the enemy boat.

But none dropped their bombs.

"Shit," said Moody.

"They're too close," said Pete. "Inside the five-mile line, just like us."

"So now what do we do?"

"We have to make them back up," he said. "Just a few feet." He thought for a minute, thought about what little he knew about Carlson, her fearful voice on the radio in shaft alley. Now that they knew they were safe from the drones, an armed boarding party was starting to climb out of the Typhon submarine, methodically loading two small inflatable boats and putting them over the side.

"How . . ." she said, but Pete was already climbing back down the ladder to enter the *Polaris*.

"Where are you going?" she said.

"Take this," he said, handing Moody his shirt. "I have to make a call."

He ran aft, aided by the angle of the ship, running downhill all the way. The angle had grown steeper, and the smell of seawater, and the sound of it rushing in, permeated the ship.

Through the missile compartment and into the engine room, almost falling as gravity aided his sprint aft. He opened the door into the tunnel and ran into the turbine room.

Water was up to the deck plates. Some of the turbines were still running, but the noises were unhealthy. The symphony of machinery he'd heard earlier, machines lovingly maintained by Ramirez, was now discordant. Gears were grinding, and steam was hissing from the turbines and pumps that were in their death throes. Pete continued running aft, to the ladder to shaft alley. Looking down, he saw there was just about a foot of space remaining above the water; he hoped the radio was still dry and functional.

As he stood at the top of the ladder, he also considered that the water might not be seawater—it could be coolant leaking from a damaged reactor, which would be lethally radioactive. It might also be alive with electricity, through the bared wires or deranged generators that were submerged beneath it. But there was no time to check, and he was running out of options. He took a deep breath, and dropped down the ladder.

The water was up to his chest, and got deeper as he fought his way aft. When he got to the alcove where the radio was hidden, only his head was above water. He reached in and pulled it out. He pressed the red button and spoke. "Typhon, this is *Polaris*."

He waited a moment, hearing nothing but static. He was about to give up when a response came.

"Hamlin, this is Captain Carlson. Is that gushing water I hear? Are you coming around now that you're about to sink?" The voice was clearer than he remembered it, perhaps aided by their proximity.

"No time to argue," he said. "You need to surface and send a boat over here so we can surrender to you. Moody is ready."

"I see her waving that flag. A boarding party is on the way."

"Thank god," said Pete. "We've got sick people onboard. Very sick."

There was a pause. "Nice try, Hamlin," she said. "I'll have to see that for myself."

"Send your doctor."

"I'll see if he's available," she said. "I think today is the day he golfs." She disconnected.

He shut off the radio and climbed out of shaft alley. He ran forward, through an engine room that was now almost completely dark.

At the watertight door, Doctor Haggerty met him: somehow he always knew when Pete was in shaft alley. He looked panicked. "Are we sinking?"

"Looks that way," said Pete.

"We've got to get out of here! Aren't we right next to Eris Island?"

"How did you know that?" asked Pete.

The doctor shrugged nervously. "I've been paying attention, glimpsing at our position on the chart when I can. We've got to get to that island!"

Pete stared hard at him.

"And we need to help Finn," the doctor added.

"You're right. Let's go."

They ran forward to the escape trunk, uphill all the way, fighting the steep angle of the ship. When they got there, they found Finn sitting calmly on his steel bench, seemingly re-signed to going down with his ship. He looked awful; his days locked in the dark had taken their toll. His skin was sallow, his eyes sunken. He looked, Pete confirmed, like a very sick man.

"Wake up, Captain," said Pete.

"Look who's here," he said, opening his eyes. "What's going on?"

"Port call," said Pete. "The doctor and I thought we'd take you out for some fresh air."

"I don't know if I can today, I'm pretty busy."

Pete was already unbolting the grid that had kept Finn cap-tive. He was dripping wet, and water pooled around his feet as he worked. The grate dropped to the deck with a clang. The captain started to climb down.

"No," said Pete. "We're going to use your little room here, if you don't mind."

The doctor climbed up the ladder. Pete handed up three hoods from the locker, followed by a tightly packed inflatable raft.

"Grab that one, too," said the captain, pointing to a tightly bundled canister wrapped in the same Day-Glo orange nylon. "That's the motor."

Soon all three men crowded into the escape trunk with the two bundles. Pete pulled up the bottom hatch behind them and turned the locking ring until it was tightly shut. It was suddenly quiet as they were sealed off from the rest of the noisily sinking ship.

"How far below the surface are we?" said the captain. "I can feel the angle."

"I think about twenty feet right here," said Pete. "The forward trunk is completely out of the water. The engine room is almost completely flooded. And we're getting deeper."

The captain moved deftly around the trunk, verifying that all the valves were lined up correctly, then he handed each of the men a yellow hood. "Put these on. They'll help you get to the surface."

Soon they each had a hood on, and gave a thumbs-up. Finn opened a valve, and the trunk began to fill with water.

"We'll fill it up first!" he shouted above the noise. "Then we'll equalize pressure, and we'll swim out."

The water was soon up to their knees, and it was hard not to feel panic as they sat in a small steel chamber that was rapidly filling with water. Pete felt his heart pounding as the waterline reached his neck. The doctor looked even more stricken, his eyes wide with fright through the clear plastic of his hood.

"Will that raft hold all three of us?" Pete shouted over the sound of rushing water.

"It should," said the captain. "I used to look at that thing when we were eight hundred feet deep in five thousand feet of ocean—always made me laugh. I couldn't think of a situation where it would ever be useful."

"Those engineers at Electric Boat think of everything."

The water finally stopped pouring in. "The pressure is equalized," said the captain. "We can open the escape hatch now." He pointed down, into the water.

"I'll go first!" said Haggerty, not giving them a chance to discuss it. He then dived below the waterline and disappeared. They heard a clank outside as the doctor egressed.

"You're next," said the captain.

"Are you sure?" said Pete.

"Go," he said. "I'll meet you at the top."

Pete took a deep breath, then stuck his head underwater. In the murk, and with the ship's steep angle, it was difficult to find the escape hatch, even in the close confines of the trunk. He hit his head hard on the way under, and fought off the natural instinct to avoid diving into a dark, water-filled pipe.

But once he was inside, the natural buoyancy of the hood and his own body took over. He made his way through the open hatch and felt himself being pulled to the surface, and before he could even remember to say *HO HO HO,* he broke through, his head once again exposed to bright sunshine and clear air.

McCallister came up soon after. The orange raft popped up immediately after that, and began to unfold and inflate immediately with a hiss. They ripped off their hoods and paddled toward the raft. The captain pulled himself in first, then leaned over and pulled Pete in with a strong arm.

"Over there!" said the captain. The motor canister was bobbing a few feet away. They both leaned over and paddled toward it until the captain could pull it onboard.

He ripped off the protective casing and soon had the parts spread out on the floor of the boat. He popped out the blades of the propeller, pulled off a plastic tag that activated the battery. He then hung it off the back of the boat, on a mount that was designed for it. The final step was to thread together two small poles, the larger of which had a ribbed rubber grip: the till. It was done in minutes. He pushed a button, and Pete could hear the engine switch on.

"It's got a high-capacity battery, and only one speed," said the captain. "It'll last about thirty minutes."

Pete looked forward. Hana Moody was still standing on the front of the ship, waving his white shirt; she hadn't noticed him escaping with Finn yet. And Haggerty, he saw, was eagerly swimming away. Toward the Typhon boat.

"Haggerty!" shouted the captain. "We're over here!"

Haggerty looked back briefly but continued swimming toward the other submarine. It didn't surprise Pete at all: a final confirmation.

"Head for the shore?" said the captain.

"No," said Pete. "The other direction."

"To rescue Haggerty?"

"No—screw him. I just want to get close to them."

"Why?" said Finn. "Don't they want to kill us?"

"Probably," said Pete. "I'll explain later. But do me a favor—lie down. And try to look sick."

The captain did as Pete asked, and he turned the boat toward the Typhon sub, about one hundred yards from the *Polaris*. They were gaining on Haggerty, who was frantically swimming away from them. Pete looked down at the captain, who looked, for all the world, like a dying man.

Pete saw a woman on the main deck, looking shocked as they approached. She gave an order, and men with rifles trained their guns and shot—bullets whistled over their heads. His gambit was having the desired effect. Pete began waving his arms frantically and pointing at the lifeless body of Mc-Callister, as if begging Carlson to let them aboard. The small engine of the boat whined loudly, making it seem like they were approaching much faster than they were. In fact, they were moving against the tide and the waves, and were barely making progress. The distance and the motion of the waves, he hoped, would keep them out of the range of the riflemen.

A shot cracked against the casing of the motor, splitting it, but it kept running.

"Are you sure about this?" said the captain.

"Not at all!" Pete said. He kept the little boat pointed at Carlson.

They were close enough that he could see the concern in her eyes. Playing the part perfectly, McCallister began coughing violently, and leaned his head over the side to spit out a giant glob of phlegm. Carlson suddenly relented, shouted another order, and the ocean behind her began to churn as her submarine's massive engines turned and pulled the submarine away from them.

She was backing away from them, panicked that a deadly epidemic was heading her way in an orange life raft. Just as Pete had intended.

The huge engines worked quickly, and the drones continued to fly in their seemingly random patterns overhead. Carlson wasn't worried at all about the drones, Pete could see; she was fixated on the raft that seemed to be speeding toward her with a cargo of disease. She backed up twenty feet, then thirty. Even as they moved away, though, some of the sharpshooters' shots came closer to the raft, as the men adjusted their aim. Pete could hear bullets whistling by them in the boat, and some shots hit the water so closely that spray hit them, and drummed against the side of the raft. *Come on,* thought Pete, *cross that line.*

The Typhon submarine continued to pull backward while the sharpshooters shot at them. The drones dived over both submarines and the raft without dropping their bombs.

Then finally, as Carlson and her ship crossed that invisible five-mile line in the ocean, the drones attacked.

The first bomb exploded on the main deck of the Typhon ship with a loud pop, seemingly causing no damage on the thick metal. It had landed on the aftmost part of the deck, far from where the men were boarding their inflatables—the part of the submarine, Pete realized, that crossed the five-mile radius first. Carlson's crew looked at her in shock. She looked at Pete with a grim smile.

"Kill the engine!" said Pete, and McCallister quickly sat up, turned off their small outboard, and turned the till so that they stopped moving forward.

While the first bomb had done little damage, the other drones were attacking in a frenzy now, dropping their bombs in a fury as the marines on the main deck took cover and scrambled to get in their small boats. The big submarine continued to move backward, exposing more and more of herself to the drones' attack. The drones ignored the inflatables, told by their programming to focus on the big target.

It was fascinating to watch.

The whole Typhon boat was now under attack. Some of the bombs began to have an effect, opening holes on spots on the deck that had previously been hit and weakened. Carlson realized what had happened and cut the engines, the water no longer churning behind the boat. But she weighed thousands of tons, and her momentum was slow to reverse, carrying her farther into the free-fire zone.

In the shower of bombs that the drones dropped upon her, one fell straight into the conning tower. A shower of sparks shot into the sky, followed by a column of black smoke. The other drones took note, and poured more bombs into the wound.

As they did, each flew away in an orderly straight line, back to Eris Island to reload.

The two inflatable boats from the Typhon were now full. A few men, some wounded terribly, were swimming in the sea. Their shipmates stopped firing at Pete and McCallister as they tried to pull their comrades aboard. The submarine was mortally wounded, smoke and fire pouring from multiple holes, the ship listing badly to port.

"She's dead," said McCallister.

"You're sure?" said Pete.

"Listen," he said. "You can hear the air banks exploding. . . ."

Pete did hear it, a series of deep explosions coming from beneath the waterline. He could feel the concussion in his feet through the soft bottom of the raft. A tower of flame now roared from the Typhon conning tower.

"All that compressed air is feeding the fire," said the captain. "Turning it into a blast furnace inside. God help anyone who's still onboard."

The ship rolled suddenly all the way on its side, toward them so that they were looking into the top of the conning tower.

"We need to get away!" said McCallister. "When that tower hits the waterline, it'll sink like a rock. The suction could take us with it!"

The conning tower drifted closer to the water, and just as McCallister had predicted, once the giant opening hit the waterline, the ship sank with stunning speed.

Pete could feel the suction at work, trying to pull their little boat backward. But they had gone far enough, had the tide working in their favor, and were soon speeding toward the beach. The small boats from Carlson's sub were still pulling survivors from the water, ignoring them for the moment.

"Let's go," said Pete, pointing toward Eris. "We've got a head start."

"Do I still need to look sick?" said Finn.

"No," said Pete. "Look like a captain. And get us ashore."

He quickly pulled the till, and turned them around.

Moody, still holding Pete's shirt, watched in shock from the deck of the *Polaris* as they passed.

"Fuck you!" she shouted.

Finn's eyes were trained on the shore. But as he kept his left hand on the till, he flipped her off with his right.

Commander Carlson jumped from the deck into one of the rubber boats, landing only halfway on; the sergeant of the marines pulled her the rest of the way aboard. "Get away!" she said, pointing toward the island. The drones continued hammering her submarine behind her, which was belching fire and smoke, and groaning as it died. Her small rubber boat pulled away, and the drones ignored it. They were prioritizing, she realized. Her dying submarine was a bigger, better target. As they sped away, she saw that they were in parallel with her other rubber boat. Her XO, Lieutenant Banach, was on that one. He gave her a slight nod, and she was flooded with relief to see that he was alive. She nodded back.

She'd been fooled, she realized. And it had worked because she'd been afraid. That little boat had started moving toward them, with the sick man onboard, and she had reacted out of fear. She was a woman who had stared down death a hundred times, from torpedoes and bombs, and the multitude of ways that the deep ocean can end human life. But for fear of a disease, she'd backed the big ship up, directly into a trap. They must have been inside some kind of safe zone, she realized now, a buffer around the island. She'd been trying to fool Hamlin, but he had fooled her instead. That clever boy had tried to get her to surface outside of that, and when that didn't work, he let her drive herself right out of it. He knew what she was afraid of. And because of that, she'd lost her ship.

She wouldn't let fear drive her again.

Banach's boat veered suddenly to port, drawing her eyes to the surface of the water.

It was Dr. Haggerty, her spy. He stopped dog-paddling and waved his arms wildly at her.

She'd never seen him in person, just a photograph in his file, but she knew it was him. That type of person, she supposed, and the intelligence he provided were vital to the war effort. To any war. Trying to trick Hamlin into cooperating had been his idea; he said they could convince Hamlin that he had worked for them all along. Said the man was unstable and distraught, and that he would be easy to manipulate. So much for that, she thought, as she looked back at her burning submarine. Because she was a warrior, she despised disloyalty, despised spies, even if they were working for her. And because she was smart, she knew she could never trust the doctor.

"Shall we stop?" yelled the sergeant as they neared him.

"No!" she shouted. "To the island."

She looked back briefly at Haggerty as they sped by him. He continued waving his arms for a moment, but then seemed to realize that he'd been abandoned. He started swimming toward shore, but they were almost five miles away, and the doctor was old and out of shape. The swim would have been challenging even for an athlete. Carlson watched without emotion as his head went under, then disappeared.

CHAPTER FIFTEEN

McCallister and Hamlin waded to shore and onto a landscape that seemed vaguely familiar to Pete. They dragged the raft onto a rocky beach and hid it, barely, in a patch of weeds.

"This way," Pete said, the geography slowly coming back to him. They crested a small sand hill that marked the end of the beach, staying low to be unseen.

Over the rise, they could now see the airfield. It was riddled with craters—artillery shells from ships and cruise missiles that had once tried to pound the island into submission, before the drones had turned them away. The outlying buildings around the field had mostly been bombed into rubble. But the tower, reinforced and strategically built into the surrounding landscape, still stood tall.

Drones were everywhere. They didn't need much runway to take off, Pete knew, could rise almost vertically, so the craters on the runway had little effect. Some were resting on the tarmac, their wings oscillating slowly in the sun. One rose up and circled lazily in the sky. Pete watched, fascinated, as an empty drone, perhaps one that had just bombed the

Typhon sub, landed on the runway, crept slowly up to a free bomb on the field, and armed itself.

Not a human was in sight.

"You know this place?" asked Finn.

"I used to," said Pete. He was lost in the sight, a grand vision of modern warfare, reduced, wounded, and bruised, but still murderously effective. *Perhaps,* he thought, as he looked in vain for another human, *even victorious.*

"Look," said the captain, tapping his arm. He was turned around, looking out to sea.

The two rubber boats from the Typhon submarine were fully loaded with heavily armed men in fatigues, making their way toward Eris. In the front boat sat Jennifer Carlson.

"Let's go," said Pete. "We don't have much time."

The drones took notice of the speeding Typhon boats but didn't bomb them, as they were now well within the safety radius. The drones also ignored Pete and Finn as they headed toward the tower.

At its base, Pete found the heavy door locked. On the small keypad next to it, he pressed his thumb. Nothing happened.

"No power?" he said.

"I don't think that's it," said Finn, pointing up to the windows of the tower. "I can see lights inside. Maybe it's been locked from the inside. Or you've been taken off the access list."

"Shit," said Pete, looking back to the beach where Carlson's boats were quickly making their way toward them.

"Do we have any weapons?"

Pete reached in his pocket and pulled out Ramirez's small gun. "Just this," he said.

He turned back to the keypad and noticed a small metal disc below it. It was corroded and rusted, but he managed to slide it over.

It revealed a small keyhole.

He pulled the red key from around his neck, and showed it to Finn.

"A key?" he said.

"Yeah. You submariners love this shit," he said. He stuck it in the hole and turned it.

He heard a metallic click deep inside the door as a relay turned. He pushed, and the giant armored door glided open.

"Let's go," he said.

They ran up the stairs as the door swung shut and locked behind them.

They bounded up the stairs to the top floor, where an unlocked door awaited them. Pete looked at Finn and drew the small handgun without a word. Nodding, they pushed the door open, Pete holding the weapon in a firing position.

"Pete Hamlin," said an old man from the center of the hexagonal room. "It's about time you showed up." He had a gray beard, and wore the shoulder boards of an admiral.

"Who are you?" Pete shouted over the sights of his pistol.

"That," said Finn, wonder in his voice, "is Admiral Wesley Stewart."

Pete allowed himself to take it all in for a moment before he began speaking. The familiarity of the control room washed over him; he knew he'd spent many days in there in the past, watching the drones below. Despite the carnage outside, the control room itself was in relatively good condition, the carpet still clean, just one of the surrounding windows cracked. Electric lights still illuminated the room, and the computers beeped, clicked, and contentedly reported their data. Somewhere far beneath them, he could feel the hum of a generator in his feet. He placed the small pistol slowly in his pocket.

Admiral Stewart broke the silence. "I didn't expect to ever see both of you in the same room. Certainly not *this* room."

He turned to Pete and pointed at McCallister. "How much does he know?"

"You might want to ask me the same thing," said Pete.

"We're here for the cure," said Finn. "The epidemic."

"The disease that killed my wife."

The admiral looked at Pete with concern. "You may have come to the right place for the cure," he said. "But that disease didn't kill Pamela."

Pete was confused. It was one of the few things he thought he knew, the memory that had anchored his actions. "But . . ."

Stewart looked at him with a seriousness that gave way to sympathy. "Pete, the disease didn't kill Pamela. The drones did."

And with that, everything came back to Pete.

BOOK
TWO

THREE YEARS EARLIER

CHAPTER SIXTEEN

Pete's small fleet of experimental drones could fly, and they could even kill, accurately dropping their small bombs on targets of all shapes and sizes. But they couldn't talk. This final problem was critical. With their small, ten-pound bombs, they could work effectively only in swarms. They were designed to overwhelm their targets with sheer quantity, pouring hundreds of bombs on targets from hundreds of directions. At the same time, any kind of traditional radio communication could be jammed or intercepted by the enemy, making the drones useless or, worse, able to be turned against the Alliance. After a brief but fantastically expensive failure with laser communications—one drone convinced another to crash into a boathouse on the coast of Northern California, near the testing range—Pete left the smoldering wreckage on the beach too tired even to feel defeated. He was nearly ready to declare the entire dream a failure while it was still in the experimental phase. His career would be ruined, but the Alliance would be saved a few million dollars, and they could move on to more promising weapons platforms.

He'd begun working on the autonomous drone five years earlier. At that time, it was a highly experimental project that the Pentagon had indulged with a few million research dollars. That indulgence was largely the result of Pete's imaginative proposal, in which he envisioned an autonomous armada of low-cost drones that could dominate a battlefield, region, or, perhaps, an entire ocean. Drones had been around for decades, so putting an unmanned plane in the sky was no longer extraordinary. But Pete Hamlin prophesied a day when hundreds of them would work together with deadly effectiveness, and this promise was enough to ensure a steady trickle of research dollars.

Two years into his project, the war began, followed soon after by the formation of the Alliance. The trickle of dollars turned into a river of money. The Allies had been startled to discover at the start of the war that they'd lost control of the seas. They had giant, advanced ships, planes, and submarines, but Typhon had numbers, seemingly endless flotillas that quickly seized control of the sea lanes from their outnumbered opponents. So long had the Allies gone without a meaningful shipbuilding program that even the shipyards had disappeared, taking with them the welders, engineers, and mechanics who actually knew how to construct ships of war. The smallest Allied ship took almost a year to build. Typhon turned out a ship a day from its noisy shipyards. The paltry Allied construction program couldn't keep up with the losses they were taking at Typhon's hands. For lack of alternatives, Pete's old proposal steadily rose to the top of the Alliance, a potential way to seize the initiative without building a thousand ships.

But as the money and the focus increased, so did the pressure, and the disappointments. Pete simply couldn't get his drones to communicate intelligently with each other, a failure that was represented vividly by that smoky crater on a California beach.

Back at his hotel, he ordered room service: an overpriced rib eye steak and a beer. It was an extravagance, but he didn't want to leave his room, knowing the drone crash had made the news—he didn't want to see it on television or overhear any local speculation. While he waited for his food to arrive, he logged on to his personal computer, something he rarely did both because he was nearly always at work and because it wasn't secure. His life hadn't had room for leisurely Internet browsing.

He was about to check out college football scores when he noted curiously that his Internet browser suggested to him a series of articles about someone named Tom Healy. Healy was a Cornell professor who was making waves in popular culture with his books about honeybees. His most recent had the catchy title *Hive Democracy*. It was his browser's mistake, Pete realized with a smile, brought to him by the word "drone," common in both his work and the work of Professor Tom Healy. He almost skipped the links, but it was late, and he didn't have the energy to look up anything on his own. He clicked through and began reading. Pete read the introduction to Healy's book, and watched a video in which the professor explained the sublime, efficient ways that bees communicated.

It was called the waggle dance. Supremely simple and elegant, engineered by millions of years of evolution, the bees could communicate the exact location of a food source, or a potential hive site, with amazing accuracy. Moreover, they could actually vote on hive locations, invariably picking the best, most strategic location. All of this strictly with their movements and their vision.

At some point, Hamlin let the room service waiter in, and

the food grew cold on the room's small table as Pete continued to read.

At 3:00 A.M., he had booked his flight to Ithaca, New York.

Pete had actually been to Cornell once before, recruiting engineers for his program as he had from all of the nation's finest schools. He remembered it being filled with Gothic architecture, a beautiful place, a Hollywood set designer's idea of what a college campus should look like.

The Dyce Laboratory for Honeybee Studies was nothing like that.

It was a thoroughly utilitarian building, one story of turquoise-colored corrugated metal, with garage doors on one side and few windows. It looked more like a small-town welding shop than it did part of a prestigious university, and in fact, it was well north of the campus. There were no ivy vines in sight, no clock towers, just pine trees and rolling hills. And everywhere, a low but persistent buzzing.

"Professor Hamlin?" The professor was walking toward him as Pete got out of his rental car on the gravel drive.

"Just Pete," he answered. "I'm not a professor."

Tom Healy shook his head. "I wasn't sure," he said, smiling. "And some people get uptight about those things." The professor's appearance suited the plain surroundings: rumpled shirt, cargo shorts, thin hair grown long and combed over a balding scalp. Pete knew his rumpled appearance masked a stellar academic career: he was a world-class authority on neurobiology, a Guggenheim Fellow, a fellow of the American Academy of Arts and Sciences, and, in what he claimed was his most enduring honor, he had a species of bee named for him: *Neocorynurella healyi.*

The professor led him to his small, cluttered office and offered him a cup of tea, which Pete declined.

"Come on!" said the professor. "It's just an excuse to use some of our fresh honey! I'm not helping you until you try it."

He pulled out a small decanter, and Pete relented with a grin. The professor poured into his steaming mug a generous dollop of honey.

"God," said Pete after a taste. "That really is good."

"Told you," said the professor. "That's our 'last taste of summer,' batch, you're lucky you got here in time."

Pete put down the mug on the corner of the professor's worn desk, and pulled out his copy of *Hive Democracy* from his briefcase.

"Ah," said Healy. "Another fan."

"It was fascinating," said Pete. "Truly. Obviously I'm not the only one who thinks so."

The professor waved his hand in the air. "It's my third book on the subject, but the first time I've ever been asked on the *Today Show*. I'm the beneficiary of a provocative title, and I can thank my editor for that."

"But you believe it, right?" asked Pete. "You believe the bees actually practice democracy like we do?"

The professor nodded his head skeptically. "Actually, I think they practice it a little better than we do. They almost always make the right decision, as a group; I've proved it experimentally."

"And why do you think their system works so well?"

"This is something I've thought a lot about," said Healy. "For one thing, the bees all have a common goal: survival. They are making life-and-death decisions together. And secondly, while they don't all have the same information, they all have the same preferences. So when they truthfully communicate their information to each other, they always agree on the correct path."

Pete nodded, waiting to hear more.

"This is your area of interest, correct?" said the professor.

"It is," said Pete.

"And you're with the Department of Agriculture?"

"Yes," said Pete, almost forgetting his cover story. The Department of Agriculture had a sizable presence at Cornell, and provided large amounts of funding to the university. It was both a plausible cover story and one that would encourage Healy to cooperate.

"How long have you been there?" asked the professor.

"Less than a year," said Pete. "And I'm a consultant. Haven't really learned my way around the bureaucracy yet." He was trying to head off any obvious questions about the agency that he wouldn't be able to answer.

"I see," said the professor, nodding. "Well, you must be important. Or working on an important project. I've worked with a lot of Ag Department folks over the years, and this is the first time one of them was able to take a charter jet to see me on one day's notice."

Pete didn't respond. He doubted he could bullshit a man as smart as Healy, so he decided to let it hang there, and let the professor decide whether he wanted to help or not. While Pete's motives might be a little mysterious, the professor couldn't doubt his influence, or the power of his backers.

He sipped his tea and continued to look Hamlin over. "How about we go for a walk?" he said. "I can't leave them alone too long out there," he said.

"The bees?"

"No," said Healy. "Grad students."

———

They walked across an expanse of grass to where a path entered the woods. Pete followed the professor into the trees. The air cooled instantly when they stepped into the shade, and Pete could tell that just as the name of Healy's honey had indicated, the end of summer in upstate New York was rapidly approaching.

"How much do you know about bees?" asked Healy.

"What I read in your book," he said. "Queens, workers, and drones."

A bee flew by them in the air.

"So what kind is that?" said the professor lightheartedly, pointing.

"A worker?"

"Good guess!" he said. "Odds are very good. Queens rarely leave the hive, and drones wouldn't be flying around out here looking for pollen."

"They don't?"

"No. Drones are the only males in the hive," he said. "Their only role is to impregnate a queen. Consequently, they are the only bees in the hive without a stinger."

"Really?" said Pete. He was struck by the irony, the drones of the hive being the only "unarmed" members. Without giving away his real reason for visiting Cornell, that made him curious. "So how did the word 'drone' come to mean—"

"What it means now? In ancient times, we thought drones were lazy, because they didn't leave the hive to seek food or do any work. The term came to be synonymous with a lazy, idle worker. Subsequently, the name 'drone' was given to mindless machines. Of course now—"

"Drones have evolved."

"And the term along with them." The professor was staring hard at him now, and Pete was eager to keep the conversation moving.

"What happens to the drones after they impregnate the queen?"

"They die. The penis and abdominal tissues are ripped out after successful mating."

"Jesus."

Healy knelt down and pointed to a bee on a purple flower.

"One of yours?" asked Pete.

"It's not marked, but quite possibly." They watched it climb over the outside of the flower for a few seconds, and then take off. It spiraled into the air and flew down the path.

"My old mentor, Professor Martin Lindauer, used to actually run after the bees when he observed them. They fly about six miles per hour, so you can keep up—although it's not easy running through the woods while trying to keep your eye on a bee."

"I can imagine," said Hamlin. "Do you do that?"

"I used to," he said. "Not so much anymore." He stood up from the flower, and looked Pete up and down. Assessing him. "So you want to learn the language these bees use to communicate?"

Pete nodded. "I do."

"You know what we call it?"

"The waggle dance."

"Good!" said the professor, happy with his pupil. "That's exactly right. But the waggle dance was discovered decades ago. By Karl von Frisch. He won a Nobel Prize for it. It's been studied thoroughly ever since, well documented, debated, revised. You've got decades of research to draw from. What do you need me for?"

"My understanding," said Pete, "is that the waggle dance is how they communicate the location of food supplies. But I want to know how they make decisions as a group, decide on objectives, prioritize their work. The democracy of the hive, so to speak. That's what I want to learn about. . . ."

The professor nodded, and seemed to think it over. Another bee landed on the flower, and they again watched it collect pollen and take off, flying the same route as its sister.

"OK," said the professor. "Let me show you a few things that might help."

The path came out of the woods. At the edge of the clearing ahead was a wooden structure, looking much like a small road sign—although there were no roads anywhere near them, not even the sound of cars. Two scruffy graduate students stood by it, both with clipboards. Between them was a small video camera on a tripod, aimed directly at the board. As they got closer, Pete thought the board appeared to be moving.

Then he realized it was covered in thousands of bees.

"This is called a swarm board," said the professor. "A swarm is group of bees that has left its hive. The swarm has but one job: to find a new location for a hive. And it's a life-or-death decision." Bees came and went from the swarm, a cloud of them swirling around the buzzing mass. Pete had always pictured beekeepers draped in white, protective clothing, with pith helmets and protective face masks. But everyone present other than him seemed unbothered by the tens of thousands of stinging insects that undulated in a mass in front of them. Everyone was dressed like the professor, shorts and T-shirts, not even gloves to protect them.

"Are they looking for a new home right now?" asked Pete. "They don't look like they're doing anything."

The professor nodded. "The swarm is made up of about ten thousand worker bees. Of that, the oldest, most experienced bees—about three hundred—become scouts. They go out, look for suitable locations, and come back and communicate the location to the swarm." Pete wanted to get a better look at the swarm but didn't want to stick his face any closer.

"With the waggle dance?"

"Exactly," said the professor. "But then they collectively decide, over a day or so, what the best location is."

"And they get it right?"

"Always," said the professor.

"What makes one location better than another?"

The professor nudged one of the grad students, who was staring into space. "Will, you tell him."

"Height," answered Will. "They want to be high off the ground so animals can't get into it. Ideally, they want a small entrance, also to keep predators away. And volume. The bigger the better."

"Good!" said the professor, slapping him on the back. The professor was obviously brilliant, Pete knew from his credentials. But he also clearly enjoyed working with young people.

Suddenly a bee stung Pete on his forearm.

"Ouch!" he said, sweeping the dead bee away. It fell to the ground. The pain spread through his arm as he looked down at the small black stinger that still protruded from his skin. He plucked it out and looked at the painful red spot that the bee had given its life for.

The professor smiled. "OK, now you're really one of us!"

"You guys get stung too?"

"All the time," said Will. "We're just used to it."

Another bee landed on Pete's arm. He stayed perfectly still until it flew away.

"Feel like moving somewhere else?" said the professor.

"Sure," said Pete.

"Let's go look at their potential homes."

They walked back into the woods down another path, Pete occasionally rubbing his arm where he'd been stung. When they came into a clearing, Pete saw another wooden structure, this time a box. A lone grad student was sitting in a chair beside it, sheltered from the sun by a large multicolored umbrella. She was in a beach chair, relaxed, her long legs crossed.

"We have four boxes set up like this all around the woods," said Healy. "They're all identical, except for size. One is forty liters, the others are fifteen."

"This one?" said Pete, pointing.

"This one is not the forty-liter dream home," said Healy. "This one is the small fixer-upper."

"Do all the scouts look at all the sites?"

"No," said Healy, "and this is what's fascinating. The same scouts will visit this site over and over, bring that information back to the swarm. But in their communications, which are always truthful, the swarm will choose the right site."

"How do you know which scouts go to which site?" said Pete.

"I'll show you!" said Healy, and they marched forward.

The potential home was a small wooden box inside a three-sided shelter. But Pete couldn't tear his eyes away from the young woman in the beach chair.

"Pamela!" said Healy. "My star pupil."

She rolled her eyes at the praise.

"Tell our guest what you are doing. . . ."

"Watching and waiting . . ." she said, making a dramatic flourish with her hand. She then leaned back in the chair, folded her arms, and waited for Pete to react. She was blond, and tall—he could tell, even with her sitting down, by the length of her tanned, athletic legs. She had piercing blue eyes that she trained on Pete without mercy. He could tell that she was used to paralyzing guys like him with a glance, enjoyed the sport of it. The professor, an experienced observer of all things living, recognized what was going on and was amused.

Suddenly, she leaned forward. A bee had landed on the sill of the box, in front of the small hole that was the entrance. As it wandered inside, Pamela placed a small net in front of the opening.

When the bee came out, it was trapped. She pulled it away and gripped the bee by its wings. With her free hand she took a tiny paint brush, the kind you might use on a model airplane, and painted a tiny yellow dot on the back of the bee. She released the bee, and it flew away. The entire operation had taken extraordinary delicacy.

"That's how we know, back at the swarm, which bees come from which box. Each has a different color."

Pete felt pressure to say something, anything, to look intelligent, as Pamela leaned over to catch another scout bee that was leaving the hive.

"Doesn't that bother them?" he said. "Getting held and painted?"

"No," she said brightly, looking up at him and waiting for the bee to enter the net. "They don't even know they've been caught."

CHAPTER SEVENTEEN

Quality versus quantity is an ancient military debate. Is it better to have a few expensive weapons systems with exquisite capabilities, or vast quantities of less capable systems that can be thrown at the enemy en masse? Overwhelmingly, the history of combat teaches that quantity almost always wins over quality. Put three noisy, slow submarines against a quiet, modern submarine, and the slow submarines will probably win. Raise the ratio to 5:1, and the modern sub is doomed. It might shoot the first enemy, maybe even the second, but in doing so it will reveal its position and deplete its torpedoes. Similar logic can be applied to tanks, planes, and even platoons of infantrymen. This idea was first quantified in World War I by British military theorist Frederick Lanchester, who created Lanchester's law: all things being equal, a twofold increase in combat units will result in a fourfold increase in combat power.

World War II proved the truth of Lanchester's law again and again. The Germans produced better planes and tanks than the Allies. The Panzer and the Stuka were superior to anything the Allies could put together, especially early in the war. But the Allies' sheer quantity, driven primarily by American manufacturing might, overwhelmed any German advantage. By 1944, the Allies were producing a ship every day, and a plane, incredibly, every five minutes. The Russians, too, always believers in the power of numbers, outmanufactured their enemies to the point that any German technological advantage was negated. The spectacle of the Soviet May Day parade was an annual manifestation of this philosophy, endless columns of men and munitions. Stalin summed it up memorably with his quote: "Quantity has a quality of its own."

After World War II, however, the United States backed away from this proven philosophy. Unable to produce either vast quantities of arms or massive standing armies, due to both political and budgetary limitations, the United States banked on its technological prowess. The result was fewer and fewer platforms of ever-increasing power. This was true across all branches, as the Pentagon procured ever-more-expensive tanks, submarines, and airplanes. In a vicious cycle, as the cost of each platform went up, the number of them procured went down. Norman Augustine, former under secretary of the Army, theorized only partially tongue-in-cheek that by 2054, at the historic rate of increase, the entire US defense budget would be used to procure a single airplane. He suggested that it be used three and a half days a week each by the Navy and the Air Force, with the Marine Corps getting it once every leap year.

Study after study, and war game after war game, showed the preeminence of quantity over quality. A 2009 RAND study about an air war with China over the Strait of Taiwan speculated that the newest US plane, the F-22, was twenty-seven times more capable than the Chinese plane. The study further assumed that the F-22's missiles, eight per plane, would be 100 percent effective, every one of them finding and destroying a Chinese plane. No matter. In the study, the Chinese launched eight hundred sorties of their vastly inferior jets on the first day and won the battle easily. But still the United States went on buying its incredibly complex, incredibly expensive, and incredibly scarce weapons platforms while their enemies built weapons that were more crude, but infinitely more deadly because of their sheer numbers.

The advent of drones and the escalation of the Typhon threat forced the United States and her allies to reconsider. Unmanned craft could allow the United States to leverage huge quantities of munitions without putting millions of men in uniform. American manufacturing once again asserted itself, manufacturing thousands upon thousands of simple, low-cost drones. No single system in the drones was revolutionary; it was all tested and relatively low-cost technology. Each flew with relatively few sensors, a single bomb, and an elegantly reliable power plant. A single drone was not a formidable opponent; it was never designed to be. But hundreds of drones were terrifying. A swarm of thousands was unstoppable.

Teaching the drones the language of the bees proved the final piece of the puzzle. While it was by no means easy, Pete could see from the outset that it would work. He soon recruited many of the world's greatest apiculture experts, although not Professor Healy himself, who seemed immune to the Alliance's generous offers of support. Pamela, too, stayed at Cornell, but Pete saw her often when he visited the campus to pursue the mysteries of the bees' language.

Soon they had converted the entire language of the bees into a grammar, and that into logic that they could program into the drones. It was an extraordinarily rich language, Pete found, and one that suited their purposes perfectly. Like the bees, his drones were all identical; they shared a complete unity of purpose, and they were making life-or-death decisions. They soon taught the drones to communicate with each other clearly, without radio signals of any kind, just with the motion of their flight. Where the bees sought sources of pollen and debated new sites for their hive, the drones sought targets, and prioritized the biggest and best of them before swarming upon them and killing them.

Pete first trained two drones to talk to each other at the Atlantic Test Ranges, one drone finding another so they could coordinate an attack on a target being towed by a Navy destroyer. Two months later, a swarm of twenty drones performed flawlessly at the Atlantic Test Ranges, taking down three remote-controlled ships and penetrating a cloud of countermeasures.

In parallel with the test flights, Pete scouted locations for the Pacific drone station. The ideal spot would be located centrally, would have at least three hundred days of sunshine a year, and would be isolated, so that no one would become curious as they constructed the airfield. It seemed like fate when he found Eris Island, an obscure medical research station that was already part of the federal inventory.

Pete suddenly found himself speaking to groups of Navy admirals. Seabees would land on Eris and construct his airfield. The second group focused on hurriedly transforming the entire Pacific fleet into a submerged force. The submarine construction program accelerated, and plans were made to route surface ships to the other side of the world. If Pete's drones worked as he promised they would, submarines would soon be the only ship that could safely cross the sea.

Pete Hamlin walked through the rows of drones at Eris Island. He took a deep breath and contemplated the culmination of all his work: years of solitary research, followed by his modest research program, followed by the frenzy that came with the war and the Alliance's pressing needs. Just one year had passed since he'd discovered the language of the bees at Cornell, the final piece of the puzzle that made the whole system work. Since then, his drones had behaved like bees in ways beyond their language. Like a swarm of bees, the drones had found the ideal home, landed their scouts, and multiplied prodigiously.

Pete admired the perfect, parallel rows of drones as he walked between them, but he knew that order would soon be gone. Randomness was an important component of their every algorithm, in the air and on the landing field where they would refuel, soaking up the island's dependable sun, and rearm by ingesting bombs from the magazines that surrounded them. Randomness made them harder to track, harder to shoot, harder to predict. It was what military planners called a "force multiplier." If the enemy didn't know precisely where each drone would be, they would have to plan for them to be in multiple places at multiple times, magnifying the drones' effectiveness. Soon they would be scattered randomly across the airfield and in the sky, in a pattern that was never a pattern—impossible to predict, shoot down, or counteract.

The drones had proved themselves in test flights of growing size and complexity, but now they would take to the air en masse, a live weapons system. It gave Pete pause to think about it like that—if everything worked, these drones before him would soon take human lives. He hoped that in short order they would become a deterrent, a force that would keep the enemy at bay. But before that, if he was to be successful, they would inevitably have to sink ships and kill people.

A control room full of people, unseen behind the tinted glass of the control tower, would witness the launch in person. Beyond Pete's gaze, in the sea that surrounded Eris Island, six Alliance submarines waited somewhere, submerged, also to observe, and to keep the enemy at bay. If one believed recent intelligence reports, an enemy submarine was lurking out there, too—watching, waiting. While the Navy brass fretted, Pete hoped that was true, relishing the thought of a Typhon commander trying to describe in a terse message what he was seeing. But as Pete walked among the drones on the eve of their mass launch, he worried that one variable he'd failed to account for would defeat them like the enemy never could.

Seagull shit.

As the first squadron of one thousand drones had arrived on the island, so had a relentless flock of gulls. No one knew for sure what brought them, but it was probably a result of the increased human activity at the island, and the inevitable stream of refuse that the gulls fed on. The birds found a hospitable home on the island, and as their numbers grew, they began to defecate prodigiously all over Pete's armada of drones. The white droppings showed up dramatically on the drones' black wings, and every day the coverage grew, far faster than the cleaning crews could keep up with. It mixed with the white dust of the island and turned into a kind of paste that dried like cement. It demanded scraping, but scraping could harm the composite material that made the drones. So instead crews went from drone to drone with large, damp sponges and tried to wipe them off while the excrement was still soft and fresh. And while it did indeed look horrible, the thick splotches coating nearly every aircraft, this was much more than a cosmetic problem. The accumulated seagull residue was heavy, and could add as much as a pound to the forty-pound weight of the drones: a 2.5 percent increase in mass. The dull blobs detracted from the aerodynamics of the drones, further impacting their range and speed. Finally, and worst of all: the bodies of the drones were covered in solar cells, and Pete was seri-

ously worried that the opaque shit of the gulls might impair
their flight, perhaps even grounding them if they couldn't
charge their batteries in the bright sun.

Seagull deterrence wasn't something he had studied before,
but he found that there was a large body of work on the subject, the result of a few high-profile disasters of commercial
airlines ingesting seagulls in their engines during takeoff.
(There was also the oddity that worldwide, many airports were
located near garbage dumps, exacerbating the problem.) Following the advice of experts, they first tried scaring the birds
away with shotgun blasts and sirens, but the canny gulls soon
realized that the noises weren't lethal and returned to the island, spreading their waste all over the bodies of Hamlin's
highly engineered drones as they ignored the noise. Next, the
Alliance imported a family of spirited Brittany spaniels to
chase the birds off, but the dogs soon grew lazy in the island
heat. Throughout, Pete's engineering team took careful read-
ings of the solar cells and battery charges that confirmed that
the batteries were slow to charge and that the situation was
getting worse as gulls continued to manufacture excrement at
a rate that seemed nearly supernatural.

Pete had no doubt that once the drones took to the air, the
problem would fix itself. The drones were designed to stay aloft
for long periods of time, landing only when they needed to
refuel or rearm. Having the whole fleet on the ground at once
for the gulls to attack would never happen again, and hopefully
the continuous takeoffs and landings would frighten the birds
away. More important, the drone force would be largely
autonomous. Once the initial launch was complete, most of
the island's human residents would depart, taking with them
the bread crumbs and pizza crusts that the gulls found so
appetizing. Once the drones deployed, Pete was confident,
the bird problem would go away. But in the meantime they

had a thousand stationary drones on the tarmac, and their batteries needed to be charged, which meant their solar cells had to be clean. Which was why he was standing in the middle of the tarmac with a fake falcon in his hands.

"Are we ready?" asked Admiral Stewart.

Pete jumped, and smiled. "You startled me."

"I can tell," he said. Admiral Wesley Stewart had been Hamlin's opponent at first, an intense one at times, but he was fiercely intelligent and possessed a brilliant military mind. Hamlin was glad he was here for the launch. He realized that men like Stewart, even if they were beholden to an older style of warfare, would be vital in the coming fight. And to his credit, Stewart, once he had his orders to mobilize a submarine fleet such as the world had never seen, had fulfilled his mission with heroic speed and effectiveness.

He pointed at the bird in Pete's hands. "This sounded like something I would want to see in person." Gulls swooped and soared around them, leaving a small bubble of space around the two men but covering all the other drones that weren't immediately in reach. Pete held out the fake falcon so the admiral could take a look. Even up close it was a convincing fake, lovingly painted to look like a peregrine falcon, from its painted-on tail feathers to its menacing, sharp eyes and pointy beak.

"You really think this is going to work?"

"The brochure said it would," said Pete. The admiral laughed.

Pete turned to the tower and waved. The Robobird had arrived just the day before, so, mercifully, they'd had no time to develop a detailed procedure for what they were about to do. This would be an operation of pure trial and error. Pete was certain that, should the Robobird be successful, its success would be followed by many pages of Alliance doctrine and formalized procedures.

"Power it up?" asked the admiral. Pete nodded. The admiral pushed the green central button on the remote control he held, and its big wings began to flap. Pete was surprised at how much force it now took to hold it in place, the robot straining to take flight. Before he lost control of it completely, remembering what he'd read in the Robobird's scant instruction manual, he threw the fake bird up and away, with a motion like he used to throw paper airplanes as a child.

It immediately flew away, wings pumping, looking for all the world like a real falcon. Pete took the controller from the admiral.

The Robobird had been invented by an eccentric pair of brothers in the Netherlands. They'd originally designed it for farmers, who hated seagulls for the way they could pick a freshly planted field clean in hours. But the Robobird had quickly found a following in the aviation community, for reasons that Pete immediately understood.

"My goodness," said the admiral as the fake bird took flight.

"Pretty good replica, right?"

"I'd say so," said the admiral. "What is that thing made out of?"

"Glass fiber and nylon composite," said Pete.

"Like . . ."

"Yes," Pete said, smiling, "just like our birds."

When the bird reached altitude, Pete made it stop flapping. It banked and glided into the wind—just like a real falcon. Pete had spent his life studying machines that fly, but he'd never seen anything like this. He pulled it around into a tight loop, then with a couple of flaps propelled it upward again.

"Having fun?" said the admiral.

"Even if it doesn't scare the gulls, I'm keeping this thing," said Pete.

It was high above them now. "Let's see if can scare a seagull." Pete turned the bird into a dive and had it fly straight down toward a pack of loitering gulls.

"Here we go!" said the admiral.

The Robobird dived sharply with its convincing fake wings tucked behind it. It dropped right over the center of the airfield and then pulled up.

Fifty seagulls scattered instantly, in a squawking panic.

They landed a few dozen feet away, on another column of Pete's grounded drones, but he had the Robobird follow them; this time they flew away with even greater urgency, sensing they were being pursued. They in turn alerted every bird they passed, until the skies were filled with noisy, panicked gulls.

Some peeled off from the group and tried to return, but Pete turned the Robobird and chased them back into the fleeing group. Pete had, in ten minutes, mastered the operation of the Robobird.

Within thirty minutes, there wasn't a single seagull on the tarmac.

"I think that thing works!" said the admiral.

"And," said Pete, chasing off a small pod of birds, "it's a hell of a lot of fun."

"My turn," said the admiral, reaching for the controller.

"Take it," said Pete, hating to give it up but eager to proceed. "I'll get a crew down here to wash these drones."

The next morning at dawn he walked the tarmac once again, among the orderly rows of now pristine drones. Some of them were still damp from the efforts of the crew that had spent all night washing their black, composite skin, and they gleamed in the early sun. They seemed to throb with potential energy as they gathered up sunlight and stored it deep in their batteries. He stopped and put his hand on one of them. It was low enough that he had to kneel. Just five feet and six inches long, and almost exactly twice as wide. The long, swept wings made it look like a glider, which, in fact, it was designed to be whenever possible to conserve energy. But a small, rear-mounted propeller provided the real thrust, the killing speed. On a bright day, with no targets to pursue, it would actually gain energy in the sky, storing more power from the solar cells that covered its wings than it burned by turning the propeller. The entire drone weighed just forty pounds, and carried a single bomb that weighed ten. It could soar as high as twenty thousand feet, and fly as fast as 80 knots. In a dive, it could go even faster. Its composite material was at once featherlight and incredibly strong; it felt warm against the palm of his hand, almost alive.

That composite had been one of the biggest engineering challenges they had handled in the design phase, but even that didn't take them long. Making a material lighter and stronger: it was the kind of challenge that engineers lived for, especially when they had the benefit of attacking it with a virtually unlimited budget. Once the drones had learned the language of the bees, those engineers had to teach them every contingency, from avoiding typhoons to bombing submarines to attacking targets by crashing into them, once its lone bomb had been dropped. It quickly became a philosophical exercise as much as an engineering challenge, with generals, politicians, and ethicists joining in. At this point in the program, because of his own vast workload, Pete had to cede some control, allowing a team of Alliance engineers to encode the final program. Soon enough they'd taught the drones how to fight, how to

kill, and how to survive. Underlying it all, they'd taught them
how to talk to each other.

He saw movement in the corner of his eye; the admiral
again approached.

"You looked lost in thought," he said.

"I was."

"You should take that as a good sign," said the admiral,
pointing upward. The Robobird was making a lazy circle in
the sky, on autopilot, keeping the terrified seagulls away. "An
auspicious start to the dawn of drone warfare."

Hamlin smiled at that. "Let's hope my drones work as well
as the Robobird."

"So . . . we're ready?" asked the admiral.

"I know the machines are ready," said Hamlin. "But are you
asking me something more philosophical?"

The admiral smiled. "I know you're not fond of philoso-
phizing."

"There's a war going on," said Hamlin. "And what we
do today will make the difference."

"Let's hope so," said the admiral. But Hamlin could hear the
doubt in his voice.

"I'll show you."

They walked side by side back through the rows of drones all
awaiting the signal from the tower to start their lives. The admiral looked comfortable in his khaki working uniform, all of
his numerous medals and awards removed, only his prized
gold dolphins, the mark of a submariner, still on his chest. Although twenty years older than Hamlin, he was fit, and Pete
had a hard time keeping up without breathing hard. *I've spent
too much time behind a desk*, he thought as they approached
the base of the tower.

The admiral started to reach for a keypad that would recognize his fingerprints and give them entry, but Pete stopped him.

"Here," he said, "I wanted you to see this."

He removed a red key from around his neck, and held it up for the admiral to see.

"A key?" he asked, smiling.

"You told me how much you liked them," said Pete. "I took it to heart." He moved a small, nearly hidden access plate by the keypad to reveal a keyhole.

"For forty years, we used keys on the Trident submarines," said the admiral, repeating a story he'd told Pete several times. "To control the missiles. Three different keys in three different hands. The system never failed."

"We've got a dozen other electronic security measures," said Hamlin. "All the latest in access control. But I thought if nothing else—it can't hurt. I even painted it red, like you said the keys were on the Tridents."

"Yes, the firing-unit keys. I appreciate that, Hamlin: an unexpected tribute to an old submariner."

"Old-fashioned but reliable," said Pete as a relay deep inside the blast-proof door turned, and the door swung open.

They entered a small, cylindrical elevator that took them up the short distance to the top of the tower. The tower, while the tallest structure on the island, was not all that high, because it was positioned so well on a natural rise that gave it a commanding view of the entire island. On one side of the tower was the tarmac, covered by buzzing drones. The rest of the island fell away from that, toward the far southern end where the old medical research station still resided. On the other side of the tower, the near side, a rocky outcropping dropped straight down to the sea. A crevice ran between them and that bluff, and was sometimes filled by the sea depending on the tides and the weather.

The elevator doors swept open, revealing a control room full of diligent workers. All possessed the same sense of earnestness, and the same barely contained eagerness. The room itself was a perfect hexagon, with broad windows on all six sides. With the tower's ventilation system allowing the island's warm, dry air inside, and the vague smell of new carpet in the air, it felt almost too luxurious to be a military facility. Pete knew that during the design phase, the admiral had insisted on hiding a rack of shotguns somewhere in the control room, but Pete was glad he couldn't see them and couldn't imagine a contingency that would require them. This was a new era of warfare, one that would depend on artificial intelligence and nylon fiber more than on cordite and lead. The admiral nodded at the small group of military personnel in the room who snapped to his attention as he entered. The rest of the team, civilians, nodded to acknowledge him and Hamlin before returning to their computer screens and their calculations. They had their companies' logos on the backs of their shirts so that the various teams could be identified easily: Boeing, General Electric, Westinghouse, IBM. Together again, the military and America's industrial giants, fighting a war.

The view was magnificent. They could see for miles in all directions, even straight above them, since much of the tower's ceiling had been made of thick, blast-proof glass. Eris had begun life decades before as an obscure medical research station, little known by anyone outside the community of people who studied highly infectious diseases. A set of small medical laboratories still operated on the other side of the island—the only buildings on the island that looked weathered at all, every other structure thrown up hastily, with no expense spared, in the last twelve months. Pete had chosen Eris for some of the same reasons the surgeon general had chosen it fifty years before—it was nearly perfectly isolated, a small volcanic rock hundreds of miles from anything. In addition, it was also a true desert island, which made it an ideal candidate for Hamlin's program: nearly 365 days a year of perfect, dry weather. Even with all the climate change they had witnessed in the past years, the rising oceans and the killing storms, Eris remained an enclave of temperate weather, which was key for Pete's mission and the performance of his machines.

Not counting that odd report of an enemy submarine snooping in the area, their best intelligence told them that Typhon had thus far failed to recognize what they were up to. Admiral Stewart had been able to put his amphibious landing craft on the beach unopposed and begin the construction project that was about to culminate. Far over the horizon, a ring of Alliance ships surrounded them, out of sight, keeping the adversary at bay while they finished their work. Inside that perimeter, but also unseen, were those six nuclear submarines that lurked beneath the waves, a last line of defense and witness to Pete's achievement. If the drones worked as designed, only submarines would be able to approach closely enough to observe.

Hamlin took three steps forward, to the front of the tower, to get a better look at the drones. The sight still took his breath away.

Below them, as far as they could see, were rows of the military drones that he had designed. The glint of the solar panels on their wings made them look vaguely like dragonflies, their wings shimmering in the sun as they absorbed power.

Hamlin was pleased to hear the admiral also react, despite himself, to the breathtaking sight.

After he'd had a chance to gather himself, the admiral started asking questions.

"How many?" asked the admiral.

"One thousand," said Pete. "Many more on the way—we'll have more room after the first wave launches. We think no more than twenty percent will ever need to be on the ground here at one time; that means we could easily launch twelve thousand, just from Eris."

"Each just has a single missile?"

"Not a missile," said Hamlin. "A bomb—a rather simple bomb, in fact. But across the island are autoloading magazines. Each drone can come back, arm itself, and return to the fight, as often as necessary. Completely without human intervention."

"What if they can't rearm?"

"If the drone senses that it can't fly far enough to rearm, it will turn itself into a kamikaze . . . it just crashes itself into the target. The planners call that a 'kinetic weapon,' but it's basically just a forty-pound piece of metal falling from the sky. Enough to destroy a lightly armored vehicle or structure."

"And they're solar powered?"

"One hundred percent. If they start to lose power, they just need to find a place to touch down and charge their batteries for a while . . . like all these are doing." He waved his hand over the armada of lazily buzzing drones.

"How long can they operate?"

Hamlin shrugged. "We're not sure. We've had one in the air, circling Detroit, for eighteen months now, and it shows no sign of wearing out. And they can land and recharge—rest, so to speak. The design life is five years but we're pretty sure they can last longer than that."

"And they use infrared?"

"Multispectral targeting. Infrared and visible imager. That's in the nose. Along the underside of the wings are the MAD units."

"And they'll target anything that moves?"

Hamlin heard the hint of accusation in his voice. "Yes— for all the engineering in them, they're a 'dumb' weapon, designed to destroy anything that moves. Think of them like land mines. We avoid them until their work is done."

"And the minefield?"

Pete held out his arms. "The entire ocean. From here to one hundred miles from the American shore. Anything that shows itself will be a target."

"And that's where I come in," said the admiral.

"Correct," said Hamlin. "Submarines will be safe from the drones, as long as they stay submerged. That may be the only place. Even at periscope depth, the drones can find them."

"Using MAD?"

"That's right," said Pete. "At shallow depths, the drones will 'see' their magnetic signature."

"What about here? What's to stop them from bombing us?"

"A safe zone. Part of the reason the area is so heavily guarded by your fleet. This is where the drones come to rearm, and recharge if necessary. For this tiny island, and a five-mile radius around it, the drones won't attack. It's the one safety that's hardwired into them. Although we can adjust that distance, as you'll see."

"What's to stop the bad guys from just moving underwater as well?"

Hamlin shrugged. "We're hoping we're ahead of them on that; we know our submarines are more capable. Part of the gambit here was to get underwater faster and more completely. And the island itself is ringed by shoals; it would be nearly impossible to approach closely submerged. If they try to get close, they'll have to surface, and the drones will destroy them. Protection of the hive is the highest priority in their programming."

"The hive?"

An engineer in a lab coat approached them and spoke to Pete. "Sir, we're ready for the first wave."

Hamlin smiled and breathed deeply, excited and apprehensive at the same time. "Green lights across the board?"

"Yes, sir. All green for launch."

"No Alliance ships within twenty miles?"

"No, sir, no ships."

"No surface ships," corrected the admiral.

"OK," said Hamlin. "Arming the central computer."

Hamlin inserted his red key into a lock in the central computer and turned it. A row of lights above it came to life. He entered a passcode, and the lights turned green.

He exhaled deeply. "Launch the first wave."

The order was relayed, and everybody in the tower who wasn't monitoring a radar screen or a computer approached a window.

It started slowly. A few drones began buzzing and then slowly rose from the runway. They took off, not quite vertically but in tight spirals. Once in the sky, they began making lazy circles around the field. The tower was soon filled with the sound of their buzzing engines.

Once a few drones had taken to the air, the others followed. They orbited around each other in swooping circles, diving and swerving with an agility that a manned aircraft could never match. Gradually a cloud of them hovered above the island, with more on the ground. Their actions in the air reminded the admiral of the flocks of swallows he'd seen migrating as a child.

Suddenly an alarm buzzed, and a jolt of concern ran through the control room. Hamlin looked behind him to a row of consoles where operators busily studied their displays, then back out onto the airfield. "Individual malfunction," reported one of the operators.

"I can see it," said Hamlin, pointing out the window, something odd in the movement of one drone catching his eye.

"One of the drones is off program," said the operator behind him. "CPU is red."

"Still ascending," said Hamlin grimly.

Stewart didn't see it until it veered away from the lazy circling of its kin and headed right toward the tower.

Everyone in the tower involuntarily ducked as it buzzed overhead. It was close enough that the admiral could actually see the bomb that clung to its underbelly, like a mother bird with an egg. It was behind them suddenly, everyone turning like spectators at a tennis match to see what the rogue drone would do next.

"Bad processor," said the operator behind them.

"No shit," said Hamlin. "Is it following its self-destruct protocol?"

The operator looked at his console again. "Can't tell, sir."

"Goddammit," said Hamlin.

"Can you recall it?" said the admiral.

"We don't communicate with them like that. If we could disable them with a radio signal, so could the enemy. They're completely autonomous—they react to only two things: targets and other drones. It's supposed to self-destruct if it meets certain criteria. . . ."

The errant drone reached the shoreline, and then suddenly shot straight into the air. At about five hundred feet, it gracefully turned, and seemed to shut off power as it fell straight toward the ocean. It crashed with a surprisingly small splash.

"One drone down, sir," said the operator.

"Pull the telemetry," said Hamlin.

"Yes, sir."

Pete walked behind the operator and looked over his shoulder at the screen. He tapped a key and pulled up the data package for that specific drone, scanned the programming. He was disturbed at how much the programming had changed since he'd delegated that to others; there'd been a time when he could have spotted an anomaly instantly, he'd known the programming so well. Now, the fingerprints of a dozen others were all over it, making it opaque.

"Send me the entire package," Pete said, not knowing when he would have a chance to analyze it in the depth required.

He looked at the admiral and shrugged. "That's why they call this a test," he said. "And that's why we're building so many. We have a built-in failure rate of about one percent."

Some of the still-airborne drones flew over to the splash zone of the errant drone and swooped low, as if to investigate their fallen comrade.

"Are they . . . curious?" said the admiral.

Hamlin laughed. "No—when it crashed, the other drones registered the object with their own sensors; now they're seeking it out."

"To kill it?"

"They might, if it wasn't inside the five-mile safe zone of the island. Now they're just checking it out."

One of the drones that swooped closest to the water took off, flew back toward them and the island. It soared straight away from them in an odd zigzagging pattern, then returned to its original position in a figure eight maneuver. Above the others, it tipped its wings and dipped dramatically.

"What's it doing?"

"Telling the other drones what it saw—that's why none of them are following. It's telling them there's no target to pursue."

"With those movements?"

"Yes. There's no radio communication between the drones, which means there's nothing for the enemy to intercept, nothing to jam. We emulated the ways honeybees communicate, the 'waggle dance' they do to communicate locations of nectar to each other with really remarkable precision. Bees use the bearing of the sun as a reference angle. We use true north. The drones 'waggle' on an angle from straight vertical; the magnitude of that angle indicates how far from true north the target is."

"And the length of the waggle indicates the distance?"

"Almost," said Pete. "It actually indicates the amount of energy needed to get to the target, so it takes into account headwinds, the strength of the sunlight, all those factors. So each drone can calculate whether or not it can make it, given the state of its energy reserves."

"Fascinating," said the admiral.

A petty officer entered the control tower. "Sir, two hundred drones are now in the air, ready to commence the test."

"Very well," said Hamlin. "Reducing the safety radius to one mile," he said.

Warning lights came alive inside the control room. Pete once again used his key to complete the procedure.

"We're temporarily reducing the safety radius for this test," said Hamlin.

"I thought you said there was no communicating with the drones?"

"This is the one exception: the safety radius signal. But the drones can tell, by distance and bearing, that the signal has to emanate from this island. From a transponder at the very top of this tower, actually. It would be impossible for the enemy to jam, or duplicate, without actually sitting in this tower." He turned a small knob, and a bright green circle on his display shrunk inward.

"Release the target," said Hamlin, excitement in his voice.

"Aye, sir," said a petty officer at the corner of the room, who spoke into a microphone.

Outside, a small cutter suddenly sped directly away from the island. It startled the admiral; it looked for all the world like someone was trying desperately to escape Eris Island. But no one reacted inside the tower, and he quickly discerned that it was part of the test. It was a beautiful white cutter, seemingly brand new. He guessed it was thirty-six feet long, a rigid-hull inflatable powered by water jets. Broad black crosses had been painted on its sides and deck, and the admiral knew these were markings to aid telemetry and observation; he'd seen similar markings on missiles during ICBM test shots years before. Huge rooster tails flew out behind the cutter; he estimated it was going at least 30 knots. While he knew suddenly it was a target, as a lifelong mariner, he found himself pulling for the boat.

Hamlin had binoculars to his eyes but was smiling broadly. "Don't worry," he said. "It's unmanned."

"Drones hunting drones," said the admiral. No one reacted.

"Target is one hundred yards from shore," said a petty officer at a radar screen.

"Very well," said Hamlin.

Already the drones in the sky were reacting. They veered off, the whining of their engines increasing in pitch and volume. It wasn't the roar of a military jet but the buzzing of a stinging insect. In seconds, six of them were zooming down the wake of the cutter, accelerating urgently. Soon they were directly over it, about twenty feet above its deck, in a V formation.

"Two hundred yards," said the petty officer, counting down the distance as the ship raced away. "Fourteen hundred yards . . . sixteen . . . eighteen . . ."

With perfect timing, at the exact moment the petty officer would have said "two thousand yards," the lead drone dropped its bomb. It exploded with a flash, and the crack of high explosive reached the tower a millisecond later. The front drone immediately veered upward, and the two behind it dropped their payloads on the ship even as it was exploding into pieces and sinking. The final drones dropped their bombs on what tiny pieces of floating wreckage still remained. It was over in seconds.

The drones, even faster and more nimble now without the weight of their bombs, immediately flew back toward the tower, to the cloud of drones that whined above them. The lead drone went through an elaborate dance: swoops, twitches, and rolls. The swarm of drones beneath it reacted to whatever news it was communicating, the urgency of the engines and their movements increasing in what, to the admiral, looked for all the world like a celebration. Their shadows crisscrossed the carpeted floor of the control tower as they flew overhead.

A few of the drones peeled off from the cloud and went back to the site of the explosion, but nothing remained, not a single shard of wreckage. The attacking drones, their message communicated, flew to an unseen part of the island. *To reload,* the admiral realized.

Hamlin put the binoculars down, and looked at the admiral with an ecstatic smile on his face.

"You've just seen the future of warfare," said Hamlin, pointing straight up to the swarm of drones above them.

"Maybe so," said the admiral, pointing out to sea. "But in the meantime, you've driven us all underwater."

Eight miles away, an enemy submarine watched. Commander Jennifer Carlson was on the periscope.

"Something happening?" asked Banach, her second-in-command. He didn't yet have her patience—a hunter's patience.

"Yes," she said. "Something."

"Shall we get closer?" asked Banach.

She wanted to, badly. She could barely see the island from this distance, even with the scope in high power and raised as high as she dared. The electronic sensors in her boat were so crude as to be almost useless. But she needed to see what was going on. The island was ringed by jagged shoals, but she'd studied the charts, thought there were breaks she might slip through at periscope depth, get her right up to the beach. From there, she could snap some pictures, take some video, chart the locations of underground cables. It was sorely tempting. All submariners were born snoops. Next to shooting at things, it was the most fun you could have on a submarine, looking through the keyhole and seeing things you weren't supposed to see.

And there was definitely something forbidden there, no matter how many times her clueless commanders dismissed her concerns. According to the few charts they had of it, the island was a medical research station, and had been for decades. They even had a few ancient satellite photos of it, showing two small buildings at the south end with animal pens and a small dock flying the yellow flag for quarantine. Old italicized warnings on the chart told vessels to stay away because of the presence of contagious diseases. While it seemed like dated information, this, more than the shoals, worried Carlson. Like Banach, she'd grown up in an area that was regularly ravaged by disease, and had an almost superstitious fear of infections and viruses. Her crew, who once a week cleaned everything to a sanitized gleam, would attest to it. She preferred targets she could shoot torpedoes at. Was the Alliance creating something smaller and more sinister?

They were definitely up to something. Farther out, past the

horizon, were dozens of enemy surface ships, standing guard in a twenty-mile ring. But none of them dared come as close as she had. She wasn't remotely worried about being found out here. No one, not even her own command, expected her to operate this far out to sea, sailing the deep blue water. To them, submarines were not strategic assets; they were designed to patrol coastal waters and pluck off an occasional container ship, or deploy a landing party of saboteurs to blow up railroad bridges and other quaint targets. The Alliance submarines carried ballistic missiles; she carried a platoon of marines with rifles and hand grenades.

"Here," she said, handing off the scope to Banach. "Tell me what you see."

He turned his hat backward and stooped over, adjusted the eyepiece, and looked toward the island. He stared a bit, and then turned slowly, a complete circle, looking around them.

"No surface contacts," he said.

"They are keeping their distance," said Carlson.

He was pointed back at the island now, his eyes refreshed. "It looks like . . ."

"What?"

"Something is flying. . . ."

She took the scope back and stared on the same bearing. She now saw it, too.

"You have good eyes, Lieutenant Banach," she said.

It looked almost like a flock of birds, but she could see the sun glint on parts of them. They were too big to be birds, if they could see them at this distance, but flew with too much agility to be airplanes, swirling and looping into the air.

"Some kind of airplane?" she said.

"Surveillance craft maybe? Cruise missiles?"

"Too many of them," she said. She tilted the right handle of the scope toward her, tilting the lens to look upward. She saw nothing but clear blue sky.

When she turned the scope back down to the waterline, she was startled to see, directly in front of them, two plumes of water erupting from the sea, a deep V of spray and foam: a fast surface ship. Heading right for them.

"Surface contact!" she said. "Arm tube one, prepare to fire!" She pushed the button on the scope, marking the bearing and sending it to fire control. She was down to five torpedoes, and badly wanted to save them for something big—a carrier or, better yet, another submarine. But this little shit was heading right for them, and she might not have a choice. How had they found her? They might have sensors mounted on the seabed, she thought, or perhaps their silhouette, just a few feet beneath the surface of the clear, tropical water, had been spotted by surveillance in the air, a plane or even a satellite. The white boat was hurtling toward them, going at least 30 knots.

"Solution is ready!" said Banach. "Ready to fire!"

She watched the boat approach, still debating whether or not to fire. It was small, she noted, with a shallow draft, shallow enough to pass right over the shoals. "Prepare to fire on this bearing . . ." she said.

Suddenly, she noticed a formation of those small, odd planes flying directly behind the craft. Pursuing it.

"Wait!" she said. She looked down to confirm that they were recording the scene through the scope, for later study.

The planes were closer now, and they were like none she'd ever seen. They were small, and there was something odd about them. She realized they had no windows.

"Captain . . ."

At that moment, following some unseen cue, the planes attacked the speeding boat. The ship disappeared in a series of bright, small flashes. None of it stayed afloat long enough to burn. After a short delay, she felt the concussions of the explosions reach the hull through the water, a rapid series of dull thumps.

The planes pulled up, maneuvered excitedly, and returned to the island.

"Captain, what did you see?"

She took her eye away from the scope and looked at Banach. "I'm . . . not sure."

They stayed at periscope depth for six hours after that, Banach and Carlson taking turns on the scope. Carlson watched the sun go down, and a few lights began to twinkle on the Alliance's odd little island.

"Tea, Captain?" Banach had appeared at her side. She handed over the scope so she could have a drink. It was strong and heavily sweetened, like she preferred.

"Thank you," she said. "You might make commander after all."

"You flatter me, Captain." He adjusted the scope, took a quick swing around, made sure nobody was sneaking up on them. "Have you figured it all out yet? We're all waiting for you to tell us what is happening."

"You'll have to keep waiting," she said. "I have no bloody idea."

"Oxygen has drifted down to sixteen percent," he said. "Shall we ventilate, Captain? As long as we're up here?"

She knew it was a good idea. Her oxygen generators were overtaxed, and fresh air was good for morale. It was dark, they were quiet, and nobody seemed to know they were out there. They could raise the snorkel mast and let the ship take a deep breath of the warm, tropical air that surrounded them. But like she told Banach: she didn't know what was going on. And she remembered those satellite pictures of the island, with its animal pens and medical scientists. Maybe breeding murderous germs and bacteria . . .

"No," she said. "Not this time."

CHAPTER EIGHTEEN

After defeating the seagulls, the commissioning of the drone station at Eris Island was a triumph. The success rate was higher than their most optimistic projections, the failure rate negligible. In the first few weeks, the drones took a deadly toll on enemy shipping, both military and civilian. Silent, grainy video from the drones was shown on breathless newscasts and widely viewed Internet clips. The clips were always roughly the same. An open, featureless ocean. A ship comes suddenly into view, far below. The ship would seem to grow rapidly as the drone swooped down, details becoming visible, the outlines of the cargo containers or the flash, rarely, of defensive gunfire. A single bomb would fall and explode with a silent white burst, momentarily drowning out all the visuals with the washed-out lightning of its high explosives. Then other drones would come into view, and the screen would become awash in white as they dropped their explosives in force. When the explosions dimmed and an image returned, what had been a ship was transformed into an oil slick and jagged wreckage, and drones were everywhere, drawn to the kill.

Enemy countermeasures were even less effective than Pete had predicted. Automated gunfire from bow-mounted guns would throw clouds of twenty-millimeter shells into the sky. Clouds of chaff would surround ships under attack, distracting the drones and degrading their sensors. But drones could overcome every countermeasure with sheer quantity. Whatever the enemy could come up with that could defeat ten drones couldn't defeat twenty. If it could defeat twenty drones, it couldn't defeat a swirling, relentless swarm of fifty. Enemy tactics evolved quickly from attacking to impairing to evading, until finally, inevitably, submerging.

Within weeks, the only military ships in the ocean were submarines, carefully staying hidden beneath the waves. Civilian shipping ground to a halt. A month after the initial launch, the second wave of a thousand drones flew all the way from Detroit to Eris on their own, at a lazy pace dictated by the shining sun and the thermoclines they could soar upon. Unburdened with bombs, they were light and efficient as they made their way west. Cities along the route had viewing parties to watch on rooftops and in football stadiums, and they cheered as the stream of drones passed overhead while high school marching bands and country musicians played patriotic songs. Watching the drones fly by made Allied victory seem inevitable.

With the station at Eris working so well, Pete immediately began planning the drone station in the Atlantic; several suitable locations had already been scouted. He would fly there at once to begin the work. But first, he had to stop on the mainland for a piece of pressing business.

His wedding.

By then they'd known each other for a year, although you could hardly say they'd dated. Pete had been consumed by the drone project, seeing Pamela mostly from the screen during chat sessions on his tablet computer. She'd broken up with him briefly as a result. That's when he begged her to meet him in Hawaii. At the head of the Kealia Trail, he'd proposed to her, not at all sure what her answer would be.

While neither wanted a huge ceremony, Pete kept delaying the wedding anyway, overcome by obligations as Eris neared completion. He felt a twinge of guilt about it. But Pete was spending his days with military men, including many naval officers and chiefs who'd missed every milestone of family life. Missing a child's birth was so common among the submariners he knew that it barely merited comment. So this made Pete feel better, along with the constant reassurances from everyone he was around about how important his work was.

But by the time he left Eris Island, he was determined not to let Pamela down again. They had a small outdoor ceremony in Calabasas County, near San Diego. Pamela was a vision in a white dress she'd bought, with typical thrift, for four hundred dollars at a department store. At the time of their wedding, it had been two months since they'd seen each other. They stayed at a hotel near the submarine base that night, and Pete gave her a string of Mikimoto pearls that he'd bought at a Navy Exchange. She expressed shock, saying she'd never owned anything so nice or expensive. Pete put them on her, which gave him an inordinate amount of pleasure, fastening the clasp with shaky hands at the back of her neck.

She gave him a small present wrapped in silver paper. He opened it and revealed a Lucite block, with the ten stages of the honeybee's life forever trapped inside.

"I didn't know what to get you. . . ."

Pete turned it over, looking at every angle of the bees, watching the thick honey pour back and forth in its tiny vial.

"It's perfect," he said. "I love it."

———

They flew to Mexico for a two-week honeymoon. Pete had volunteered to handle all the planning, because it felt like he should do something. He planned the entire trip, and paid for it, with one trip to an Internet travel site. At the resort, they fell into an easy routine of waking up early to claim the best lounge chairs around the pool, and then eating breakfast and drinking coffee while watching the sun rise. They eavesdropped on the other honeymooners at the bars and napped together in the afternoons.

Three days into the honeymoon, they returned to their room from the pool, pleasantly drunk from an afternoon of margaritas and sunshine. An envelope had been slipped under their door. Pete watched Pamela cringe at the sight of it.

"It's probably nothing," he said.

"I'm actually shocked they left you alone for three days," she said.

It was a note from the Pacific Command. Pete had received an invitation to speak at Stanford University. Everyone knew he was on leave, but they wanted to make sure he was aware of what would be a great opportunity. It would the first stop of a victory tour, a chance to gloat in front of many of those who had condemned the program, and him. For just a moment, he considered declining because of his honeymoon, but in the end he didn't fight hard. It was too tempting to resist. There would be many people in the audience who had doubted him, and maybe doubted him still. He asked Pamela, told her he would be gone no more than forty-eight hours, and she, of course, gave her approval because his enthusiasm left her no choice. He boarded a military charter to Palo Alto and assured her that she'd barely notice his absence.

Pete had another motivation to return briefly to the project, one that he didn't reveal. He'd received a disturbing report about some of the drones flying far from their assigned patrol areas, and desperately wanted to investigate the claims. He'd received some of the programming transcripts already but was having a hard time penetrating the code, which had been heavily modified by the Alliance team charged with the final program. Pete was no programmer, but at times it seems like the code had been almost deliberately made complicated, to make it impossible for him to troubleshoot. He needed more data, but couldn't get the access he needed from his hotel room.

It was impossible, he knew, for the drones to malfunction that way, to function at all that far from their operating areas. But supposedly some activist on the coast of Oregon had filmed a drone. The government had quickly taken the video down, squashed the report, and detained the purveyors. Some of his more hawkish friends in the Pentagon promoted the idea that it was a Typhon drone, requiring an even greater investment in their drone program. Whatever it was, Pete wanted to find out more, and that was impossible with an unsecured Internet connection at an all-inclusive resort in Puerto Vallarta, Mexico.

The crowd at Stanford was made up of nerdy engineers and aggrieved college students, with significant overlap between the two groups. The moderator was the university president, who introduced Pete cordially but with a stern, disapproving undertone that Pete was pretty sure he had rehearsed in a mirror. Such a presentation would have been unthinkable even just a few months before, when his program was described in the same way people decades before had described Ronald Reagan's Strategic Defense Initiative, or "Star Wars": it was not only immoral, they said, it was impossible, a crushingly expensive, destabilizing overreach by militaristic fanatics. The threat of SDI had helped bring about the end of the Cold War, as the Soviets knew they couldn't keep up with American technology. Hamlin and his colleagues envisioned that the drones would have the same kind of transformative power.

Introduced to the crowd, which filled Memorial Auditorium, he let the polite applause die down before speaking.

"As long as weapons have flown into the sky," he began, "we have tried to remove human pilots from the process." He clicked a button on his remote, and an antique engraving of a hot air balloon appeared on the giant screen behind him. It stopped Hamlin for just a moment. He'd only reviewed these slides on the screen of tablet computer. Seeing the high-resolution image on a screen so many times larger was slightly breathtaking. He could see details he'd never noticed before in the engraving, the tiny soldiers pointing, the puff of smoke coming from the boiler that was generating hot air to give them flight.

"This was true even before airplanes. In 1849, Austria tried to bomb Vienna with unmanned hot air balloons. Some of these, incidentally, were ship-launched. On August 22, 1849, Austria launched about two hundred unmanned balloons. This, the first aerial drone attack, contributed to the end of the Venetian revolt."

He started clicking through slides, his pace reflecting the rapid advance of technology. "Development kept pace with every advance in aviation. Remote-control biplanes were tried in World War I, generally with disastrous results. Remote-control single-wing planes were tried in World War II, without much better luck. Joseph Kennedy, Jr., JFK's older brother, was actually killed in a test flight of this program. Our enemy, the Germans, went a different route in an attempt to bring

unmanned weapons to the skies: rocketry. Their success, and
the success of rocketry in general, stalled drone development
for many years."

He put a new photo up, his first in color: a cigar-shaped
missile with stubby wings and the word TOMAHAWK painted
on the side. "As technology improved, the dream of unmanned aerial weapons took a new turn: cruise missiles. But
these weren't drones; they were weapons in and of themselves.
They could be used once, and then they were destroyed
along with, hopefully, their target. They couldn't perform any
other missions, like surveillance, and they could never return
to base."

New slide: a small, fragile-looking plane painted in desert
camouflage. "Attitudes changed dramatically in 1982, when
Israel deployed these, the Scout UAVs, with great success in
their brief, triumphant war against Syria. While the Scout was
unarmed, its use as both a decoy and for reconnaissance
proved invaluable. For the first time, the drone had proved itself on the battlefield. The US military took notice."

"Technology raced ahead," said Pete. "Soon, it was obvious that drones could do nearly everything a manned plane
could do. It could do many things better, like stay in the air
for many hours and fly deep into harm's way without risking
an American pilot. The only thing holding back the wholesale
deployment of drones were doctrinal conflicts, and squeamishness about the use of unmanned aircraft. It took another historical event to eradicate this squeamishness."

He advanced the slides again, this time showing the World
Trade Center, smoke pouring from both towers. "On Septem-
ber 11, 2001, all that changed. We had a new kind of enemy, and
needed a new kind of weapon." New slide: a new drone, bigger than the previous, and for the first time, it was holding on to
a missile. It had odd, downward-facing tail fins, and a bulbous

nose. It was immediately recognizable as an unmanned craft: there were no windows.

"This is the Predator," said Pete. "On February 4, 2002, the Predator fired a Hellfire missile in the Paktia province of Afghanistan, near the city of Khost. It killed three men, the first time the CIA had ever used the Predator in a targeted strike. The modern era of drone warfare had begun."

He flashed through a few slides, showing the rapid evolution that took place after the success of the Predator and its successor, the Reaper. Drones got larger, more heavily armed, and, critically, more automated. "Drones were no longer just an acceptable alternative," he said. "They were a central part of military strategy and tactics." Finally he showed a photo of the airfield at Eris Island, a thousand drones arranged in the sun.

"Modern drones, unlike the Predator, are completely autonomous. They use a complex algorithm to assess targets, and the viability of an attack. Bigger targets are more valuable than smaller targets. Faster targets are more valuable than slower targets. If a drone can't kill a target by itself, it will gather help until a kill is assured. If it sees a viable target and can't rearm in time, it will actually crash itself into it."

He paused dramatically. "It is the Internet of weapons systems." It was a metaphor he'd carefully chosen for this Stanford audience, at the place where so much of the actual Internet had been born. "It's distributed all over the world. It's survivable. If any one piece fails, the other pieces fall into place, making the system impossible to destroy."

He showed a brief video clip of drones taking off and landing, ingesting new bombs in what even to Pete was the creepiest part of the entire cycle. That video stopped, replaced by an old black-and-white photo of a military ship. The long, flat deck gave it away as an aircraft carrier. Crosshairs marked the center of the ship: the photograph had been taken through a periscope.

"This," said Pete, "is the *Shinano*. She weighed sixty-five thousand tons, and on November 29, 1944, she was sunk by the United States submarine *Archerfish*. Until recently, she was the biggest ship ever sunk by the United States Navy."

The old imperial carrier disappeared and was replaced by modern video of a container ship—a giant one. She was cruising across a featureless ocean, unaware of what was about to happen to her, or that her death would be shown to a roomful of college students.

"This is the *Taymal*," he said. "A container ship of the type I am sure you recognize. This is an enemy ship, fully laden with enemy cargo bound for an enemy port. Seven hundred and forty thousand tons in all, with about thirteen thousand containers. One side effect of our campaign is that nearly every enemy merchant ship is full, because their fleet is so depleted."

This film, unlike the ubiquitous war porn they'd all gotten used to on the news channels, was not filmed from a nose camera onboard a drone. Rather it was filmed by a surveillance plane far above the battle that happened to be tracking the progress of the *Taymal* when the drones showed up, a fortunate accident. So, far more clearly than normal, they could see the full deadly formation of the drones as they arrived at a lower altitude, ready to attack. It was spectacular footage, and Hamlin had been saving it for an occasion like this.

Soon after the lead drone came into the frame, there were quick flashes of light as the first bombs dropped. A few of the neatly stacked containers were knocked askew. Another bomb exploded, and a container fell overboard with a large silent splash.

The ship made a panicked turn to starboard, but evasion was impossible. The drones that had dropped their payloads peeled off to reload and alert their brothers, and soon the sky was filled with drones, each dropping bombs with killer precision. A fire broke out in the forward part of the ship and spread rapidly aft as a fuel tank was penetrated.

Suddenly, men could be seen scurrying around the deck, trying to control the damage. Pete heard the audience gasp. Up to that point, it had just looked like machines versus machines. Even though he'd watched the clip a hundred times, Pete hadn't noticed the crewmen before, too small to be noticeable on his computer screen, but here, expanded on the auditorium's giant screen, they were impossible to ignore. Their movements were panicked, and at the same time, valiant. They were scurrying around trying to save the ship, themselves, each other. One man, in flames, fell into the sea.

The *Taymal* slowed and stopped, and began to sink. It listed severely to port, causing more of its containers to tumble overboard. The crewmen continued running around, fighting until the end, even though it must have, at that point, seemed as inevitable to them as it did to the audience in the thickly cushioned chairs of Memorial Auditorium. They were doomed.

Soon the *Taymal* was halfway under, then completely submerged. A dozen stubborn containers bobbed upon the sea, but these, too, were bombed by the drones until no trace of the ship, cargo, or crew remained.

The lights came back on as the video ended, and Pete looked out at the shocked crowd. He cleared his throat.

"Eight minutes," he said. When he'd practiced the speech, without noticing the tiny men onboard the *Taymal*, this phrase had sounded so much more triumphant. "Eight minutes was all it took to sink one of the world's largest cargo ships. Without risking a single American life."

He wrapped up without even hearing himself speak. The moderator asked if there were any questions.

A gray-haired man raised his hand and stood. A helper rushed over with a cordless microphone. "That operation was completely autonomous?" he asked. "Was it directed by anyone on the ground?"

"Completely autonomous," said Pete. He cleared his throat, getting back into his rhythm after the disturbing video. "Obviously many of the details of the program are classified, but that is one thing that we want our enemies to know. The drones will seek them out, and the drones will destroy them. It takes no intervention from a ground crew of any kind."

Next question: a young woman with a peace sign on her shirt. "Wasn't that a civilian ship?"

"There are no civilians in that part of the Pacific," he said. "Anyone at sea in that area is a combatant and will be treated accordingly."

An unhappy murmur went through the crowd, as Pete expected. A shaggy young man in a denim jacket stood up and shouted without waiting for the microphone.

"What about the drones attacking us, on American soil?" he yelled.

"Impossible," said Pete, his tone dismissive. "Numerous safety features are built into the drones to prevent just that."

"Bullshit!" said the man, causing a stir in the crowd. Pete didn't mind; he'd been protested before. Tie-dyed pacifists, of course, but also the standard anti-government crowd, who were convinced that the government drones would spy on their mountain cabins and take away their guns. The shouting protestor continued. "Drones are attacking mainland, civilian targets, and the reports are being suppressed by the Alliance!"

Pete shook his head with a wry smile. "Simply not true," he said. "If drones were hitting anybody on the mainland, I would be the first to know about it. And I haven't heard a thing."

"All of you!" said the man, turning to the crowd. "Look for the video now, before it gets taken down!" he said. He was holding his phone in the air as if the audience could see the images on it. Uniformed military guards suddenly began moving toward him. *Where did they come from?* Pete wondered.

"Look for it!" he yelled as he was led away. "In the last three days, drones have dropped bombs five times on the West Coast! We have video of a drone patrolling in Sequim, Washington. We have reports that people were killed just this morning in Puerto Vallarta, Mexico!"

Pete froze at the mention of the resort town where Pamela waited. The crowd erupted; shouts of approval countered by jeers. Most people in the room reached for their phones, some to film the guards dragging the man out of the auditorium, others to look for the video he had referenced.

Chaos reigned in the audience. Pete walked numbly backstage, where he was strangely alone, the crowd noise dissipating behind thick curtains. He pulled out his phone and searched for "Sequim drone" on the Internet. It was listed in a dozen places, but it had been taken down in every place he looked. Six thousand people had watched it on YouTube before it disappeared: *This video no longer available.*

He texted Pamela, and called her: no answer.

He called the resort's front desk: no answer.

Finally, he called his masters at the Alliance. He got through to an officer in the situation room, who after several terrifying minutes on hold, put him through to the tactical duty officer in the Alliance war room.

"Are you on a secure line?" asked the major.

"No," said Pete.

"Get somewhere where we can talk," he responded. Pete could hear the stress in his voice.

"I'm the OIC for the entire drone project," said Pete. "You have to tell me what's going on."

There was a long pause as the major thought it over.

"There appear to have been some catastrophic failures, among a small number of the birds."

"Fatalities?" said Pete, his voice catching.

"No," said the general, a slight note of hope in his voice. Pete felt relief flood his body until the duty officer finished his thought. "None on US soil."

Pete hung up the phone and walked out a side door, around to the front steps of the auditorium. A few of the protestors eyed him, but none confronted him directly, perhaps because of the dazed look on his face. He sat on the steps until his watchers from the Alliance found him and hustled him into a waiting car.

CHAPTER NINETEEN

They flew Pete to a drab Alliance office building near Atlanta, and for two days they debriefed him. Quickly, Pete could tell, they deemed him unreliable. The funny thing was, in the entire time, no one told him directly his wife was dead; no one said a word about it. They showed him photographs of the destroyed resort. They showed him a breakdown of all the people killed, listed by nationality. Pamela was on the list, just one name among many. They explained, in abstract, how the human remains would be disposed of and the cover story that they'd come up with: natural gas explosion. It was in their eyes, he could see it; they knew that his wife was among the dead. But it was as if everyone assumed that someone else had said the words to him, a legion of psychiatrists, engineers, and generals. No one offered a word of apology. Or asked him for contrition.

Another sure sign of his fall was the reduction in his access. He wanted to look at the drone programming, to see where it could have gone so wrong. There was no way a drone should have traveled that far, and that far inland. There had to be a glaring error somewhere in the program, and he was certain he could find it if they would just let him. But the Alliance suddenly isolated him from the drones, from the team, from any of the technology that he once knew so intimately. It was a new level of autonomy, Pete thought wryly. Now the drones operated without even the participation of their creator.

Suddenly idle, with more spare time than he'd had in years, Pete began looking for reports of other rogue drones. He had a solid Internet connection in the temporary office where they'd stashed him, and he could see the videos as they popped up. He watched them until they were suppressed, usually within minutes. A bomb dropped on a ferry near Seattle. The video showed screaming commuters in suits scrambling to climb the sides of the boat as it turned over. Another bomb fell on a cargo terminal in Los Angeles, setting it on fire. That clip was of unusually good quality, showing the lone drone swooping in gracefully, dropping its bomb, then peeling away. Most were on the West Coast, although Pete saw a reliable clip from as far inland as Reno, Nevada, where a drone dropped a bomb on a truck stop, igniting a spectacular fire as the fuel tanks exploded. The drone then recognized how far it was from Eris, and the impossibility of rearming, and went into self-destruct mode, flying directly into a semitruck that was trying desperately to drive away on Interstate 80.

Pete was shuffled in and out of a number of remote offices, always well away from the drone program. At first he thought he would be assigned to a place where he would be closely watched. But instead, the Alliance, in its bureaucratic wisdom, just gave him a series of meaningless assignments where he could do little harm while still remaining under their control.

All were within the Alliance's vast research apparatus. He worked on a team studying the effects of paint colors on a submarine crew's mental health: dark orange was best, red the worst. He worked briefly on a program that was evaluating the use of airships as surveillance platforms: their slow speeds and steady movements allowed for a kind of high resolution that wasn't possible from planes or satellites. After that, he was given orders to a research detachment in Frederick, Maryland. He scanned his orders at a hotel bar as he drank his third overpriced martini. Something to do with the flu.

The next morning, he walked the two blocks to his new office, hoping the cool air would mitigate his hangover. He checked the address twice when he arrived. The military leaders of a past era had sought to intimidate and impress with their structures, the Pentagon being the ultimate example: a city unto itself in a mythic, magical shape. The Alliance, Pete had learned, sought the opposite; they wanted to disguise and obscure the true scope of their power by distributing their vast resources across anonymous leased offices and buildings across the land. Like the drones, the Alliance sought security in redundancy, and vast, wide distribution. Such networks, Pete well knew, were almost impossible to kill. The building where Pete reported had just six stories, of which the Alliance occupied only the top floor. The ground floor contained a Subway sandwich shop and a dentist's office. One of the other tenants in the building was a financial advisor, whose darkened windows and security door looked far more secretive than the Alliance office where Pete found himself that morning, with its unlocked front door, unmanned reception desk, and new carpet smell.

Inside the suite, he found his way to office 16-E, where the door was locked. There was a keypad, but he had no code. He

rang a buzzer, and could hear movement inside. He could tell
the door was solid; he'd been behind enough serious security
doors to recognize one when he saw it: the heavy weight, the
precise balancing, the hidden hinges. He heard a click within
the door, and he pushed it open.

Inside were two men, looking up at him somewhat suspi-
ciously from their drab metal desks. They were at opposite
ends of the small office, as far apart as they could arrange:
Pete sensed instantly that the two men didn't like each other.
A large, tattered world map had been hung from the center
wall, a series of colored pins pressed into it. Above one man's
desk was a small flat-screen television, tuned to one of the
news channels that was favorable to the Alliance, with the
sound muted. The screen periodically seized and pixelated, as
if the cable connection was poor.

"You the new officer in charge?"

"I am," he said. "Pete Hamlin. Pleased to meet you. Is this
the whole team?"

The younger man stood and raised his hands dramatically.
"This is it. I'm Reggie Strack," he said, walking over with a
hand extended.

"You're the doctor?"

"I am—your resident physician. Epidemiologist. Serving
the Alliance by combatting the flu."

"How long?"

"Fighting the flu? My whole career. But I've only been working for the Alliance six months." He had an earnest look, and
a friendly, open manner.

The other man had made his way over. "Steve Harkness,"
he said. "I'm an Alliance communications specialist." Harkness was the kind of young man who exuded ambition. His
clothes were casual, but neatly pressed and well tailored, the

kind of garments worn by a man who occasionally expected, or hoped, to be photographed. "I'm here to get the word out, raise awareness both about the flu and the Alliance's efforts to help the sick and find a cure."

He stopped. Pete was aware that both men were sizing him up, deciding whether or not they could trust him.

"So," said Pete. His mouth was still dry from his hangover, his voice scratchy. "Is this a real disease, or a propaganda operation?"

Harkness winced at the word, but Strack laughed. "It is a real, frightening disease," he said. "*And* this is a massive propaganda operation."

Pete did the minimum amount of work he could do to get by, and spent the rest of his time alone to mourn Pamela. While he still wanted to figure out what had gone wrong, he was glad in a way that the Alliance hadn't assigned him to anything to do with the drones. He loathed himself for his part in Pamela's death, and had vivid nightmares in which he would follow a drone, in his mind, from Eris Island, where he had probably cheered its departure, to Mexico, where it dropped the single, ugly bomb that ended her life. He tried to fight it off, but he couldn't help but imagine her final moments. Was she beside the pool, in one of the prized lounge chairs near the bar? Or was she in the water, lazily paddling back and forth as the men poolside watched her through their sunglasses? Maybe she was wading in the ocean, up to her knees in the sea, and saw the drone fly in. Perhaps she thought it was Pete's plane in the distance, returning him to their honeymoon. He imagined her squinting at it curiously when she realized that this plane had no windows.

Pete's team had weekly meetings in Silver Spring with other
research groups, where they presented their findings to an in-
different panel of officers led by General Cushing, who always sat in the middle of the group and nodded his head, his
strong hands folded in front of him. He rarely spoke, but when
he did, the room always fell respectfully silent. He had a chest
full of ribbons on an Army uniform, ribbons that Pete could
tell, even from across the room, were regular Army commendations, not Alliance. He had a combat infantry badge and
jump wings, and the ribbons themselves were the kind that
you saw only on regular military officers. Alliance ribbons had
a smooth appearance, colors that looked like they had been
chosen carefully by focus groups and laid out by designers. Real
military ribbons had a knotty, disorganized look, like combat
itself, a random assortment of colors and patterns, here and
there adorned with dark stars or a bronze V that Pete learned
stood for Valor. Just as Alliance officers were being given military commands to demonstrate that they were all, in fact, one
team, combat officers like Cushing were being given Alliance
commands. He scowled continuously at their weekly meetings,
like it was a duty he had accepted grudgingly, and he couldn't
wait to get back into a position where people were shooting at
him.

Their weekly meetings took place every Tuesday, along
with three other detachments. Each group was given fifteen
minutes to talk, five minutes for each man on the team. Pete
had no idea how many of these meetings the generals had to
sit through in a week, how many well-polished five-minute
speeches they had to endure. It was amazing, sometimes,
how much information a man could cram into five minutes,

and at times it was amazing how little. But the schedule never varied.

Strack, in his five minutes, would detail the latest outbreak numbers, emphasizing that the problem was uncontained. Harkness would describe, and occasionally show, the media campaigns that his group had created to promote hand washing and the idea that only the Alliance could find a cure. After they were done, Pete was offered a chance to elaborate, a chance he always declined, opening up five minutes on the agenda to someone more eager than he to kiss the ass of a table full of generals.

It was a forty-mile drive from Silver Spring back to Frederick. In bad traffic, it could take well over an hour, and Pete usually welcomed the time alone in his car. "Alone with his thoughts," would be inaccurate. He preferred to be without thought entirely, his guilt-ridden mind wiped clean at least for a moment. Inching along in traffic was one of the few places he could actually achieve this thoughtless state. Most times he didn't even turn his radio on.

Somewhere near Germantown, he got off of I-270 to get a cup of coffee. Traffic was inching along, and no one was expecting him back at the office anyway. Even off the interstate, though, traffic still crawled. It was starting to rain a dreary, light mist, and Pete wasn't able to let his mind drift the way he wanted to in the stop-and-go traffic.

He came to realize that this was no normal traffic jam brought on by the daily commute; something was going on. Cops at intersections were directing traffic; barricades lined the road. Crowds of people were walking, all in the same direction he was driving, all traveling at roughly the same speed, allowing Pete to track the small groups that walked hand in hand down the sidewalk. It was the same kind of foot traffic you might see before a sporting event, a walk to the stadium— except this was a weekday, and these people didn't look excited, they looked grim.

Many of them wore surgical masks.

He came to a complete stop by a low, brick building: the Germantown Community Recreation Center. Hastily made signs declared that PEOPLE WITH SYMPTOMS SHOULD NOT GET VACCINATED—SEE YOUR DOCTOR. Officials in masks directed people to various lines that came out of the doors and wrapped around the building. They were handing out masks, so everyone in line was wearing one. Paramedics waited lazily by ambulances; volunteers took down information with clipboards. Pete could see, inside the center's double doors, hundreds of people in a dozen lines, or maybe it was just one line winding throughout the building. On the sidewalk near him, a mother was frantically talking to a bewildered volunteer. Her child, a girl maybe four years old, stared at Pete, only her eyes visible above a mask that was far too big for her small face.

A car behind him honked. Traffic had opened up. He pulled forward and found his way back to I-270.

Back in the office in Frederick, Pete flipped through Strack's presentation from that morning.

"Do you realize you're looking at my slides?" said Strack.

"I do," said Pete.

"You're going to ruin your reputation around here if you start participating."

"It looks like it's getting worse," said Pete, stopping on a chart with the last six months of data.

"That's why you're in charge," said Strack. "You read a bar graph like none other."

Pete smiled. "Is it getting . . . deadlier? It seems like, looking at these numbers, the mortality rates are climbing."

Strack shrugged. "The flu is one of the deadliest diseases in the world. Other diseases—lots of diseases—have higher mortality rates. Like Ebola. Or rabies. If rabies is untreated, you die, almost every time. But year after year, for most of modern history, the flu kills more people than anything else in terms of sheer numbers. And historically, it thrives during times of war, when people are traveling all over the place, food supplies and medical supplies are scarce. The 1918 flu pandemic, a direct result of World War I, might have killed a hundred million people: five percent of the world's population. So yes . . . if that's what you're asking me. It's real."

"I wasn't asking that," said Pete.

Strack laughed. "Of course you were, don't be shy. It's hard to know what to believe right now, god knows. Hell, we're at the heart of the bullshit machine right here in this office. But I've got the data, I've been to the hospitals, I've looked at the blood. This is real."

"But just because it's real—"

"Doesn't mean it's not propaganda," said Strack. "Which is why, I'm sure, we've been given these luxurious accommodations and a communications specialist. And you."

"So it *is* deadly. But is it anything new?"

"The flu is always new, that's the devious nature of it. Each strain is unique. But overall—no. It's not remarkably different in deadliness or virulence than any flu we've seen in the last hundred years. More deadly than some historical strains, less deadly than others. But no question we should be wary of it. Which is how I'm able to get to sleep at night."

"How so?" said Pete.

Strack shrugged. "I'm not a dumbass. I know we're milking this for propaganda value somehow, keeping the people in a panic. But maybe the work I do—*we* do—will help prevent the spread of it. Maybe we'll stumble on something that helps keep influenza at bay from now on—it wouldn't be the first time that a war effort has led to some concrete, lasting good. So that's how I sleep at night."

"I see."

"How about you?"

"Me?" said Pete. "I don't sleep at night. Ever."

Strack chuckled nervously, but stopped when he saw that Pete wasn't laughing with him.

Pete broke the silence and shoved a stack of a paper toward Strack. "Look at this."

Strack looked them over. "Evacuations?"

"Mostly in coastal areas. To prevent the spread of the flu."

"Where did you get these?"

"I've been requesting them for weeks, finally somebody slipped up and sent them to me."

"But these don't even . . . these areas have nothing to do with the flu. There's no correlation at all."

"I know," said Pete. He'd already made some crude comparisons between the evacuations and Strack's latest projections.

But they did correlate to areas that had been hit by drones, at least according to the radical blogs he was following now from Internet cafes across town.

"Weird," said Strack. He squinted at the data again, and then back up at Pete, with newfound respect. "So let me ask you a question. As long as we're being chummy with each other."

"Go ahead," said Pete.

"Why *are* you here? I mean, I looked you up. I know you were the hero of the drone program for a while. You've done more network news interviews in your life than anybody I know personally. Way more than Harkness, which I'm sure galls him, by the way. So how did you end up in this backwater of the Alliance?"

Pete thought it over for a long moment. "I think in part they put me here to get me out of the way. They didn't think they could trust me anywhere near the drones anymore."

"But why *here,* though? Why working on an obscure flu project? You used to be one of the chief badasses in the Alliance. Surely they could use you somewhere else."

"Have you ever heard of Admiral Hyman Rickover?" asked Pete.

"No."

"He was the father of the nuclear submarine. An engineering genius. Dreamed it up, fought for a decade to make it a reality while virtually everyone in the Navy and the Pentagon told him he was crazy. He's a hero of mine."

"Did he send you here?"

Pete laughed, something he didn't do much anymore, but Strack had that ability. "No. But he once said something I think about a lot. 'If you're going to sin, sin against God, not the bureaucracy. God will forgive you but the bureaucracy won't.'"

"So which did you sin against to end up here?"

Pete paused. "Both. But my point is: don't make the mistake of trying to attribute too much logic to the bureaucracy. There might not be any good reason I'm here. I think they probably thought I could do very little damage here, while at the same time they could keep an eye on me."

Strack shook his head. "As much as I hate to admit it, I don't think you're giving them enough credit."

"How so?"

"You're an inventor, right? You invented the drones. Now they want you to invent a flu epidemic. You convinced everybody that the drones were a game changer. They want you to do the same thing with the flu."

Pete looked down at Strack's slides again and pointed.

"Not me," he said. "You're the resident genius here, Strack."

The young doctor held his arms up. "That's what I keep telling everybody!"

"Are you the only one working on a cure for this thing?"

He shook his head. "No, not at all. My mission is really the epidemiology—the actual victims, the rates of transmission, things like that. Empirical data about the actual disease."

"But somebody's working on a cure, right?"

"Of course," said Strack, shuffling through some papers on his desk. "Teams everywhere, in every Alliance country. But if you ask me, based on the reports I'm getting, the most promising work is being done *here*." He handed Pete a black-and-white aerial photo of an island. "This is our most productive research station. They're working in almost total isolation, and we have reason to think they're getting close."

Pete stared at the photograph of the barren island. The photograph was old, taken before his work there, before they'd carved out the airstrip and erected their tower. But he still recognized the kidney shape, the rocky bluff at the northern end, and the two flat buildings on the other side.

"I'm waiting for them to send me there," said Strack. "Maybe they'll send all of us, the whole team."

"I've already been there," Pete mumbled in shock.

"You have?" said Strack, confused. "When?"

Just then the door burst open and Harkness walked in, his blue suit immaculate, a broad smile on his face.

"Hello, team! What are you guys up to?"

"Defeating the enemy," said Strack, turning back to his computer.

"Good," said Harkness, failing to read the sarcasm. "I've got

good news . . . they just doubled our funding. And they're moving us across the hall to a bigger office, getting three more
people on the team!"

"What happened?" said Pete.

"West Coast governors are freaking out. Two hundred
people have died in San Diego this month." He was beaming.

CHAPTER TWENTY

The new office reflected the rising importance of their project, with twice as many desks and even a small kitchen. The smells of fresh coffee and new carpet blended together pleasantly, along with the murmuring of the new team members, whose names Pete struggled to remember. Strack's tattered world map had been replaced by a digital Mercator projection of the world that took up an entire wall, with red pinpoints of light to indicate flu hotspots. Harkness's single flickering monitor had been replaced by a bank of six flat-screens against another wall, all of which he controlled and watched with rapt attention.

Pete came upon Harkness on one of those first days, watching the news on an Alliance-friendly channel as the anchor recited the dangers of the flu and the strides the Alliance was taking to defeat it. Pete was fascinated to see that Harkness was practically mouthing the words as she spoke, as if reading a script that he had written.

Pete watched for a few moments before speaking. "Do they . . . ?"

"Work for us?" Harkness said matter-of-factly, not taking his eyes from the screen. "No, not anymore. We used to do that. But we found that the really fire-breathing Alliance guys in the media did a better job on their own. Honestly, they are purer and more driven to the party line than guys on our pay-roll were."

In fact, the woman on the screen did stare at the camera with studied intensity as she spoke. She was blond with blue eyes, red lips, and teeth so white that they seemed almost predatory. She was stunningly beautiful. Harkness, pleased by Pete's interest, grabbed a remote and turned up the volume so they could listen.

"Travelers returning from Hong Kong should be quaran-tined," she said. "It's just common sense. Our soldiers have to observe twenty-one days of isolation when returning from hot zones. If it's good enough for them, why not for the rest of us?"

The camera turned to a tired-looking academic type who started to respond but was soon cut off by the gorgeous anchor.

"Here, look at this," said Harkness, pointing to a screen right below the newscast. Against a black background, fifty words were jumbled together like a huge crossword puzzle, ex-cept all the words were changing in size and position. The biggest word, in large red letters in the middle of the screen, was FLU. Around it were dozens of associated words, like PANDEMIC, OUTBREAK, STOCKPILE, and INFECTION. Suddenly, HONG KONG appeared in small letters at the edge of the cluster. Harkness eagerly tapped the screen.

"There, see? It's trending now."

"Is this a representation of the words in her broadcast?"

"No," said Harkness. "It's all the terms associated with in-fluenza discussions, across the whole Web. These are the top fifty words, so you can see Hong Kong just broke through."

As he spoke, the words grew bigger and moved closer to the center of the cluster.

"Just because she said it?"

Harkness shrugged. "It was trending before, we knew that. But it doesn't hurt. A mention by her, on a broadcast like that, all the chattering voices want to chime in."

"And that's good for us?"

"Absolutely," said Harkness, nodding vigorously. "We need people to be aware of the dangers, and these dangers necessitate quarantines."

And quarantines have other uses, too, thought Pete. *They allow people to be gathered up and locked away without trials or lawyers. They keep people afraid, and compliant.* But he kept those thoughts to himself.

Pete stood there for a little longer, watching the cloud of words shift and change in front of them—there was something hypnotic about it, all these flu-related words moving around each other, forming patterns, growing and shrinking as the whole world tried to figure out what to do about the epidemic.

Harkness worked tirelessly as the epidemic spread, always carefully inserting the story of a potential cure. The war (and by implication, the enemy) had brought them the flu, the storyline went, but the Alliance would bring them the cure. For all his faults, he was the perfect man for the job, a relentless worker coupled with ruthless ambition. Pete soon learned how to read those screens along the wall, and saw that their work was having the desired effect, keeping people at once terrified and hopeful, and convinced that only the Alliance could save them.

While Harkness worked to create the mythology of the cure, Strack worked day and night, too, doing what he could to bring about an actual remedy. He had visualizations on his computer similar to Harkness's, but instead of words and trending topics, Strack dealt with deaths and mortality rates, secondary infections and quarantines. His screens were more difficult to interpret than Harkness's, but he assured Pete that despite whatever level of Alliance bullshit accompanied it, the flu was very much real. And, he said, for the time being, damn near unstoppable.

Pete looked closely at the sporadic communications he got from the rest of Strack's extended team, especially those on Eris Island. The war was making it difficult to communicate, and impossible to get them the supplies they needed. Nonetheless, they were making progress on a cure, the reports said. Harkness dutifully sanitized the reports, elaborated where necessary, and published the results in their weekly meetings. Pete himself began presenting during his allotted five minutes, explaining how they were using their new resources, where the anticipated trouble spots were. He'd adopted Strack's philosophy: they were curing a disease, and no matter what, that was a positive thing.

One morning, Pete came into their new, lavishly appointed office to find everyone hushed. Strack was standing at the front of the group, with Harkness at his side. He held a message in his hand in a red TOP SECRET folder.

"We've been waiting for you," said Strack.

"What happened?"

"They did it," said Strack, so quietly Pete could hardly hear him. "They've got the cure."

"And it's just in time," said Harkness. "They're evacuating the island."

"What?" said Pete. "Why? That place is a fortress."

"They're almost starved out. We can't get them supplies, and we've got intel that there might be enemy submarines in the area. Typhon puts commando teams on their subs, this is what they're good at: raids, search-and-destroy missions. If they land a team on Eris Island, those researchers, and everything they've done, could be at risk."

"They'll never get a detachment on that island," said Pete. He felt an old pride rising up in him. "It's unapproachable. The drones will get anything on the surface, and shoals on all sides prevent a submerged boat from getting close. That's why we picked it."

"We can't take that risk," Harkness said. "The military detachment on Eris evacuated weeks ago. We're sending a small plane out to get the medical team. It's probably already in the air."

Pete walked across their large new office, to the map of the world that covered almost an entire wall. With his finger, he traced the journey of a West Coast plane to the spot where Eris Island would be, if it showed up on the map. "Flying at night, I hope," he said, almost to himself.

"They did it," said Strack. He was brimming with pride. "They really did it! We found a cure!"

"And the information pump is primed," said Harkness. "As soon as that plane gets back on Alliance soil, the story will start to flow: the Alliance has cured the scourge of our age."

Harkness walked to his stack of consoles and pushed buttons on a remote until all the major news sites were on-screen. Every channel was talking about the flu. Hospitals were turning away patients in Jacksonville. Schools were closing in Indiana. Public swimming pools had been ordered closed by the surgeon general.

Pete was still staring at the world map. He looked at his watch and did some rough math in his head. "It's almost sunrise on Eris Island," he said.

CHAPTER TWENTY-ONE

Commander Jennifer Carlson was in the wardroom enjoying a rare moment of solitude when the phone buzzed at her knee. She jumped; her instincts were humming. *Maybe it's the storm,* she thought; the rare squall blew through the area around Eris and made the ship rock in a way that she hadn't felt in weeks. The heavy weather seemed to announce that something was about to happen, and she wasn't inclined to ignore her instincts. They had served her well.

Because of her past success, Typhon had grudgingly allowed her vast free rein. Even her marines had stopped asking her when they might form a landing party and start blowing things up. Instead, they just continued to work out in the makeshift gym they'd created in the crew's mess, ate constantly, and cleaned their many, many weapons. Carlson had heard that Alliance boats carried no small arms, some philosophical statement on the purity of the deterrent nature of their submarines. It was typical of their mealymouthed moralism, she thought. Carrying rifles and grenade launchers would be too dirty for them, but nuclear warheads were somehow acceptable.

Almost all blue-water shipping had been eliminated by the scourge of the drones, so other Typhon sub skippers had taken to the brown waters off the coasts, picking off an occasional cargo barge or garbage scow, or lobbing a cruise missile at a factory. She had stayed near Eris Island, certain that at some point, the war would turn on that tiny speck of land. This despite the fact that they hadn't gotten a whiff of anything from the Alliance since she tried to kill that enemy submarine with a life raft.

Once every two days, they came to periscope depth to shoot trash and receive the broadcast from command. Increasingly, those messages were from impatient admirals wondering what she was doing out there. She didn't give two shits. Sooner or later, she knew, the Alliance would try something important at Eris Island. And she would blow it to hell.

"Captain," she said, picking up the phone as it buzzed a second time.

"Captain, please come to the bridge." She could hear the excitement in the officer of the deck's voice. It was Lieutenant Banach, and he wasn't prone to overreacting. She rushed to control.

The ship was bobbing at periscope depth, the diving officer and the ship's automated system doing an admirable job of keeping depth control in challenging conditions. They had come shallow as a matter of routine. In addition to shooting trash and transmitting messages, they ventilated briefly, bringing fresh air onboard. She was still wary of Eris and the medical work they did there, so she always insisted that the ship be upwind of Eris Island and at least ten miles away when they took a breath, lest they inhale some dangerous microbe invented by their enemies.

They'd also been delayed slightly by the storm, not wanting to stick their nose up in rough seas. Coming to PD was always fraught with danger. Like an animal at a watering hole, the submarine was at her most vulnerable at periscope depth, slow and exposed. While their titanium hull made them invisible to the magnetic detectors of the drones at periscope depth, if they broached the surface, and the deck of the submarine came out of the water, they would be visible to the drones' other sensors. The swarm would be on them in seconds in a frenzy. But periscope depth was also when you could see the world through human eyes, via the finely crafted lens of the periscope, a sensor far more deadly than any of the electronics they'd been entrusted with. When she stepped on the conn, Banach stepped aside immediately and yielded the periscope.

"Do you see it?" he asked as she focused.

She took a moment, waiting for a rogue splash that had fallen across the lens to fall. And there it was.

"I do," she said, although it was difficult in the early dawn light: a plane, flying close to the ocean and painted in dappled gray camouflage. Her officer of the deck was to be commended for spotting it. She automatically centered it in the scope, pushed a red button on the right handle, entering its position in the fire control system.

"Alliance?"

"It is," she said. "A small transport plane, though, not a combat plane."

"What a fool!" said the OOD. "At that speed and altitude? In this part of the ocean? Permission to ready a missile, Captain." He had already raised the surface-to-air missile mast, behind the scope.

"Wait," she said, smiling grimly even as she looked through the scope. She felt the roll of the ship in her feet, rare at this latitude, and it spoke to her. "His low altitude and speed are deliberate," she said. "He's trying to look like a drone heading for Eris. He wanted to land before sunrise, but was delayed by the storm, just like we were."

She heard Banach step to the chart and confirm it.

"He's smart," he said. "An hour ago, it was completely dark, and we would have thought just that: that he was a drone, even seeing it on radar. But I saw the asshole."

"Hmmmm."

"Don't we still want to shoot it?" he asked.

It was tempting. At this range, with a clear visual, they would knock that plane right out of the sky. All she had to do was point the missile, and push a button. But something stopped her, a hunter's instinct for a bigger prize, a risk worth taking.

"No," she said. "Let's wait. If he's going to Eris, he's not staying there—he's going to pick something up."

"You're sure, Captain?"

"I'd rather shoot down a full plane than an empty one."

"Aye, Captain," said Banach. He stepped to the chart and began plotting a course toward the island. "When do you think he might leave Eris?"

"My guess? Sunset." She smiled. "To the island at ahead flank, on this bearing."

"Aye, aye, Captain."

Dr. Manakas waited in the dark for the plane, but it was delayed by a rare bit of bad weather near the island. His mind created images as he stared in the darkness and worried; at one point he thought he saw a man over the hill, watching them. That was impossible, he knew; they were the last human beings on the island, the military detachment having long since left. But he kept staring, and when dawn finally arrived, the man (or mirage) was gone.

The plane landed soon after. The doctors who remained on Eris, eight in all, cheered as it touched down and deftly dodged the pockmarks on the runway. The plane was smaller than Dr. Manakas had expected, painted with splotches of camo, barely bigger than the drones that investigated it curiously before darting away.

They greeted the dashing pilot as a hero, even more so when they learned that he'd brought food: a cooler of steaks, two dozen eggs, potato chips, and real Coke. They'd been living on leftover Army rations and instant coffee for a month. They cooked on the charcoal grill that had been languishing for months for lack of real meat.

"We were expecting you before sunrise," said Manakas as they ate steak and eggs for breakfast at the picnic table outside the research building. He was careful to say it away from the group, not wanting to convey his concern.

"Bad storm fifty miles east of here," said the pilot. "Delayed me about an hour while I went around it."

"See anything out there?"

"Nope," he said, looking past him to the ocean. "Not a thing."

But Manakas could hear the note of resignation in his voice.

They were scheduled to leave the island at sunset; they had all day to prepare. But they had long since staged the small amount of personal gear they were allowed to take, stuffed into seabags and dusty suitcases. The results of their research were packed more carefully, in five tightly sealed watertight plastic containers. They were transparent, and you could see the rainbow of hanging files within some, hard drives and carefully swaddled vials and beakers in others. The five plastic containers made a small tower inside the plane, a monument to years of effort. The plane was loaded quickly, so they just sat and waited for sunset, and watched the drones.

The medical team had learned every habit and sound of the drones, as they were the only type of life that could thrive on Eris Island. They knew the buzzing sound of an engine revving up prior to takeoff; they knew the difference in the engine note of an unarmed bird returning to the island and the more baritone sound of a drone fully weighed down by a bomb. They knew the sound of the dance they made in the sky, the herky-jerky noise they made as they moved rapidly back and forth. And they knew the cool, liquid clicking of a drone that was picking up a bomb. The pilot was fascinated as he watched, and asked for explanations from the researchers of drone behavior that they had long since become bored with.

Dr. Manakas, the head of the detachment, was leaving behind a cache of personal effects in his small office; they'd told them that weight would be limited on the small plane. He had packed a few photographs, the ones of his wife and children that had sustained him. He had a shelf full of novels that he loved but would leave behind. A closet full of lab equipment that had served him so well would also be abandoned. He would even miss the view, he thought as he looked through the window behind his desk. It was starkly beautiful, in a way—rocks, water, and sky—and looking in that direction, the view wasn't too polluted by drones or their bombs. He hadn't taken enough time to enjoy that view, he realized. Had been too busy trying to find the cure. But they had done that much, at least.

"Are you ready?" It was his protégée, Dr. Sandra Liston, from Columbia, a brilliant doctor ten years younger than him, who did more for the cure than any of them. She was beautiful, with jet-black hair that had grown long during her two years on the island, and legs that were toned from the hikes she took up the island's leeward hills every day before break-fast. In one of his books along the wall, Graham Greene had written about the "love-charm" of bombs during the blitz in London during World War II. As the noose tightened around Eris Island, Manakas knew exactly what Greene had meant.

Inevitably, after a year on the island, he and Liston had begun sleeping together, a poorly kept secret in their tiny com-munity and a failing that seemed to be largely forgiven by their peers despite their families at home. Somewhat more re-cently, he had fallen in love with her, and that, he knew, was a better kept secret and far less forgivable. He had told San-dra one night, as they lay on the bed in his tiny room, moon-light washing over them, the sound of surf coming through his open window. She hadn't been able to say it back to him. They both knew that one way or another, the beginning of their escape marked the end of their affair.

"I'm almost ready," he said to her. "Go ahead. I'll be right out." She nodded and left him to say goodbye to his small of-fice.

He sighed and waited until he saw everyone board the plane—he had to make sure he was the last one to leave. What he was about to do might well be construed as treason, and he didn't want to implicate anyone else, although he was at peace with it. He pulled out a thick manila envelope from his desk, one that was filled with a sheaf of papers that summa-rized their work and a flash drive that contained all the key findings and DNA sequencing. It wasn't everything, but it was enough, a summary of the trickiest parts, and should be enough for a skilled team of doctors to replicate their results. He just could not, as a doctor and a man of science, see their entire body of work leave Eris Island on a small plane in the middle of a war zone. If what he left behind fell into enemy hands, then so be it. At least it might still cure somebody. He looked at the envelope and tried to think of a way to label it, so that anyone coming into the office would know it was worth salvaging. Finally he pulled out a red marker and wrote across it in large letters: THE CURE.

He left it centered neatly on the middle of his otherwise empty desk.

Commander Carlson called the submarine to battle stations an hour before sunset, ordering the officer of the deck to stay on the scope continuously. They weren't within sight of the island, but they were close enough to be wary of drones. If their scope was spotted, and attracted a swarm, that might be enough to alert a clever transport pilot. Carlson had positioned them right along the flight path on which the transport plane had come in, and there they sat, going in a slow clockwise circle, waiting for the sun to set. She'd checked; it would be nearly a full moon for them that night, a lucky break. And a curious decision by the Alliance, to fly any kind of important mission with visibility so good. They must be in a hurry, she thought. Or confident that no enemy subs would venture this close to Eris Island. The control room was blood red, all the regular lights turned off to aid the officer of the deck on the nighttime scope.

She saw something, a glint of the dying sunlight on a wing. She blinked, and flipped the scope to high power to confirm.

"Contact," she said, pressing a button on the scope to mark the direction.

"It's on the bearing to the island," said Banach, excitement in his voice.

"Raise the missile mast," she said, and heard the switch thrown behind her.

She turned the scope and watched the mast rise up: a black, thick tube with concave oblong hatches on either end of it. It looked something like a nineteenth-century cannon, but was really just a watertight container for the three surface-to-air missiles inside. It looked wildly out of place, as if it had been bolted onto the submarine. Which, indeed, it had. Historically, submarines had always been vulnerable to attacks from the air, especially from helicopters, which turned the predator into prey. Choppers could dip sonar into the water, blanket the sea with sonobuoys, kill submarines with airdropped torpedoes and depth charges. A fast submarine went 30 knots; a slow helicopter could travel at 150 knots. Helicopters were the only natural enemy a submarine had.

At their last refit, however, their boat had been equipped with a missile launcher armed with three pencil-shaped heat-seeking missiles inside. It rose from the conning tower just like a periscope. When they pushed the firing button, the missile would take off on a bearing they selected, looking for the in-frared signature of anything that was generating heat. Ideally, the engine of an enemy aircraft. The system was originally designed to be a defensive weapon, to use in a counterattack against an ASW helicopter. *But, what the hell*, thought Carlson. If there's a plane full of Alliance VIPs, she was going to shoot it down. *You don't get medals for playing defense.*

The weapon was useless against drones—their little solar engines didn't generate enough heat to register in the missile's homing mechanism. And the launcher came with only three missiles, so even if it did score a hit against a drone, it would soon run empty as the swarm came down on them. Once, Carlson had been part of a group that tested a variety of defenses against an earlier generation of drones. They tried every projectile, laser, and missile that Typhon could come up with. The most effective thing, to her amusement, was the most primitive: a deck-mounted Gatling gun. Hundreds of dumb bullets flying through the air actually did well against a few drones, shredding them to pieces. But the problem, everyone in the fleet knew, wasn't one drone. Or even three drones. The problem was a dozen drones, or fifty drones, and all their friends.

"Visual?" asked Banach.

"Yes," said Carlson. "Something." She could just see it, a reflection of sunlight on the wing. "Ready the launcher."

The ugly concave doors on each end of the missile mast flipped open, and she could feel the dull *thunk* in the handles of the periscope. The launcher swung toward the bearing she was facing. It was getting dark fast; she hoped she would be able to see the target well enough to make the call. While every OOD had fired dozens of missiles in the simulator, they had fired only one real missile, on the range. She remembered the satisfying blast of flame from the launcher, the way the missile seemed to dip dangerously close to the ocean as it took off, the way it screamed toward the target on a bright, sharp triangle of fire. They had surfaced immediately after, and they could still smell the sharp tang of rocket fuel in the air.

She blinked to clear her vision. The control room was silent as they waited for her command. Finally, the target came close enough that she could make out the cockpit. A cockpit with no windows.

"Drone," she said, disappointment in her voice.

"Shit," said Banach.

"Lowering number one scope," she said, turning the ring. "Lower the missile mast." She kept her hands up on the ring as it went down, stretched her back and blinked her eyes. "We'll go back up in five minutes," she said. "After he passes.

We'll keep looking. All night if we have to. Let's get some tea up here. Sooner or later, we'll get our chance."

The transport plane took off ten minutes after sunset. Only the drones remained on Eris, taking off and landing, ingesting their bombs and dancing for each other. It was dark onboard, but still Liston and Manakas didn't hold hands, or even sit next to each other. They sat across from each other and pretended like nothing was wrong.

Eris disappeared immediately as they took off; within seconds it was all water, in every direction. It was a long flight to the mainland, and Manakas vowed not to look at his watch at least for the first few hours. They'd chosen the small, slow plane deliberately, he knew, to mimic the movement of a drone to anyone who might spot them on radar. But up in the air, the plane felt slow and vulnerable. It rumbled, but none of the research team spoke after the first few minutes. A few fell asleep immediately, and Manakas envied them.

He stared out his window. Moonlight was glinting on the surface of the ocean, illuminating the interior of the plane with a dim, blue glow. They were flying into a vast nothingness, a tiny pod of doctors who had studied the flu a thousand miles from home. *Home.* He thought about what that even meant, what must have changed since he'd left. What had changed in him.

Something caught his eye as he looked out the window; a flash on the surface. It was easy to see in the darkness. He saw two flashes, diverging, then realized that one of them was just a reflection on the ocean surface. His heart sank as he knew instantly what it meant. Thank god he'd left that envelope; he could take some solace in that. At least their work wouldn't be in vain. The flash focused into a V-shaped jet of pure white flame, propelling a missile toward them at the speed of sound.

Manakas turned and looked at Dr. Liston across the aisle, wanting her face to be the last thing he saw before he died. She saw the pure sadness in his eyes and forced a smile, trying to make him feel better.

CHAPTER TWENTY-TWO

Carlson surfaced her submarine among the wreckage, after verifying that no drones were in the immediate area. She kept the ship rigged for dive and took a minimum number of the crew topside, in case they needed to submerge quickly. But she wanted to see the wreckage herself, verify the kill, and pick up anything that would make for useful intelligence. Or a good trophy.

She climbed onto the main deck while Banach drove the ship from the control room; she wouldn't even put anybody on the bridge, wanted to be able to submerge quickly if they had to. Among her team topside were three of the marines, including their sergeant. One of them held a long, curved hook, exactly like those used by lifeguards, to pull any compliant survivors from the sea to be interrogated. The others carried the short carbines that they so loved, in the unlikely event that a survivor wanted to fight to the end.

But, as she expected, no one had survived. Only tiny traces of the plane remained, a few thin seat cushions floating in the water, some empty plastic bottles, a tire from the landing gear.

They steered silently among it, the flashlights from the commandos illuminating the detritus.

"Confirmed kill," she said, almost to herself.

"I wonder what they were doing," said the sergeant.

Carlson shrugged. "Me, too. Not delivering the mail."

She heard a slight scraping along the hull beneath her feet. One of the commandos shined his light on it.

"I don't see anything," he said.

She squinted. It was almost impossible to see, but she could hear it. Then she saw it; a transparent plastic container, bobbing at the waterline.

"There!" she said. She sensed it was important. Two of the marines got down on their bellies and tried to reach it, but it was impossible. The sergeant tried with the big metal hook, but there was nothing to grip on the plastic container.

Suddenly, the radio on her belt clicked to life. "Drone," said Banach from the control room. "Port beam."

Shit. "How far out?" she said.

"Maybe ten minutes," said Banach. "Heading straight for us."

"Shall we secure, Captain?" asked the sergeant.

"No!" she said. "Get that box!" He resumed frantically batting at it with his hook, but it was futile.

"Looks like four drones in all," said Banach on the radio. "In attack formation."

Carlson looked at the sergeant. "Get that box," she said again.

Without a word, he handed her the hook, nodded, and dived off the side of the submarine.

"What the hell?" said Banach from control. He'd heard the splash. "Do we have a man overboard?"

The sergeant grasped the floating container with both hands and kicked himself over to the side of the sub. Carlson lowered the hook around him, so it grabbed him beneath his arms, just as designed. The two other commandos got behind her and helped pull him up, plastic container in hand.

"Visual on drones!" said Banach. He had the 4x magnification of the scope on his side; they still couldn't see or hear them topside, but Banach's visual meant they were very close. "Get below!"

The commandos ran for the hatch, plastic crate in hand. Carlson followed them, her eyes to the dark sky.

At the hatch, they tried to go below, but the crate wouldn't fit.

"You've got to be shitting me," she said. The commandos were frantically turning the crate, trying to find an angle at which the rectangular container would fit down the round hatch.

She could hear the drones.

"Move!" she said, stepping between the commandos. She tore the lid off the sealed crate, threw it into the sea, and dumped the contents of the container into the submarine. A torrent of paper poured down the hatch.

"Down, down, down!" she yelled. The first drone was in sight now. The marines jumped down the ladder, landing and slipping on the pile of Alliance paperwork. Going last, she slid down two rungs of the ladder, and slammed the hatch behind her.

Without waiting for her order, Banach performed an emergency dive. Water poured around the hatch as she spun the locking ring, sealing the ship shut. They had just made it. Banach, she knew, would have submerged with them still topside if that's what he needed to do to save the ship. She had trained him that way.

After a few minutes, Banach made his way aft, wild eyed.

She saw him do a quick count of everyone before he met her eyes with relief.

"Disappointed?" she said. "You almost got to take command."

He nodded. "Maybe next time, Captain."

"Any damage from the drones?"

"We heard the lead drone drop its bomb. Hit the surface of the water and sank without detonating."

"Good," she said, the adrenaline rush subsiding. She held her arms out, indicating the pile of paper at her feet. "Get somebody down here. We need to start scanning this shit."

CHAPTER TWENTY-THREE

The three original members of the team, Hamlin, Strack, and Harkness, were all sitting at their desks awaiting word about the flight to Eris Island.

Harkness had the propaganda machine ready, waiting to unleash it the moment the plane touched down safely. He passed the time by nervously watching the ever-changing word clouds on his monitors as they told him what people were saying about the flu and the Alliance, and no doubt fantasizing about how the displays would change when the cure was announced. Strack nervously shuffled papers at his desk, the latest mortality reports, also no doubt hoping that his daily diet of statistics was about to change radically.

As for Pete, he busied himself with rough calculations using approximate speeds of transport planes. He didn't know the exact plane or its speed, of course, but had a feeling it might be trying to approximate a drone, meaning it would travel very slowly—at least until it was a safe distance away, or closer to areas that the Alliance controlled. He kept adding variables to the equation, wind speed and rates of fuel consumption for a plane fully loaded with passengers, but soon the results all started converging on a single number. It was a complicated problem but allowed Pete to use his extensive knowledge of military aircraft, and gave him a comforting refuge to occupy himself. His slowest estimate had the plane touching down on US soil in twelve hours. The fastest: six.

That's why Pete felt a stab of dread when he heard someone buzzing their office door for access after just three hours. He knew it had to be bad news.

Especially when General Cushing himself walked in.

They all stood up, automatically. Cushing was in a dress uniform, a step more formal than what Pete saw him in weekly at their Tuesday briefings in Silver Spring. He carried nothing but his hat. His face was grim. He was alone, without the aides that were as much an insignia of his rank as the stars on his collar.

He looked them over for a moment before speaking, and cleared his throat. "They're gone," he said.

Harkness almost jumped. "Gone? What do you mean? General?"

"Missing without a trace," he said. "The plane from Eris Island. Missing and presumed dead."

"Shot down?" asked Hamlin.

"We have no direct evidence of that," said the general. "But they were a warplane, on a strategic mission, flying unescorted in a war zone. They went missing a few minutes after takeoff. Draw your own conclusions."

Strack went pale. All that work in pieces over the ocean, or drifting to the bottom. Colleagues of his, too, now dead. Scientists killed by the war machine they had all tried to avoid.

Harkness, too, looked stunned. More than Strack, he looked bewildered. A huge, enthusiastic consumer of his own propaganda, he couldn't believe the Alliance could suffer a defeat like this. "Maybe it was a mechanical failure," he said, wanting to believe it.

"Maybe," the general said. "Doesn't make a difference to me. To us."

Pete looked up at that. Even as his two colleagues digested the news in their own way, he realized that the general wasn't there just to deliver bad news. He was there to tell them what was next. And he was staring right at Pete.

"What now?" he asked.

"There's a chance there's still usable information on the island. The plane was small, and the medical team couldn't bring much with them. They were supposed to bring just the essentials, and destroy everything they left behind. But they didn't have much time. Maybe they left something useful behind. If they did, we have to get it. We need it, and we need to keep it away from our enemy."

Pete shook his head. "You'll never get close, General. And neither will Typhon. It's surrounded by drones, and shoals, and thousands of miles of open ocean. If there's anything of value on Eris, it couldn't be in a safer place."

"No fortress stays secure forever."

Again Pete noticed that the general was staring just at him, not the other two members of his detachment. He wasn't surprised. A realization dawned on him. In a way, it confirmed a feeling he'd had ever since he learned that the flu research was being done at Eris—he would return to Eris. It was his destiny.

"You want me to go there."

"You're the only man who can," said the general. "You're the only man in the Alliance with a working knowledge of the drones, the island, and the epidemic."

"How?" asked Pete. "Want to put me on the next transport plane? Because that didn't really work out so well."

"Not a plane this time," said the general. "A submarine. The *Polaris*."

The thought of flying a plane there had seemed reckless to Pete, but the mention of a submarine sent a chill through him. All the stories he'd heard about life onboard a nuclear submarine—the stale air, the bad food, the claustrophobia, the constant risk of death. He'd personally worked on the drones' anti-submarine algorithms, and the MAD sensors that made them work. He'd rather take his chances on a plane, where at least the end would come quickly.

"It won't work," said Pete. "The drones won't let you approach on the surface, or at periscope depth. The shoals won't let you approach submerged."

"We think there's a way in," said the admiral.

Pete shook his head in disbelief. "It's a suicide mission."

"I feel that way about every submarine patrol," said the general. "But we've spoken to the best minds in the submarine force. They think there's a way."

Pete laughed out loud. "Sorry, but you're talking to a guy who knows better, General. I picked that island, I've studied the charts probably more than any man on earth. I programmed the drones that surround it on how to kill submarines."

"We think there's a way," the general said again.

Pete scoffed, looking at his two colleagues for support. "Care to share the details?"

"In due time," said the general. "But first . . . we have to teach you how to drive a submarine."

The door to their office burst open again, and a small man in a khaki uniform limped inside. He was wearing a black leather patch over his left eye, the same half of his face covered in pink wrinkled scars, the distinctive scars of a man who'd lived through a ferocious fire. He had the oak leaves of a commander on his collar, but the front of his uniform was devoid of military decoration save for two things: the gold dolphins of a submarine officer, and below that, a war patrol pin. His nametag said ASE.

He nodded at the general and then stared down Pete with his one good eye. Pete felt an old, rebellious urge to say something sarcastic, to show he wasn't intimidated by this show of military brass.

"Is that pronounced 'aze'?" he said. "Like purple haze?"

"No," said the submariner. "It's pronounced 'ace.' As in: I've killed a bunch of people."

CHAPTER TWENTY-FOUR

Pete stared at the sonar screen, his eyes burning from fatigue. The two bright, parallel bars of the degaussing range came into view, as he knew they would.

"Dive, make your depth six hundred and thirty-two feet," he said.

The diving officer acknowledged the order, and Pete felt the angle in his feet as the ship dived. He pictured the bottom of the ocean rising toward them as their depth increased. It was flat there, he knew, and sandy. But he still didn't want to touch bottom.

"Left five degrees rudder," he said, steering the ship slightly, putting it right in the middle of the range. They were easing toward it, right on track. When they lined up perfectly, he gave his next order.

"Ease your rudder to left two degrees." There was an unusually strong current at the range that day, pushing them sideways, or making them "crab," in the words of Commander Ase. The small rudder would keep them moving right on track, right down the middle. Unless something went wrong.

Right on cue: a screeching alarm, a swirling red light. "Stuck dive planes, sir!" yelled the diving officer. They suddenly tilted forward steeply. Pete had to grab on the periscope ring over his head to stay on his feet.

"Right full rudder!" he ordered. "Switch to manual control!"

The diving officer complied, but the ship continued to dive. The big rudder was having the desired effect, the ship would dodge the electrified walls of the degaussing range, turning right in front of the entrance at Point Alpha. But he wasn't sure they would miss the ocean floor.

"Emergency blow!" announced Hamlin. "Forward main ballast tanks!"

He grabbed the right-hand lever and pulled it toward him. He heard the tanks gasp as the valve turned and high-pressure air shot into the forward MBT and expanded, instantly expelling thousands of tons of seawater. The angle of the ship came off instantly, the huge air bubble in the tank over-whelming the force of the stuck planes. For a moment, the ship was level; then the angle started going up. "We caught it!" said Pete. He went from leaning forward to leaning back-ward as he watched their depth change. The ship was now soaring toward the surface.

The diving officer counted down their depth as they as-cended. "One hundred feet," he said. "Ninety . . . eighty . . . seventy . . ."

The angle leveled off suddenly as the ship broke through the surface, and crashed back down. They were bobbing on the surface.

"Sir, the ship is broached," said the diving officer, stating the obvious. Pete could hear waves breaking against the side of the hull.

Immediately, drone alarms began screeching from the ESW console. The floor shuddered as bombs rained down on them. "Emergency deep!" shouted Pete as alarms indicating fire, explosions, and flooding lit up the control room. He scanned the alarms, prioritizing, identifying a reactor scram as his most pressing concern because it would kill their propulsion.

Then, with a pneumatic sigh, the control room shuddered and the alarms went silent. The lights surrounding them came on, revealing that they were not in the control room of an actual *Polaris*-class submarine. They were on a simulator, a perfect replica of a control room perched atop hydraulic pistons and a bank of computers that could simulate every possible catastrophe. It belonged to the Navy's submarine school in Charleston, South Carolina, but it seemed to Pete that every other student had been sent home so the facility could be devoted entirely to his brief, intense apprenticeship.

Commander Ase limped to the edge and dropped a small steel gangplank that linked the simulator to the surrounding, three-story platform.

"Well, I didn't hit the bottom that time," said Pete as Ase made his way in. His heart was racing.

Ase nodded. "Aye, that's true," he said. "But you'll be on the bottom soon enough. After the drones take care of you."

"So what was I supposed to do?" said Pete, too tired to sound frustrated.

"You're supposed avoid the bombs," said Ase. "These submarines cost a lot of money. *Reset!*" he yelled into the shadows. The simulator shook with a *thunk* as unseen operators prepared it for another run.

And so they ran it again, Pete trying to squeeze the ship through the degaussing range during fire, flooding, every variety of stuck planes, and attacks from both above and below.

When not on the simulator, he was in the classroom, learning from a string of submariners, all of whom seemed to worship Ase, about all the systems that would keep him alive and get him to Eris Island. Even in his exhaustion, Pete soon learned to appreciate the elegance of the submarine's design, the engineering that had gone into it. Every feature and system had evolved over time, many in battle, to make the ship at once both safe to her crew and deadly to the enemy. His education in aeronautical engineering was more useful in the process than he'd expected. Underwater, the submarine moved more like an airplane than like a surface ship, as the water moving over her control surfaces positioned her just like the air flowing over a plane's wings. Thus he was comfortable with the principles that kept a submarine submerged. Ase and his followers rarely spoke about how a submarine operated on the surface.

Much of his training revolved around great submarine disasters. They called it "lessons learned," and in fact, the fleet did an admirable job of adapting their machines and their tactics by studying the wreckage of their martyrs. But it was more than that. His instructors in Charleston were indoctrinating Hamlin into a brotherhood. And part of being in that brotherhood, he learned, was an understanding that every time you left port in a submarine, you were going in harm's way.

The USS *Thresher* was the first great nuclear submarine lost, commissioned in 1960 and lost in 1963, with all 129 men aboard. It was during a post-overhaul dive trial, about two hundred miles east of Cape Cod, Massachusetts. The ship was in constant communication with the *Skylark,* a submarine rescue ship that cruised above her, a safety measure that ended up doing no good at all. At test depth, one thousand feet beneath the surface, flooding began in a place and for reasons that were never determined. At that depth, Pete learned, the force of the water would have been like a cannon, the noise alone would have been debilitating. For reasons not completely understood, the ship's emergency blow system failed to save them. There was some speculation that the rapidly expanding pressurized air froze the valves that were designed to channel it. At 0915, the worried commander of the *Skylark* transmitted on the "Gertrude," his underwater telephone, the message, *"Are you in control?"*

In response, the *Thresher* transmitted back this garbled, incomplete message: *"Nine Hundred N."*

Those were the last words anyone ever heard from them.

The second disaster Pete studied was another US nuclear boat, the *Scorpion,* lost under more mysterious circumstances in 1968. The boat had been diverted to observe a group of Soviet ships near the Azores in the Atlantic. Commander Francis Slattery, the commanding officer, radioed on May 21, 1968, that he had made contact with the Soviet group and was sur-veilling them at 15 knots and a depth of 350 feet. No one would ever hear from him again. When the boat was five days late returning home to Norfolk, Virginia, the Navy finally announced that there was a problem and initiated a search. Ninety-nine men disappeared along with the boat.

There were a number of theories about the fate of the *Scor-pion.* Some thought the ship had been done in by one of its own malfunctioning torpedoes. Many others, given the nature of the mission, suspected the Soviets. Incredibly, for a ship that was lost under such mysterious circumstances, the US Navy actually had audio of it sinking. SOSUS arrays, highly sensitive hydrophones mounted to the seabed at critical places throughout the world, had recorded it. Hamlin's education in submarine disasters finished with that tape, as an instructor pointed out the sounds of air banks bursting and bulkheads collapsing as the great ship imploded on her way to the bottom of the sea.

One disaster they never spoke of in Charleston was the more recent fire onboard the *Regulus,* the sister ship of the *Polaris.* Pete thought maybe it was too recent, that the men around him might have known sailors onboard, many of whom did not escape with their lives. He remembered seeing news video of it limping into port at the time, damage visible to its sail and hull, scorch marks and jagged metal. He remembered a later report that the ship was deliberately destroyed, having been declared a total loss, too damaged to repair. But the men with dolphins on their chests in Charleston never mentioned it. The *Regulus* disaster was still a tragedy, Pete thought, not yet mythology.

The evening after Pete heard the sound of the *Scorpion* being crushed by sea pressure, he waited on the conn of the simulator for his normal four-hour shift. He reviewed procedures as he waited; there was some problem with the computers and they had to wait while the entire software package was reloaded by the simulator's operating crew. Commander Ase leaned on the rail and watched him as he paged through the procedure for flooding. First immediate action: ahead full. Maximizing speed maximized the flow of water across the planes, the force that would pull them to the surface.

"What did they teach you today in the classroom?" said Ase, emphasizing the world "classroom" with disdain.

"More submarine disasters," said Pete. "Lessons learned from the *Thresher* and the *Scorpion*."

"Lessons learned?" He laughed theatrically at that, the sound echoing in the cavernous space that held the simulator. "What did they tell you to learn from the *Thresher*?"

"Don't screw around at test depth," said Pete.

Ase nodded appreciatively, but it was hard to tell if he really approved, his scarred face frozen in its permanent sneer. "That's not bad," he said. "Good advice, actually. But I'll tell you the real lesson."

"Please do."

"It was an unlucky boat! They had a scram pierside in Puerto Rico in '61. Then the diesel wouldn't work, then the battery crapped out. Got so hot inside they had to evacuate the crew. The *Cavalla* had to pull alongside so they could draw electric power from her. If that had happened at sea, they would have sunk. In 1962, a tug ran into her in port; she had to go to the yards in Groton to get that fixed. You want a lesson from the *Thresher*, there's your lesson: stay off unlucky boats."

"I'll do my best," said Pete. "What about the *Scorpion*? What's the lesson there?"

"The lesson of the *Scorpion*?" Ase pointed a long finger at Pete. Pete noticed for the first time that even the tip of his finger was scarred, the skin waxy and wrinkled, the nail deformed. "Here's the lesson of the *Scorpion*. Don't ever trust the Russians," he said. "No matter what anybody says."

The simulator reset with a thud, startling Pete.

"OK," said Commander Ase, rapping his academy ring against the metal guardrail on the platform. "Let's get to work."

Pete drove the simulated ship down to the depth of the range, 632 feet.

"All stop," he ordered. The engine order telegraph dinged its acknowledgment as the ship slowed, creeping right into the range.

Pete zoomed in on his console, checked the motion of the ship. Current was a negligible .2 knots. That was, Pete knew, the exact value of the historic average current in that area, although you would never know it by the consistently apocalyptic conditions they usually thrust upon him in the trainer. The ship drifted into the degaussing range as Pete waited on the balls of his feet for the next, creative disaster to befall them.

A yellow light came on the diving officer's panel; the lights dimmed slightly.

"Degaussing is active," said Pete. He looked out into the darkness, where somewhere Ase and his crew of tormentors were preparing to spring something on him.

The ship slowed slightly near the exit of the range. "Make turns for three knots," Pete ordered, needing the slight additional thrust to maintain ship control and complete their passage through the range.

The yellow light went off. "Ship is clear of the range," Pete announced.

He waited, but still no disaster. He walked to the chart. It wasn't the first time they had allowed him to get this far, but it was rare, so it took him just a second to recall the next step.

"Ahead two-thirds!" he said. "Right fifteen degrees rudder."

The ship sped up and turned, driving Pete to the position where they'd determined they might squeeze through the shoals at periscope depth, the seven o'clock position, if due north on the island's clock was high noon. "Make your depth one hundred feet."

At the shallow depth, Pete slowed and executed a slow right turn to clear his baffles: peeking behind him to make sure no enemy boat had crept up in their sonic blind spot. Sonar reported no contacts.

He stepped to the conn. "Dive, make your depth eight-zero feet," he ordered, at the same time turning the orange ring of the port periscope. The cylinder rose up smoothly, and Pete flipped out the handgrips as it came up, quickly putting his eye to the soft rubber eyepiece.

He was staring in the ocean now, looking up as far as the scope would let him, turning slowly, watching as they ascended. Even a fishing boat dragging nets could screw things up, although he doubted in real life a fishing boat would be operating here, in the land of the drones. But the simulator crew had never let realism stop them before in their endless pursuit of creative disasters that could stop Pete on his quest.

The view through the scope was a perfect simulation, taking into account weather and time of day. It was calm and bright. Pete watched the water get lighter as they came shallow, expecting the whole time to hear that a fire had erupted in the engine room, or a scram had shut down their power plant, or that a torpedo had appeared out of nowhere and was screaming toward them.

But nothing happened.

The scope broke through, and Pete executed three slow turns, verifying (once again to his surprise) that they were alone. "No close contacts!" he said. And he trained the scope on Eris Island.

It was right where it was supposed to be. Drones flew above it, some lazily making their way toward him. Pete knew that they were randomly searching, that they hadn't seen his scope at this distance. And the degaussing had made the ship invisible to their magnetic sensors at periscope depth. They moved slowly toward the small break in the shoals. Pete's heart raced; they'd never allowed him to make it this far.

Right before the shoals, one of the drones drifted right on top of them. Pete knew immediately they'd been seen. It soared into the sky. At this proximity to the island, it attracted a legion of followers.

"Right full rudder!" he ordered. He was too close to the island to go deep, however. The ocean bed was right beneath him. An attack formation of five drones was heading directly toward them. Pete braced himself for the impact of their bombs.

The simulator stopped moving with a pneumatic gasp. The lights came on around them. Pete heard Ase approaching first, and then saw him at the edge of the platform, throwing over the small bridge onto the simulator.

"I thought the degaussing would make me invisible?"

Ase shrugged. "I guess it didn't take."

"Didn't take?" said Pete, his frustration rising. "What am I supposed to do? Swim out there and fix it?"

"Calm down," said Ase. "You did fine. I would just recommend verifying the effectiveness of the degaussing before you make your approach to the island. That range hasn't been used in five years. If it doesn't work, you can always make another pass."

"Verify it?"

"Give the drones a peek before and after you degauss. Do it while you can still go deep and evade if necessary, see how they react. That's all, Hamlin."

"OK," said Pete. Ase was being unusually constructive in his criticism. It was every bit as unnerving as his quiet approach to the degaussing range. Pete found himself bracing for the next catastrophe.

They did three more runs, these a more traditional series of flooding, fire, and every variety of ship control casualty. Pete had learned that the outcome of the training wasn't necessarily to bring the ship through the degaussing range every time. Indeed, he was convinced that given the complexity of some of the casualties being thrown at him, recovery was often impossible. Rather, they were looking to see if he had completely absorbed the procedures and the doctrine that they were throwing at him all day, so that even in a catastrophic situation, he was still making logical choices, making the best of whatever bad options he had.

"You're getting there," said Ase, after a particularly challenging run through the range in the simulator. He was sitting on the dive chair with a clipboard, going through his critique.

"High praise," said Pete. He'd been in Charleston for four weeks. The last week they'd abandoned the classroom entirely, and he'd spent full days in the simulator, eight hours with a short break for lunch. At night, it was back to his room to study procedures and try to relax enough to fall asleep.

"Well, don't let it go to your head," said the commander, smiling with the half of his face that still worked. The dim lights in the simulator exaggerated the ripples of his scars. He was truly a frightening man.

"Want to do that one again?" asked Pete. "Maybe throw in a couple of helicopters?"

Ase shook his head. "Nope," he said. "That's it. You can practice more when you get to the boat."

Pete was startled. He'd stopped asking when he was actually going to report to *Polaris*. "When is that?"

"You leave tomorrow for the coast."

Pete nodded, trying not to look nervous in front of Ase. "Tomorrow."

"Yeah. Pack your shit. The driver will be there at 0600."

"Will do."

"Here," said Ase. He pulled a tablet computer that had been hidden beneath his clipboard. "That contains your orders, and the patrol order for the *Polaris* that takes effect when you get onboard. You're the only one that can open that thing, but you'll have to show Captain McCallister when you report."

"You know him?"

"He's a good man," said Ase. "Smart."

"Is he lucky?" asked Pete.

"Up to this point," said Ase, not quite smiling.

The silence grew as Ase continued to stare at him. The support crew had left, and all the lights on the surrounding platform were off, making it invisible. The simulated control room was now a small cube of dim light suspended in darkness, supported by unseen forces. Soon, Pete realized with a chill, he'd be sitting in a real submarine, suspended in an endless ocean.

"I was out there," said Ase after a long pause.

"Out there?"

"Where you're going. Near Eris Island. We'd caught a whiff of a Typhon submarine on a SOSUS array; they sent my boat out there to check it out. I was skipper onboard the *Regulus*. Heard of it?"

Pete nodded. "Were you there . . . ?"

Ase did his scary half smile again. "Yeah, I was there during the fire. We went out there to sniff around for this enemy boat, and soon enough we found her. She was noisy as hell, the way those Typhon boats all are—we heard her from five miles away. They don't build them for stealth. A fifty-hertz tonal in a sound channel on the towed array . . . remember what all that means?"

Pete nodded. The enemy ship's electrical system operated on 50 Hz, unlike the 60 Hz of Alliance ships. A 50 Hz tonal, or any of its harmonics, was one of the surest sonar signatures of an enemy boat. A sound channel was caused by different temperature layers in the ocean, causing sound to travel many times farther than it normally would, like light being reflected by parallel mirrors.

"We worked hard to get close, creeped up on her baffles," continued Ase. "She went quiet, drifted in and out, but we had a solution we were pretty confident in. By the time I was ready to shoot, we'd been at battle stations for twelve hours.

"We shot two torpedoes with a twenty-degree spread. Instead of running away, she turned right toward us. Launched a couple of countermeasures and came right at us. Her countermeasures worked, our torpedoes peeled off. And then she shot one of her torpedoes right down our throats."

This was news to Pete. He'd only heard about a fire on the *Regulus,* a heroic damage-control effort. No one had ever told him that the boat had been hurt in battle.

"Her torpedo went right by us, exploded about a hundred yards past. We were so close to each other, it was like a knife fight in a telephone booth. The torpedo missed us, but the shock wave blew out one of our main seawater valves—the engineer called away flooding in the engine room. I fired two more torpedoes back at her and came shallow, trying to slow the flooding."

"You surfaced?"

Ase shook his head. "Hell no. There were drones everywhere. We stayed at periscope depth and hoped they wouldn't see us. She did the same.

"Anyway, my boys did good work, flood control worked, we slowed the flooding soon enough, but we'd taken a tremendous amount of water onboard—we had to stay shallow while we pumped it off. And it seemed like my torpedoes had done the job; nobody was shooting back at us. We thought we were lucky with the drones, too; none had spotted us at that point with just our periscope raised, although we could see them darting around in the distance. I thought we might live to fight another day. Then the OOD called me to take a look." He took a lengthy pause, as if he were once again looking out a periscope.

"It was a life raft," he said. "Drifting right toward us. The goddamn thing just appeared in the ocean. One of those big, orange, covered ones, a completely enclosed inflatable. At first I thought maybe we'd gotten lucky and sunk the bastard, even though we hadn't heard an explosion, and they abandoned ship. We were just starting to debate what we should do about it, whether we should take them prisoner or leave them adrift, when it got close enough for me to see it was empty. I stared for a minute longer than I should have, trying to figure out what it meant. Then the drones saw it."

"Shit."

"The Typhon boat had positioned themselves with the current and launched the raft so it would drift right toward us."

"Why didn't they shoot you with a torpedo again? You were sitting ducks."

He shrugged. "Maybe they wanted to conserve their torpedoes. I think they didn't want to give away their position again; we would have shot right back. Who knows? Maybe they just wanted to see if the lifeboat attack would work."

"And it did?"

He nodded. "The raft kept drifting nearer, and by the time the drones spotted it, it was right next to us. We couldn't dive, the engine room was still flooded. The down angle alone would have fucked us, about eleven tons of seawater rolling forward. Propulsion was screwed up because of the flooding, with the emergency propulsion motor we could barely make three knots against the current. The first bombs landed on the raft, blowing it to hell. But everything on that raft was made to float—the drones just kept hitting it, shredding it. Finally, one of them hit the scope."

"While you were on it?"

He nodded. "That's how I got this," he said, tapping his eye patch. Pete winced at the click of his mangled fingertip on the leather. "Blew the optics right though the scope, shot the glass into my eye."

"Jesus."

"A second bomb fell a few feet underwater, hit the conning tower and exploded, breached the bridge trunk. Started a fire in external hydraulics. That's about five hundred pounds of pressure, caught fire immediately. We lowered everything, submerged, even though that made the flooding start again in the engine room. Took local control in shaft alley, guys standing waist deep in water, controlling the planes with wrenches while the control room burned. Killed half my crew," he said.

"My god," said Pete. He'd never heard any of this.

Ase shrugged again. Pete realized he'd told the story many times, both in the brightly lit halls of power where he had to explain the disaster to his admirals, and in the dimly lit bars of Groton and Norfolk, where submariners told their real stories.

"We managed to get the fire out. Limped back to Pearl, at periscope depth the whole way. Saved the boat, somehow. Not that it mattered. It was too much to repair. As soon as they finished their investigation, they dragged her out to sea and scuttled her."

Pete took it all in. It was the most Commander Ase had ever spoken to him.

"You know why I'm telling you all this?" he asked.

"So I know to lower the scope during a drone attack?"

"Yeah, I do recommend that. Highly. But in general—fuck the drones. The drones are like the weather, or . . ." he said with that weird smile curling onto his broken face, "the current. It's something out there you all have to be concerned about, something you should use to your advantage, just like the Typhon boat did. But that's not the reason I told you that story. That's not what you need to know."

"What do I need to know?"

"There's an enemy submarine out there. And somebody onboard really knows what they're doing."

CHAPTER TWENTY-FIVE

Commander Carlson carefully dried and scanned every page of the documents they'd plucked from the sea. Almost all of it was readable, although that didn't mean it was understandable. Much of it she'd read while holding the damp sheets in front of a hand dryer in the crew's head.

It was medical research, she could tell that much. Something about the flu, which made sense given the history of the island. She knew about the flu, they all did, they'd been getting increasingly serious messages about hygiene and hand washing, and they'd all been required to get flu vaccines during their last port call, vaccines that clearly no one expected to be effective. That was confirmed in the captured documents—the scientists wrote about the futility of the present vaccines, and the virulence of the new strain. There were frightening classified briefs from the Alliance about the spread of the disease, the death rates, the unrest in the cities where it was doing the most harm.

She concluded that the crate of paper she'd grabbed represented some of their earlier work. Some of it contained dates.

The earliest date was three years before, the most recent about a year earlier. But she could tell, even without any medical training, that they were getting close to a cure. There was an excitement in the more recent documents, a certainty that an answer was at hand.

She wrote a brief, one-page memo that summarized their findings, the dates that the paperwork spanned, the paragraphs and charts that seemed the most important to her untrained eyes. She consolidated these into about a five-page message, with the relevant scans attached, and sent it to squadron headquarters. It was as large a message as she dared send; she didn't want to stay at PD any longer than necessary in the zone so close to the island where she chose to linger. They came to PD and sent the message to their satellite in a sixty-second, encrypted burst. They submerged the instant they received confirmation that the message had been received by the satellite.

Then she went to the wardroom, shared a microwave pizza with Banach, and waited for two hours, the amount of time she thought it might take for her bureaucracy to partially digest the information.

At sunset, they rose again, and a message was waiting for her. The OOD held the scope while she went to radio, reading it one line at a time as it came out of the printer.

Jennifer Carlson was a woman who had seen much during the war. But what she read on the message made her jaw drop. She walked back down to the wardroom, where Banach was enjoying a post-pizza cigarette.

"Sorry," he said, starting to snuff it out on his plate. He knew his commander didn't like smoking, and he did it only when she wasn't around.

She waved her hand dismissively. "I have word from our illustrious leaders."

"Did they congratulate us on shooting down the plane? Or chastise us for deviating from doctrine?"

"They express their congratulations," she said, reading the message. "And they confirm that it was a high-value kill."

"Oh?"

"The Alliance is sending out another rescue mission to the island, this time by submarine."

"Smart."

"The boat they are sending is the *Polaris*," she said. "She's on her way."

Banach raised an eyebrow at this. "They know exactly which boat is coming? They know the name? How could they know that?"

"Because," said Carlson, holding the message in front of her. "We have a man onboard."

CHAPTER TWENTY-SIX

They flew Pete on a commercial plane from Charleston to St. Louis, where he boarded a military transport. The pilots seemed mildly put out to be hosting him, in the way military pilots always did, barely saying a word to him on the flight from St. Louis to Spokane, Washington.

At the Spokane airport, Pete was met on the ground by a military vehicle that was flying a small Alliance flag from the right corner of its hood. The drivers, however—two sergeants—were regular Army, and had numerous battlefield commendations. They weren't talkative, with Pete or with each other, but they seemed happy to have him, to have duty on the mainland, for which Pete, as their cargo, got part of the credit.

"Seat belt, please, sir," said the driver as Pete settled into the small backseat. As soon as it clicked, they were off with a roar of the vehicle's heavy engine, heading west.

Pete realized that he'd been in the Alliance's bubble for a long time. Outside the walls of the military bases where he'd spent so much of his time in the past few years, it seemed like things were starting to break down. In the hardscrabble towns outside of Spokane, a few people stared at them accusingly from their porches as they passed. Almost every store was closed. A few gas stations were open, but cars were lined up, most of them parked: they looked like they were waiting for gas to arrive. Lines also snaked out the doors of government clinics and pantries. A light mist began to fall, obscuring the view. The people in lines stood still, their faces blank, oblivious to the rain. Not long ago, Pete had associated poverty with obesity, a bad fast-food and junk-food diet accompanied by plentiful television and video games. The poor had transformed, he saw, back to an earlier version of want, where they looked gaunt, like images of dust bowl farmers during the Great Depression. Soon they were in the prairie, and Pete fell fast asleep as the sergeants murmured to each other about battles fought and comrades lost.

When they crossed the Northern Cascades and neared the coast, the area became increasingly militarized. A vehicle similar to their own sat alongside the road, charred, burned out.

"What happened to them?" asked Pete.

The solider in the passenger seat looked back at Pete without saying anything. He pointed to the sky.

After three hours of driving, they stopped suddenly on a deserted strip of highway, and the soldiers checked their tablet computer.

"Orders are updating," said one of them.

"We should be OK," said the soldier who wasn't driving. "Looks like we're meeting your boat in Bangor. Puget Sound is deep enough there for your ride, but pretty far inland. Improves our odds."

They waited ten minutes until the tablet beeped. The driver read the orders, and then handed it to his partner to verify.

"We've got an hour to kill," he said. "Looks like they want us to do the rest of the drive in the dark."

"Sounds good," said Pete. He was about to ask the soldiers if they had any food, but they had both already fallen asleep in their seats, trained, like soldiers everywhere, to sleep whenever an opportunity presented itself.

After fifteen minutes, he let himself out of the vehicle to urinate, and to stretch his legs. He walked a few feet away, not sure if he would be violating some kind of Army etiquette by peeing too close to their vehicle. It was a still, cool night, and Pete noticed for the first time that the soldiers hadn't even pulled over: they'd stopped in the middle of the highway. It didn't seem like any kind of martial arrogance; he assumed they must have good reason to believe that no other drivers were coming along. And, come to think of it, Pete hadn't seen one in a while, in either direction. Not even another military vehicle. The interstate must be closed to civilian traffic, he realized.

Something caught his eye to the north, in the sky. A dark form, flying silently toward them. He felt the hair stand up on the back of his neck, and fought the urge to shout out to his companions until he was certain.

It swooped low, and then curved back into the sky, too high for him to see in the blackness. He kept his eyes up, and saw it again, blocking out its silhouette in the stars.

It was a vulture.

He exhaled loudly with relief. Any other time in his life, the appearance of a lone vulture on an empty highway might fill him with silent dread, a dark omen. But under the circumstances, he almost laughed with relief.

The vehicle behind him erupted with alarms. The driver threw his door open.

"*Get in!*" he screamed.

Pete dived for the door. Before he even had the door shut, they were spinning their tires, speeding down the highway.

The soldier in the passenger seat reached up and silenced the alarm in the overhead console that was blaring. "Drone," he said. "Directly behind us. Flying west."

"What the fuck were you doing out there?" said the driver.

"Taking a piss," said Pete.

"Did you see it? Why the fuck didn't you say something?"

The driver had switched on a center console that showed the drone as a tiny, bright green blip to the east in the center of a small screen.

"Gaining on us," said the passenger. "Radar says he's going about one hundred knots."

"That means he's not armed," said Pete. "That's too fast for an armed bird."

The two soldiers looked at each other, assessed Pete's knowledge without saying anything to each other.

"So you think we should just go back to sleep?" he said. They were roaring down the highway, hitting potholes with jarring force.

"No," said Pete. "It's in suicide mode. Unarmed, far from home. He's going to try to crash into us."

"I've heard about that," said the soldier in the passenger seat. "Kamikaze mode."

"Well, fuck me," said the driver. He was scanning the road-side, looking for some kind of natural cover, but there was nowhere to hide.

"Wait until he's in his dive!" said Pete. "Once he starts free fall, he doesn't alter course. Everything shuts down."

"You're sure about that?"

"I wrote the program," said Pete.

"Did you also write the program that's supposed to keep them from attacking on Alliance territory?"

"Five hundred yards," said the soldier in the passenger seat, looking at the radar screen. "But he's climbing."

"It wants to gain altitude before diving," said Pete.

"So what should I do?"

"Keep driving straight," said Pete. "Let it commit to a solution."

They roared down the highway. The driver suddenly veered to avoid a massive crater in the center of the road. Pete could feel the vehicle coming up on two wheels. They crashed back down.

"That's a new one," said the driver. "Not on the chart. Probably where our friend there dropped his bomb."

"Bombing what?" said the other sergeant.

"Unlucky farmer?" he said. "Who knows. Maybe a mule or a goddamn enemy possum."

Other alarms began beeping on their overhead console. "One hundred yards and diving," he said. "Heading right for us."

"Keep driving," said Pete. He was counting down in his head, running the numbers, knowing the drone wouldn't correct its free fall in the last ten seconds of flight. "Slam on the brakes when I say so. . . ."

They could see on the radar that it was directly behind and above them. They still couldn't see it. Pete watched the two dots on the radar screen converge, their truck and the enemy drone. The two dots were almost on top of each other.

"*Now!*" he said.

The driver slammed on the brakes, and the truck skidded to a halt, going completely sideways. They sat for one pregnant moment, and then the drone crashed directly on the stretch of road in front of them, right outside the driver's side window. There was no explosion, as the drone carried no fuel. Just sparks and the concussion.

They waited a moment, made sure there were no more blips on the screen, and then all three men got out to look at the wreckage.

Debris was scattered everywhere, centered on a small crater the drone had created in the asphalt. None of the pieces had any kind of markings or identification on them. Both sergeants took pictures. It was the closest Pete had been to a drone since leaving Eris Island. After a few minutes of catching their breath and walking around the wreckage, they got back into the truck without a word.

The driver drove slowly around it, into the median, to avoid the destruction.

The soldier in the passenger seat was the first to speak. "Those things are bigger than I thought."

"We're almost there," said the driver. They'd driven about another hour since the drone attack and were approaching the submarine base. They'd slowed down to an almost leisurely pace to make the rendezvous at the exact right time, which seemed painfully slow after their brief one-hundred-mile-per-hour sprint.

The soldier in the passenger seat turned and shook Pete's hand. "We're not going to hang around after we drop you off, I'm afraid, so let's say goodbye now."

Pete took his hand.

Suddenly they were at the head of the dock. They exchanged documents with two men in a machine gun nest that was topped by a heavily camouflaged metal shield. He waved them on and then ducked back below his cover after a quick survey of the sky.

"Go," they said to Pete. "Good luck."

He jumped out of the vehicle with his seabag, and as soon as he did, his companions sped away inland, as fast as they could drive.

Pete looked around. The soldier in the machine gun nest was deep inside his shelter, invisible.

"Is there a submarine around here somewhere?" Pete yelled toward him.

"That way," said the soldier. His hand appeared out of the shadows, and pointed down the pier.

Pete didn't see a submarine, but he started walking in that direction anyway.

After a few minutes it came into sight, a dark shape emerging from the ocean. When he got to it, the brow and a single set of lines were the only things that connected the vessel to shore. Water still dripped from the dark steel of its hull; Pete got the impression that it had surfaced just moments before his arrival. A man waited for him topside, in a full captain's uniform.

"Welcome aboard," he said.

"I'm happy to be here," said Pete, extending his hand. The captain was wearing regular Navy ribbons; Pete thought he probably wanted him to notice that.

"I'm Captain Finn McCallister," he said.

"Pete Hamlin," he answered, taking the captain's extended hand.

An alarm screeched belowdecks. "Let's get going," said the captain. "Sounds like they're near."

"Who?"

The captain looked at him like he was making a bad joke. He pointed at the sky, just like the soldier who had driven him there a day before.

"The drones?" asked Pete.

"Of course not," said McCallister, striding toward the ladder. "The drones are perfectly engineered to defeat the enemy and protect the Alliance. But all the same we should get submerged before they start dropping bombs on our heads."

CHAPTER TWENTY-SEVEN

At the bottom of the ladder, a young officer was waiting for them, a weary smile on his face and a stack of linens in his hands.

"Lieutenant Ramirez will show you to your bunk," said the captain. "He's your new roommate."

"There's a uniform here, too," said Ramirez, patting the top of the stack. "So you can look like a submariner. We even put your name on it."

"Sorry for all the trouble," said Pete.

"Don't apologize," said Ramirez. "This is the first time I've seen the sky in five months. I'll be forever grateful." He gave the hatch a longing glance as the captain spun it shut, preparing the big submarine to go to sea again.

"I'm going to control," said the captain. "I need to get us to the dive point as quickly as possible. As soon as we get in deep water, I'll bring you to my stateroom so we can have a look at your orders."

"Aye, aye, sir."

"In the meantime, Ramirez will show you around."

"Come on," said Ramirez, no longer interested in lingering now that the last sliver of sky had been shut off to them. "First stop, our stateroom."

As it turned out, it was right around the corner.

There were two bunks, one of which had been stripped bare revealing its thin, Navy-issue mattress.

"Here," said Ramirez, handing him the stack of sheets and pillowcases. For the first time, Pete noticed that a pamphlet was sitting on top: WELCOME ABOARD THE USS *POLARIS*.

"What's this?"

"That? A little bit of a joke. A thing we used to hand out to visiting bands of Cub Scouts and Rotarians. A memento of happier times. But there *is* some info that might be useful to you in there. Ever been on a submarine before?"

"Never," said Pete. "Spent a lot of time in the simulator in Charleston. But this is my first time on a real boat."

"You get used to it after about five years," he said. The fatigue from all the years showed in Ramirez's face, but his smile was genuine. Pete thought Ramirez was one of those guys who could suffer through anything, probably a job requirement for a career in the submarine force. Or maybe he was just glad to have somebody new to talk to.

"Well," said Pete. "Hopefully this won't take that long."

There was a sharp knock on the stateroom door, and a strikingly beautiful woman appeared, with commander's insignia on her collar.

"Already hanging out in your stateroom?" she said. "Looks like Ramirez's bad habits rubbed off on you fast." She had shoulder-length blond hair and a turned-up nose. Her body was small but powerful, athletic, reminding Pete of a cheerleader. Her eyes were hard, though, and she stared Pete down.

"Yes, ma'am," said Ramirez, unfazed. "Now that I've shown him his rack, I'll show him where we watch movies and take showers."

"That will cover a normal day in your life," she said with a snort. She extended her hand to Pete. "Commander Hana Moody," she said. "I'm the XO."

"Pete Hamlin," he responded.

"I know," she said. "You must be important."

"Not at all," he said. "It's all about the mission."

"Which is?"

There was a pause as she waited for Pete to disclose something. Anything.

"Ma'am, I'm not really at liberty to say. I haven't even reviewed my orders with the captain."

She tossed her head and exhaled loudly. "Jeez, some manners from you. A guest on my ship, given this prime bunk, and you're keeping secrets from a superior officer."

"Yes, ma'am," he said. "Once I tell the captain, it will be up to him to share with anyone on a need-to-know basis."

"I'm familiar with the requirements," she snapped. She was looking him up and down now. "Ever been on a submarine?"

"Never," he said.

"Are you Navy? Alliance?"

Pete shook his head. "I'm not at liberty to say."

"Jesus, you're a pain in the ass. I'm told you have officer of the deck training?"

"Correct, ma'am."

"Then I guess we'll treat you like an officer. We can use the help."

"Only got four on the entire crew right now," said Ramirez. "Captain, XO, me, and Frank."

"You're forgetting somebody," said Moody.

"Oh, the doctor!" Ramirez said in a teasing way, as if he knew it would irritate her.

"He gets a stateroom to himself and no duties on the watch bill," she said. "But you won't get off that easy. I'll need to observe you before putting you on the watch bill, of course."

"Of course," he said, and their eyes locked.

"It'll mean spending a lot of time with me," she said. "Hours and hours."

"Looking forward to it," said Pete.

She laughed loudly. "Sure you are, hotshot. All right—I'm going forward to take the watch from the captain."

She turned and left without another word.

"She's pretty hot, right?" said Ramirez.

"Sure," said Pete.

"Beautiful," Ramirez said a little wistfully. "But deadly."

They spent a few minutes talking about hometowns, and what was going on ashore, as Pete unpacked. Ramirez was eager for news about the epidemic and the Dallas Cowboys. He had a girlfriend who had dumped him recently, and clearly he still pined for her. She hadn't written to him in months; Ramirez worried about her.

Pete pulled out a Lucite block, one of the only personal items he'd thought to pack.

"What's that?" said Ramirez.

Pete handed it to him. He turned it over in his hand. "Is that a honeybee?"

"It is," said Pete. "At every stage of its life cycle. There's the larva," he said, pointing. "The pupa, the adult."

"Very cool," said Ramirez, staring at it curiously.

"It was a gift," said Pete, feeling it necessary to explain.

"Let me guess," said Ramirez. "From a girlfriend."

Pete shook his head, trying to hide his sadness.

"Wife?" said Ramirez.

Pete shook his head again, and carefully took the Lucite block away.

"Ex-wife?" said Ramirez.

Pete didn't have it in him to clarify, so he let that stand.

Ramirez shook his head ruefully. "Join the club, my brother. The Submarine Force Lonely Hearts Club."

Pete placed the honeybee memento above his desk, and continued unpacking.

After a few minutes, a sound-powered phone on the wall of the stateroom chirped, and he was summoned to the captain's stateroom. On the way there, he passed a muscular lieutenant with HOLMES on his nametag. He nodded gruffly in Pete's direction, his only acknowledgment. *I guess not everyone here is happy to have a new shipmate,* he thought.

"Come in, shut the door," said the captain when Pete arrived. He scooted over to make room in the small stateroom.

"Aye, sir."

"Listen," said the captain, as they both sat down. The cramped quarters made for a kind of instant intimacy. "I suspect you're a civilian—maybe I'm about to find out. So, if that's true, why don't you call me Finn, and I'll call you Pete. At least when it's just the two of us."

"Sure . . . Finn."

The captain smiled broadly at that, as if he was pleased and surprised at the effort. "OK, let's take a look."

Pete pulled out the small tablet that he'd been holding, and powered it on. He swiped his finger across it, and the patrol order came to light. The first few pages were all boilerplate, long descriptions of responsibilities and secrecy requirements. The captain scanned through it all quickly, swiping ahead with the confidence of a man who had read a great many patrol orders and knew how to get to the good parts. He watched the animated projections of the epidemic, his eyes growing wide. Finally he got to a paragraph that offered a summation of the mission and he read it, and Pete watched him go back to the top and read it again before he offered any kind of reaction.

"Eris Island," he said. "You can get us in there?"

"I can," said Pete. "It won't be easy, but I can."

"One time we got within about two hundred miles and it was hot as hell. Drones everywhere."

"We'll stay submerged as long as possible. Degauss and cross the shoals at PD."

The captain nodded while making eye contact. "And that's where we'll find the wonder drug?"

"Yes, sir," said Pete. "We hope so."

The captain tapped the icon on the screen that contained Pete's personnel file. "I'll read this in a minute, after we get through the nuts and bolts here, but are you a doctor? A scientist?"

"I'm an engineer," said Pete. "With extensive experience on Eris Island and with the drones. That's my expertise."

"Aha," said the captain, nodding, thinking it over. "There's someone I'd like to share this with," he said.

"You have that authority, sir."

The captain picked up a microphone over his desk, and turned a switch. His voice boomed across the ship. "Doctor Haggerty, report to the captain's stateroom."

He hung up and waited for the doctor to arrive. Pete knew that somewhere close, Commander Moody was fuming at being kept out of the loop. He wondered how she would take it out on him.

Later that night, Ramirez took Pete to the wardroom. "I've shown you where to sleep, now I'll show you where to eat. That should about cover it."

It was a somewhat formal-looking room: wood panel cabinets, a glass case with actual silver serving platters on display, and eight chairs arranged around a table with the captain's chair at the head, the only chair with arms.

"That silver is from the USS *George Washington*," said Ramirez, pointing at the cabinet. "The first ballistic missile submarine. The first to carry a *Polaris* missile."

Pete stared through the glass at the elaborately etched silver tray, a long, flat-decked submarine carved upon it. "Beautiful," said Pete.

"Hard to imagine an era when they served food on silver like that onboard a submarine."

Pete looked around and confirmed what Ramirez was saying. Any formality in the wardroom had long since given way to a kind of grubby practicality. Very old magazines were stacked across the table. A well-worn steel coffeepot had the power of place in the room, right next to the door. Giant, unillustrated bags of Navy-issue snack foods were arranged on a side counter—cheese balls and corn chips. Little boxes of cereal were stacked like bricks against one wall. After years at sea, it seemed, the *Polaris* had given up on the burden of formal meals.

"Breakfast?" said Ramirez, holding up a tiny box of Apple Jacks. "Or lunch?" he said, poking a bag of the bright orange cheese balls.

"How about just coffee?" Pete responded, sitting down across from him.

"We have that," said Ramirez. He began to make a fresh pot.

"How often do you get resupplied?"

"As often as we can," said Ramirez. "Which ain't that often. We meet a tender up north . . . every year it gets farther north. Every six months if we can pull it off. Each time the food gets worse, the supply parts get harder to come by. Unfortunately, they made this boat so well that it just keeps running."

"Why so far north?"

Ramirez looked at him as the coffeemaker began its noisy burbling cycle. It was a hard, assessing stare.

"The drones," he said.

"The drones?"

"If we go far enough north, we're less likely to get one of our own little bombs dropped on us. Every year we go farther. Two months ago I was on the bridge when we met the tender. We were so far north that with my binoculars I could actually see ice in the water."

"Jesus."

He shrugged. "Of course, we're not supposed to say that. But I can tell you that we haven't heard a whisper from an enemy ship out here, submarine or otherwise, in over a year. But every time we get near the surface, those drone alarms start screaming."

The door burst open, Frank Holmes in workout gear carrying a stack of papers. He was followed by a man Pete hadn't yet met. It had to be Haggerty, the doctor. Ramirez quickly stopped talking.

"What's going on in here?" said Holmes with a large smile on his face. "A non-qual lounging in the wardroom?" He began feeding classified papers into a shredder that sat at the corner of the room, which groaned as it tried to digest them. Pete fought his engineer's impulse to tell Frank to slow down, he was feeding too much paper into the machine at once.

Ramirez shot Pete an evil grin that said, *watch this.* "Hey, Frank . . . whatcha doing?"

Frank turned around, still feeding his sheaf of paperwork into the shredder. "I'm deleting these old targeting documents," he said.

Ramirez burst out laughing. "That kills me every time!" he said. He looked at Pete. "He says he's deleting stuff when he shreds it."

"Whatever," said Frank with a shrug. "Same fucking thing." He clapped his hands as the shredder finished chewing through the last document.

"So," Frank said to Pete. "Who won the Super Bowl? Was it awesome?"

"Tell us it was," said Ramirez. "Even if it wasn't."

Pete learned in the wardroom that part of his onboarding required a cursory physical examination from Haggerty. He followed the doctor to sick bay after he finished his coffee.

"Any contagious diseases?" Haggerty asked, reading from a clipboard.

"No," said Pete.

"No coughing, diarrhea, sore throat?"

Pete shook his head.

"Don't be offended," said the doctor. "We have to ask everybody."

"I'm not offended at all," Pete answered.

The doctor turned and reached in a drawer for a small plastic cylinder. He wrote a tiny serial number on it and handed it to Pete. "Here, wear this on your belt: your personal dosimeter. It will keep track of how much radiation you receive from the reactor. Don't worry, it won't be much. I read them once a month, and all of us have negligible doses, even guys like the captain and Ramirez who have been here for years." He pointed to a row of binders, one for each crewman, past and present.

Ramirez's was thick with paper, one sheet representing every month onboard.

"Thanks," said Pete, undoing his belt to attach the device.

"It's a hell of a thing," said the doctor.

"What's that?" said Pete.

"Your mission. Our mission. You really think the cure is out there?"

Pete shrugged. "You're a doctor, don't you believe in cures?"

He smiled wryly. "Of course I do. I'm just not sure I still believe in patrol orders."

After his physical, Pete met Ramirez back in the stateroom.

"Home sweet home," said Ramirez as he walked in.

"How long have you been at sea?" he asked, remembering the folder with Ramirez's exposure tracking.

He squinted his eyes, as if deep in thought. "Five years and two months. Longer than anybody except the captain."

"And you've been engineer the whole time?"

He nodded. "Yep. And Frank is weapons officer, Moody is XO. That's it—four watchstanders. The ship was designed to operate with no fewer than six, originally, but here we are."

"What about the doctor?"

"Not a watchstander. Technically, he's not required to learn a watchstation as the science officer, but it would be, you know, good manners if he did. I hear most doctors on other boats do it."

"That's the plan for me?"

Ramirez nodded. "You should be able to complete the qualification in a couple of weeks with all your simulator time. Everything is pretty much automated. But it'll still be nice to have another name on the watchbill."

"I'm looking forward to it."

"Just don't get too good. They'll never let you leave."

Pete laughed. "Is that what happened to you?"

Ramirez nodded. "Yeah. For a while I sent messages requesting a transfer—my sea tour was supposed to end two years ago. They stopped even giving me the courtesy of a response. And I stopped asking—don't want to look disloyal. In the current environment."

He held Pete's gaze.

"Meaning?"

He could tell Ramirez was assessing him, not completely sure if he could trust Pete.

"The captain and I—we're Navy guys. He went to the academy, I was ROTC at Texas A&M. Frank and Hana—they're Alliance officers. Pure Alliance."

"True believers?"

"Exactly. They distrust everyone and anyone who isn't drinking the Kool-Aid. And they don't mind letting their bosses know about it."

"And that includes you?"

"Absolutely. *And* the captain."

Pete thought about that.

"What about the doctor?"

Ramirez laughed. "Who knows where he comes from. Medical school, I guess."

"So why did you volunteer for submarines?"

"That's a question I ask myself a lot these days," said Ramirez. "My father was a submariner, I guess that had something to do with it: a captain."

"What boat?"

"The *Alaska*. An old Trident. Here," he said, "let me show you something."

He reached into his desk and cleared some papers and books out of the way, revealing a small safe. He spun the dial and opened it up. Nestled among a dozen bottles of medicine was a small nine-millimeter pistol.

"This was my dad's," he said, pulling it out. "At sea, he slept with it."

"The drugs, too?"

"No," he said. "I happen to be the controlled medicinals custodian, one of my many collateral duties, that's why I've got a safe."

"So why did your dad sleep with a gun?"

"He said that the captain of a Trident submarine was the most vulnerable part of the entire strategic weapons triad. So the minute the boat went alert, he put the purple key around his neck, and this pistol under his pillow."

Pete took it and hefted it. He dropped the clip. "It's loaded," he said.

"Well, he couldn't very well stop a mutiny or a KGB take-over if it was unloaded," he said.

"Are you allowed to have this?"

He shrugged. "Not technically. No real small arms allowed on the boats anymore—just a few Tasers and billy clubs. The doc is the only other one who has the combination to the safe, we do a monthly inventory of the drugs together. He never says anything."

"Maybe he thinks it's a cigarette lighter."

Ramirez shook his head vigorously. "God no. Cigarettes would *really* get me in trouble."

Pete spent the next days learning the ship's systems, usually with Ramirez but also standing watch with Moody, Frank, and the captain. Ramirez had been right, the ship was easy to learn, the systems supremely well engineered, and with Pete's technical acumen he soon learned them all. While he didn't have the competence they'd all gathered after thousands of hours on the conn, the simulator and the attention of Commander Ase had served him well, and he was soon trusted enough that they signed his qualification book and made him an officer of the deck. They honored the occasion in the wardroom with a real meal, a chicken that had been saved deep in the freezer for a special occasion, and a bottle of wine that the captain brought down from his stateroom. Only Moody wasn't present, as someone had to stand watch in the control room.

"To our new watchstander," said the captain, raising a glass. "By my calculation, this should give each of us twenty-five percent more time in the rack, and Hamlin seventy-five percent less."

They clicked their glasses together and drank.

"What now?" said Ramirez.

"Now—we have a mission to complete."

"Are we getting close?"

The captain nodded. "We're getting close."

Suddenly the phone buzzed at his knees, a direct line to the control room. He picked it up.

"Captain."

He nodded as he listened, his brow furrowing with concern. "OK. I'm on my way up."

"Something wrong, Captain?"

He nodded. "We've got a submerged contact. Moody thinks she's following us."

The next two weeks were a blur of evasive maneuvers, countermeasures, and stifling tension. But they couldn't shake the shadow boat. Pete watched a change come over the captain as he tried to evade the enemy boat, but couldn't. One

night prior to taking the midnight watch, he spent some time
with the captain to discuss the situation in the wardroom.

"You're certain it's the enemy?"

He nodded. "No Alliance boats would get this close to
Eris—trust me. It's crazy to get this close, and if I didn't have
your assurances that you knew some backdoor in, I wouldn't
be trying it either."

"Why don't they shoot us?"

"I've thought about that," said the captain. "Maybe they
want to see what we're doing. Maybe they want to shoot us
after we pick up our cargo."

"So why don't we shoot them?" Pete asked.

At this, the captain's demeanor darkened. "Have you been
talking to them?"

"Who?"

"Hana and Frank," he said. "They think I should just fire
two torpedoes at her, make all our problems go away."

"They haven't said a word to me about it," said Pete. "But
why *don't* you?"

"At this range—they'll shoot back immediately. And they'll
hit us, sure as shit. Firing a torpedo at them is a murder–
suicide. As long as we've got a chance to evade, and complete
our mission, I'm going to keep trying."

"Unless they shoot us."

"If they shoot at us first," said the captain, "I've got a torpedo in tube one with their name on it. We can say goodbye
to each other as our torpedoes cross paths."

The next morning, the captain called them all to control. He
looked like he hadn't slept all night. Ramirez and the captain
stood on one side of the plotting table, Frank and Hana on

the other. Pete stood to the side, equidistant between the adversaries.

"OK," he said. "We're going to try something new. We're going to launch the MOSS."

Hana rolled her eyes. Frank looked to her for approval, then snickered.

"The MOSS, Captain?" Moody was incredulous. "That thing is archaic. It's a waste of time."

"What's the MOSS?" Pete asked.

"It's a submarine simulator," said Ramirez. "Basically a fake submarine we launch from a torpedo tube. It broadcasts our same acoustic signature. The bad guy follows it." But even Ramirez didn't sound optimistic.

Moody continued. "Captain, respectfully, we'll never fool a modern boat with that thing."

"We'll rig for ultraquiet," he said. "Then we'll launch countermeasures and push out the MOSS. While Typhon is trying to figure it out, we'll peel away to the north. If we're quiet enough, and the MOSS works like it's supposed to, we'll slip away."

"Waste of time," said Hana again, frustration in her voice.

"You have any better ideas, XO?" said the captain. They were glaring at each other.

"I do, *sir*," she said, emphasizing the word. "Instead of firing that dusty MOSS, launch a real torpedo down their throats. If you want to evade, a torpedo in the water will make that a lot easier. Let's get the first shot off in this fight."

"She's two thousand yards away, Hana. At this range, she'll fire right back on a dead bearing."

"So we evade!" she said. "That's what you're planning on doing anyway! Let's take a shot and then evade!"

"I've made my decision," said the captain. "Frank, load the MOSS in tube three, and prepare for battle stations."

"We're not going to discuss this anymore?" said Moody.

"Discussion is over," said the captain. "Now, follow your goddamn orders."

For a second, they all stared at each other. Then Frank stormed out of control without a word, while Hana continued to glare at the chart.

Frank pushed his way past the doctor on the ladder on the way out. He'd been standing there the whole time, listening.

CHAPTER TWENTY-EIGHT

Commander Carlson kept waiting for the shot, but it became clear to her that the Alliance boat was trying to evade her, not willing to engage in any suicidal actions: smart. In the meantime, she would follow. She was proud of shooting that little plane down, and she would stick to that philosophy. Better to shoot the enemy ship on her return trip from Eris Island.

Polaris was a good, quiet ship, with a skilled captain, she could tell. Acoustically, they had two things she could hold on to. At very close ranges, inside of one thousand meters, they could hear a 60 Hz tonal. It could be anything electrical that was sonically sorted to the hull, broadcasting that slight electric whine into the sea. It traveled a very short distance, its high, narrow frequency attenuating quickly in the ocean. But it was distinctively man-made and therefore invaluable, a sound they could pluck from the cloud of natural noises that surrounded them: the roar of the ocean, the tides, the shifting of the ocean floor, and the mournful cries of whales a hundred miles away. Moreover, it was distinctively Alliance, as the

Typhon boat operated on a 50 Hz electrical system, so they could quickly distinguish any of their own noise from the enemy's.

Secondly, they had discovered a sound made from the ship's reduction gear, a slight chirp. It could have been a chipped tooth along one of the many gears, and it clicked reliably with every full rotation of the screw. This sound had the added advantage of being directly related to the speed of the reduction gear, and therefore, the speed of the ship. Over many days of tracking *Polaris,* they had even constructed a formula to convert the frequency of the chirping to the speed of the ship.

Both noises disappeared entirely outside of about two thousand meters, so they worked hard to stay inside that range. It was difficult because the *Polaris* tried all the standard evasion techniques, changing speed and course often. *Polaris* was hampered here by the fact that Carlson knew their destination: Eris Island. Still, sometimes they drifted out of range. When they did, Carlson had a third sound she could count on to reel the *Polaris* back in: the voice of their spy. It almost felt unsporting to rely on it, but there you go. War is hell.

Carlson was in control with Banach and two of her officers whom she trusted only slightly less. They were staring at the small-scale plot in the corner, looking at their estimate of the *Polaris*'s course and speed. Suddenly a starburst of noise lit up their sonar display. Banach quickly put headphones to one ear.

"They're launching countermeasures," he said, quickly putting down a red X on the chart at the position of the launch. "And another," he said, making another red X.

"They're up to something," said Carlson. The Alliance had basically two categories of countermeasures, things that spun in the water, and things that fizzed; they looked to be using both. The goal for both was to create a large acoustic cloud that the *Polaris* could escape behind, the same way infantry used smoke grenades on the battlefield. Carlson wasn't too worried; she had too many good cards in her hand. But she was curious.

"Target zig," said Reese, her youngest officer, on the phones with sonar. "Target has turned to the south," he said, taking the information from the display in front of him.

Carlson looked at the plot. Over days, the ship, despite all its maneuvering and attempts to evade them, had steadily made its way toward Eris. Maneuvers like this weren't unusual as they tried to shake her. But the countermeasures were a new twist; the large amount of ambient noise they were creating was weakening the acoustic grip they held on their prey.

She walked over to the sonar display, the narrow band read-out stacking dots on top of each other. The dots represented the actual data from sonar. If they stacked in a perfectly straight line, it indicated that they had a good-quality solution: they knew the *Polaris*'s course and speed. But the newest dots were starting to stray, bending toward the right.

"Target is speeding up, too, no?" she asked.

"Yes, Captain," said Reese. "Turned to starboard and sped up."

She clicked on the screen and looked at the data. The 60 Hz tonal was loud and clear. But the clicking of the reduction gear had disappeared entirely.

"Ship is rigged for silent running," said Moody. She was looking at an electronic status console in front of her. All unnecessary machinery had been stopped to make the ship even quieter. This included fans and air conditioners, so the temperature was steadily climbing in control. They were all at their battle stations. The doctor was in sick bay, "counting

Band-Aids," as he said. Frank was in the torpedo room, while Ramirez was in the engine room. The captain, Pete, and Moody were in the control room. Pete was in the dive chair, directing the rudder and the stern planes. "Countermeasures are in the water and activated."

"Very well," said McCallister. "Launch the MOSS."

They felt nothing in their feet, no rush of water or change in pressure—it wasn't like when a torpedo was ejected from the ship. They had pumped open the outer doors of the torpedo tube, and the MOSS simply swam out.

"The MOSS is launched," reported Moody.

"Very well," said the captain. "All stop."

Pete rang it up, and the engine room answered immediately.

"Left five degrees rudder," said the captain. Pete turned the yoke in front of him. "Sir, the engine room has answered all stop. My rudder is left five degrees."

"Very well," said McCallister. "We're turning away. How long until the MOSS broadcasts?"

"Five minutes," said Moody.

Everyone in the control room looked at their watches.

The MOSS swam from its torpedo tube powered by a small electric engine. Unlike the ship it was born to imitate, its propulsion machinery was almost silent, the energy flowing from a chemical battery rather than the spinning of turbines and the pumping of water through a nuclear reactor. Five minutes into its journey, it began broadcasting a recording from a transponder in its nose. The sound was carefully designed to sound like a *Polaris* submarine, with a 60 Hz tonal and a broadband signature in the back of that like the *whooshing* of steam through pipes. While the MOSS was tiny, it was noisy, purposefully so, creating an acoustic profile that was slightly louder than the ship it was leaving behind. It was a decoy, and like a hunter's wooden duck floating on a lake, it had to attract attention without being obvious.

After five minutes of broadcasting, the MOSS turned on its programmed course. It turned right and sped up slightly, to 8 knots. Its acoustic twin, the real submarine, turned left at this same time, and the distance between the two grew.

After forty-five minutes, its battery exhausted, the MOSS died. A small valve slid open, filling a center chamber with seawater. Its mission complete, the MOSS sank to the ocean floor.

"The MOSS is broadcasting," said Moody. The *Polaris* was now just drifting, its screw not turning, as silent as the big ship could be.

"I see it," said the captain, tapping the screen in front of him. He looked at the narrowband profile that had suddenly appeared on his console, the 60 Hz tonal a bright line that was peeling away from them. He switched displays to see broadband sound, and watched the line tracing away from them that marked the "steam ring," the signature of a very nearby submarine, the actual sound of high-pressure steam moving through pipes. It was a faithful duplication of their own noise being broadcast by the MOSS. "So that's what we look like," he said, almost to himself.

Moody came to his side. Despite her lack of faith in the plan to evade, she was excited, and determined, as always, to succeed. "Look!" she said excitedly, pointing at the display of the enemy boat. "They're turning! They're following the MOSS!"

"Make turns for three knots," said the captain. "Let's drive slowly away before they figure it out."

Carlson allowed them to swing right to follow the sound, but the hair was standing up on the back of her neck. Something wasn't right.

"Captain?"

Banach was standing beside her. Just as she had finely tuned instincts about enemy submarines, like any good XO, he had developed good instincts about his commander.

"I don't know about this . . ." she said.

"Why? We can hear them clearly. If anything, it's louder."

"Exactly," she said. "And faster. So why no noise from the reduction gear?"

He furrowed his brow at that.

"We're following that sixty hertz because it's all we've got."

"Correct," said Banach. "It's all we've got. We haven't always held both signals."

"It's going completely straight now, at a higher speed."

"Maybe they've given up," said Banach. "Perhaps they are abandoning their mission. Because of us."

She snorted at that. "No," she said. "You poor thing. It's been so long since we've been in port, you've forgotten what it feels like to be seduced." She swept through the sonar display, looking on all bearings for another sound, anything. But there was only silence, except for the 60 Hz beacon in front of them, the clearest they'd heard their target since they first acquired it.

Then, after forty-five minutes, it disappeared entirely.

"Shit!" said Carlson.

"I don't understand," said Banach, sweeping the cursor on the display through the ocean. "It just disappeared!"

"A drone of some kind," said Carlson, already heading for the main plot. "We've been duped."

She tapped her finger on a spot on the chart precisely between their current position and the spot where the fake *Polaris* had first turned and sped up. "Here!" she said. "Drive us here!"

"Left full rudder!" said Banach. The big ship turned to port.

"We've been driving away from them for almost forty minutes," she said. "Assuming they are going very slow . . ."

"Maybe a mile or two?"

"If they were driving directly away from us," she said.

"Have we lost them?" said Banach.

"We lost them," she said. "They outsmarted us, fair and square."

"We're almost in position," said Banach.

"All stop!" she ordered. "Rudder amidships!"

As her big ship coasted silently through the ocean, she closed her eyes and pictured the drone submarine to her north, and her prey somewhere to the south, an entire ocean to hide in.

Banach started to talk, but she stopped him with a finger to her lips, her eyes still shut.

Suddenly, a bright blip appeared on the sonar screen.

"Transient!" said Banach. "Bearing two-zero-zero."

"Drive to it," said Carlson, relief flooding through her even as she felt a slight sense of shame. Just as she told Banach, the *Polaris* had outsmarted them fair and square. The only reason they were able to find them again was because at this critical juncture they had a friend onboard. A friend who helpfully dropped a heavy wrench into a dry bilge, sending a pulse of sound into the sea that traveled for miles and miles.

"I think we did it!" said Moody.

The captain nodded grimly. "Ahead one-third," he said. They were three miles away from the enemy boat, the farthest they'd been since they first spotted her. At this distance, they would be invisible, even at the slightly higher speed.

"Engine room answers ahead one-third," said Pete.

Frank appeared in control. "Did it work?" he said.

"Maybe," said the captain. He fought the urge to speed up even more, the desire to open distance faster balanced by the greater noise the ship would create.

"No sonar contacts!" said Moody as the enemy disappeared entirely from their screen. The captain checked his watch.

"The MOSS will die soon. Then they'll know."

They drove a few minutes more at five knots, seemingly alone according to the blank display in front of them. Then the enemy reappeared.

"She's there!" said Moody. "And faster, by the look of it."

"She figured it out," said the captain, "when the MOSS died. Doesn't surprise me. Sped up and backtracked. I would have done the same thing. She still doesn't see us."

"Speed up?"

"No," said the captain. "Let's just try to slip away."

They watched the Typhon sub move on sonar, created a solution that showed her moving, just as the captain had predicted, right down her old track. Not pointing directly at them as she had for days. The bright dots stacked up neatly.

And then suddenly the enemy veered.

Moody sat down and quickly worked out a new solution.

"Target zig." She looked up. "She's turned toward us."

"Dammit," said the captain.

"Speed zig," said Moody. "Speeding up."

"Ahead two-thirds," said the captain. "Make turns for eight knots."

"Too late," said Moody, fine-tuning her solution on the display. In minutes, the Typhon boat was again following them so closely and so tightly that on sonar it looked almost like they were towing her. "They've got us."

"Goddammit!" shouted Frank. Pete winced. He realized

they'd all been whispering everything since they went to battle stations.

"How?" said Moody. "How did that happen?"

Pete turned around to look. For the first time, he saw real resignation in the captain's eyes. Moody stared at the captain, but Frank stared at Pete; everyone seemed to be accusing everyone else of giving the ship away.

Soon enough, Ramirez had made his way to control, and the conversation grew heated.

"Every time we start to get away," said Moody, "they know right where to find us."

"Exactly!" said Frank. The captain ignored him.

"Something is giving us away," he mumbled, looking at the chart.

"Or someone," said Moody. Her eyes were locked on the captain's, bright and wary.

"What exactly are you saying, Commander Moody?"

"I'm saying that the Typhon boat seems to know our every move. We were completely silent back there, and she turned right toward us."

The captain shook his head. "It has to be something . . ."

"Maybe a transient?" said Ramirez.

"Did you hear something?" snapped Moody.

"No," said Ramirez. "But obviously *they* did."

"Let's look at the sonar recordings," said Moody, already moving toward the screen and deftly changing the display. "Every individual hydrophone. We know when it happened— about thirty minutes ago."

She moved the cursor backward in time, and they all stared over her shoulder at the picture the computer had rendered, turning noise into green waves of light and dark.

"There!" she said.

At first, Pete didn't see it, but she changed the resolution and it came into view. A bright spike at precisely the time the Typhon boat had turned toward them.

"What the hell?" said the captain. "Something that loud would have traveled for miles!"

"We didn't stand a chance," said Frank.

Moody was still feverishly turning knobs on the central console. She threw a small switch and began playing the actual audio through the control room speakers.

It sounded like a whirring, the universal sound of the ocean, an ear to a seashell. Then suddenly, there was a bright spike of noise. It actually made Pete wince. It sounded like a hammer on a steel pipe.

She moved the cursor, turned up the volume, and played it again, this time staring at the captain.

And then she played it again.

"All right," said McCallister. "Enough."

She played it again.

"Knock it off, Moody!" he said.

"Why stop now?" she said. "I think we're finally getting somewhere here. Let's narrow it down by hydrophone."

She clicked through a few more menus, and suddenly there was a small line graph for every one of the twenty-six hull-mounted hydrophones that lined the exterior of the ship. She pointed to the one where the spike was the biggest, twice as big as the adjacent sensor.

"There!" she said. She tapped the number beneath the graph. "Hydrophone twenty-three."

"In the engine room," said the captain. They all looked at Ramirez.

"What?" he said.

"Did you hear anything?" said the captain.

Moody let out an exasperated sigh.

"No . . . I was in maneuvering the entire time with the doors shut—"

"Captain, I demand you arrest this man," said Moody.

"Fuck you!" said Ramirez. "I was back there keeping the ship running while you were developing your paranoid fantasies."

She slapped the screen so hard, Pete thought she might break it. "Fantasy!" she screamed. "What is this?! Somebody is banging on the damn hull, giving us away, and you're the only guy back there!"

She turned again to the captain, gathered herself, and stood up, almost at attention. When she spoke, her words had a formal steadiness to them. "Captain, I'll ask you again: arrest this man for treason. For mutiny."

Ramirez locked eyes with Pete. His defiance had faded now; he looked genuinely worried that the tide was turning against him. The word "mutiny" hung in the air almost as jarringly as the sound spike on the twenty-third hydrophone.

The captain stared Moody down. "I'm not arresting anyone."

"Then I'm taking command of this ship and arresting you both," she said.

Frank slowly pulled something from his pocket. Hamlin realized that they had planned this.

Ramirez suddenly bolted from the control room. McCallister started to follow, but Frank pointed his Taser at the captain's chest.

Seconds later, alarms began wailing.

Moody and Pete jumped forward to the control panels and began cutting them out, announcing them out of habit.

"Radio is disabled!" he said.

"Fire in the four-hundred-megahertz generators," said

Moody, cutting out the alarm. They were almost right next to each other on the panel. "He's sabotaging us," she said, directly to him.

"Ahead two-thirds!" said McCallister. "Rig for general—"

Before he could finish the order, Frank Tased him. The captain fell to the ground, writhing in pain.

Hana stood up and announced to Frank and to Pete, and to the recording of the deck log, "I am Hana Moody, and I am now in command of the *Polaris*. I have the deck and the conn."

"Aye," said Frank. He was resetting the Taser and smiling as McCallister groaned at his feet.

It had all unraveled so fast. Pete realized that Moody and Frank were now waiting to see how he would react.

"I'll find Ramirez," Pete said. And before they could say anything else, he flew down the ladder and out of control.

Radio was trashed, he saw as he sprinted by. The screens of the computers were caved in. A small fire extinguisher had done much of the damage, Pete could see, as it still jutted out of one of the shattered monitors. The small generator room for the 400 MHz machines was a soggy ruin. The fire-suppression system had put out the fire with a thick coating of foam, but the machines were destroyed. Lights shut off as he ran, the electrical system trying to protect itself from the carnage.

Just before reaching the door to his stateroom, he heard a gunshot. The sound was deafening in the confined space.

He burst through the door to see Ramirez slumped against the bulkhead, shot in the head. Leaning over him, the doctor was placing the old nine millimeter in his hand, trying to make it look like a suicide. He turned to see Pete standing in the doorway.

Pete rushed toward him, but the doctor stood up and trained the gun on him.

"What?"

"Don't move, Hamlin, or I'll do the same to you. Which would be a shame because we need you."

"I guess you're not really a doctor."

Incredibly, Haggerty looked a little insulted by this. "Of course I'm a doctor."

"Why did you kill him?"

"He was going to try to stop their stupid little mutiny. And that wouldn't do. This mutiny might be helpful to us. He and the captain were the only guys smart enough for me to worry about, and now they've both been neutralized. As for you, I still need you. I need your mission. I need your orders."

Pete suddenly lunged toward him, but the doctor was surprisingly fast. He brought the butt of the gun down on the top of Pete's head, bringing him to his knees. He was now staring right into the face of his dead friend.

He expected to hear a shot, ending it all just like it had for Ramirez. But instead, the doctor fished something out of the small, open safe. A minute later, he felt a needle sinking deep into his neck.

"There," said Haggerty. "This will make you forget just about everything."

Haggerty moved fast, knowing he had only minutes before he was discovered.

Almost everything in the stateroom belonged to Ramirez, of course, and while there were stacks of engineering documents that he was certain were classified, he had no way of telling which of the indecipherable tables and charts would be valuable to his masters at Typhon. They all looked the same to him. Deeper into the pile on his desk, he found a trove of pictures of Ramirez's girlfriend, and he threw these to the floor.

Hamlin's desk was almost bare, he was furious to discover. But above it, something caught his eye.

He pulled down a smooth Lucite block. Entombed inside it were insects. Honeybees, actually—each stage of life of a honeybee. It had to be Hamlin's, he knew; he'd been in the stateroom hundreds of times and had never noticed it before. But what did it mean? Did the honeybees contain some kind of secret code? Perhaps inside them there was some kind of microchip, or memory card? He pocketed the block, the only thing he took with him.

On the way out, he checked Hamlin's pulse to make sure he was still alive, and placed the warm gun in his hand.

CHAPTER TWENTY-NINE

A loud crash below their feet snapped Pete back into the present. He was back in the control tower on Eris Island, with McCallister and Admiral Stewart.

"What was that?" said Stewart. Finn stepped to the glass and looked down.

"Carlson and her crew," he said. "They're trying to shoot their way into the tower."

Pete joined them at the glass.

"We don't have much time," said Stewart.

"Can they get in?"

"Eventually," said Stewart. "It's blast-proof and bulletproof, but they'll shoot through it sooner or later."

"And we'll never fend off that entire crew of marines once they get in," said Finn.

Pete's head was spinning, trying to figure out a plan, even as all his memories came flooding back.

Suddenly, the noise from below stopped. Stewart and Finn ran to the other side of the tower. Pete hesitated, then followed them to the glass.

Carlson and her men had given up on the door. They'd climbed to the low rise of exposed rock toward the sea, the bluff that faced them. They began shooting at the windows. Each crack was deafening, and each strike made the windows crack and splinter. They dived to the floor and covered their heads.

"That glass is bulletproof!" yelled the admiral. "But like the door—it won't last forever against a sustained attack."

Sure enough, the window that directly faced Carlson was almost completely eradicated, the floor of the control tower covered with powdery glass. Bullets were now flying through the tower and hitting the opposite window from the inside, until it, too, was gone. Suddenly there was a pause in the shooting.

The three men crept slowly to the window. Pete wondered if Carlson was pausing to accept their surrender. He also wondered if they should give it.

On the bluff, another marine was aiming a different weapon at them—a much larger weapon.

"Is that . . . ?"

"It's a grenade launcher," said Admiral Stewart. The man holding it had two bandoliers of grenades across his chest.

Carlson was pointing at them, at the damaged window. The man with the grenade launcher took careful aim and fired. The grenade hit just below them, bounced off the tower, and exploded in the air.

"They're going to lob one in here eventually!" said Finn.

"We can go below," said Stewart. "Into the bunker. It's more heavily armored down there, made to survive a missile strike. There's food, water—we could live down there for months."

"No!" said Pete.

"What choice do we have?" asked Stewart. "We're sitting ducks up here."

"No more hiding beneath the surface!" said Pete.

"Just until help arrives—"

"We *are* the help!" shouted Pete.

"Then what do we do?" shouted Finn. "Do we have any weapons? Any guns at all?"

"Actually," said Pete, "we do have a weapon. We've got the most sophisticated weapon system in the world."

They heard the curious noise of the grenade launcher again, and as if in slow motion, watched as a grenade passed all the way through the tower, in one shattered window and out another, exploding in the air outside.

"Jesus Christ!" said Finn. "Let's get below! We don't have any choice!"

Pete ran to the center console and entered codes that were rolling back into his memory. Soon, he had the display up that he wanted; an outline of the island, with a dotted line exactly five miles from the tower. He took the red key from around his neck, inserted it, and turned it. The display changed, the five-mile ring blinking. As an alarm rang in the tower, Pete turned a knob and shrank the circle to ten feet. Stewart saw what he was doing.

"You'll destroy everything!" he said.

"I know," said Pete.

As he worked, he swore he heard laughing outside the tower.

"We've almost got them!" said Carlson. She was breathless with excitement. They were against the very door to the tower. She'd seen it in pictures a dozen times, grainy satellite photographs of it, and a few times through the magnified optics of her scope, when she dared get that close. But here she was. She slammed her fist on the door to the tower, more from excitement than from frustration.

As she backed up, her marines kept shooting at it, but the bullets were having little effect, barely denting the door. The thing had been built to withstand a sustained attack.

"We'll get through it eventually," said the sergeant as he reloaded.

"Maybe," said Carlson. "But how much time do we have?"

Banach had stepped away and was looking at the rocky bluff that faced them. "Let's go up there," he said, pointing. "We can easily shoot at the tower from there."

"We'll be exposed . . ." said the sergeant.

Carlson thought it over. From the bluff, they could shoot out the windows—there was no way they were as solid as that door. Then, maybe lob a grenade into the tower. From their current position, while they might shoot their way through eventually, it could take hours. In the meantime, they could be summoning help, arming themselves, destroying everything of value, who knows?

"Let's do it," she said. "I want to kill them quickly."

"Yes, ma'am," said the sergeant, already leading his men up the rock face of the bluff.

She and Banach looked at each other. "Having fun?" she said.

He nodded. "Nice to see these guys earning their pay for a change."

They scrambled up the bluff behind the marines. As she neared the top, she saw what was left of her submarine out at sea, a few floating scraps still being bombed by the relentless drones. Just in front of it was the wounded *Polaris,* badly damaged but untouched by the swarm. She felt a pang thinking about her lost boat. But it was balanced by the relief she felt at escaping with her life, and the thrill of the hunt.

"Almost all the windows are out!" said Banach after a few minutes of shooting from atop the rise. The men inside had

stopped showing their faces; they were hunkered down, panicked, no doubt, perhaps contemplating surrender. Banach
had a small pistol out, but the commandos around them had
the bigger guns, automatic rifles and a grenade launcher that
Carlson had been only vaguely aware was onboard. She admired the efficiency of the marines as they worked, the sergeant barely said a thing as they took their positions, covered
one another, and shot accurately at the windows. There was
something medieval about it, she thought, besieging a tower
on an island. And as in any siege, time was on their side. Soon,
several windows of the tower had been completely shot out.

The marines stopped shooting momentarily, and the sergeant addressed the man with the grenade launcher. She
couldn't hear his words, so deafened was she by the firing that
had gone on all around her, but she knew what he was saying.
The same thing she might say to a brash OOD who had a torpedo in the tube, the outer doors opened, and the bearing of
the enemy. *Take your time,* he must be saying. *Make it count.*

The soldier got down on one knee, squinted through the
sight, exhaled, and fired. The grenade launcher made a satisfying *BLOOP.* The grenade flew directly toward the tower but
hit low, bouncing off the side and exploding as it fell toward
the ground. The sergeant leaned in and calmly spoke to the
soldier again, who nodded and adjusted his stance. His second shot flew directly through one of the windows they had
blown open with their bullets.

And then it passed directly through a shattered window on
the other side. It exploded harmlessly in the air.

There was a moment of silence, and then they all burst out
laughing.

"What a horrible shot!" said Carlson, laughing with the rest.

The sergeant put his hand on the shoulder of the soldier

with the grenade launcher, moved him slightly to his left, so
that his next shot wouldn't pass all the way through.

Before he could shoot, there was a sudden change that
Carlson became aware of on a subconscious level. The drones
that had been hovering all around them, watching their fun
but not participating, suddenly jerked in their flight paths, as
if jolted by a sudden and important set of new instructions. A
large contingent of them formed into a V and flew directly
toward the *Polaris*. The drones that had been directly over
their heads dipped ominously, their buzzing engines deepen-
ing by an octave as they changed course.

Almost immediately, the bombs began falling.

The first one landed in the middle of the commandos,
shattering their bodies, sending three of them rolling down the
hill. The man with the grenade launcher was cut almost in
half, leaving his weapon behind as he rolled into the sea. The
gray rock of the bluff was suddenly red with the blood of her
men.

Carlson was shocked to realize she wasn't hit, even as the
bombs continued to fall. She followed the dead bodies of the
marines, rolling down the bluff, thinking that the drones
might take her for one of the dead.

Banach followed her down. They were in that slight crevice in the rock now, between the bluff and the rest of the island, but the drones weren't fooled at all. An explosion went
off right in front of them. She was turned away, but Banach
lost an eye in the explosion; his face was covered in blood.

Banach pulled himself upright, still alive, and dragged
himself on top of her. At first she wasn't sure what he was
doing and started to get angry with him, could barely breathe
from the suffocating weight of his body on top of hers. Then
she realized that he was trying to protect her.

It won't work, she thought. The drones saw the concentration of bodies, alive and dead, as an attractive target and wouldn't stop until they were obliterated. He might absorb the first blast, maybe the second, but the drones were relentless, and her death was inevitable. Banach was so close, the whole length of his body atop her, that she could feel his weakening, dying pulse through her uniform. Each explosion forced him down harder on top of her, as if he were a lover trying to tighten his embrace. A bomb exploded directly on top of them, and his heartbeat stopped. His blood poured over her face, and her arms were pinned by the rock walls, her hands unable to clear her eyes. His dead body absorbed another blast, and then another. *How gallant of him,* she thought. But she would have preferred to die atop the bluff in the first blast, she realized, looking out at the sea.

CHAPTER THIRTY

Moody watched from the deck of the *Polaris* as the three rubber boats zipped by her on the way to Eris Island; two from the Typhon boat, and one from the escape trunk of *Polaris*. The *Polaris* boat contained just Pete and McCallister, and no guns. The Typhon boats in contrast were crammed with men, all of them carrying weapons. She could take no satisfaction in the imminent, brutal deaths of those two traitors, because it would mean that Typhon would soon take Eris Island. And the cure.

The drones continued to bomb the Typhon ship. It was sinking rapidly even as the boats escaped it. They zipped by Dr. Haggerty, who was pathetically waving his arms at all parties, seemingly shocked that no one wanted to save him. She didn't understand it. She felt a creeping, familiar aggravation, much like she had when Hamlin had arrived with his secret orders. Once again, so many people seemed to know exactly what was going on, while she did not. Haggerty went under for good at about the same time the Typhon submarine did.

She reminded herself that she was still in command of an

Alliance submarine. She'd been watching the waterline care-fully, and while only the nose of the sub still stuck out of the water, it no longer appeared to be sinking. She had to sum-mon help somehow, even with radio disabled. Maybe she could launch the emergency beacon, draw in help from the Alliance. She had two billion dollars' worth of technology under her command, nuclear missiles, torpedoes, the most advanced submarine in the world. Surely she could thwart three rubber boats.

The boats landed on the island, and she lost track of what was happening until the action began to center on the distant control tower. She heard the sharp staccato cracks of rifle shots. That sound stopped and was replaced by something lower, more powerful.

Suddenly there was a change in the air. The random swoop-ing of the drones over Eris turned into a direct flight.

Toward her.

She'd observed enough drone attacks to recognize what was about to happen. Somehow the radius had changed, she realized, putting the *Polaris* in the killing zone. Without think-ing, she executed a perfect swan dive off the side of the *Polaris,* into the ocean. The cool water braced her, gave her clarity of mind she hadn't had in days. As she came up to the surface, she was already swimming fast, athletically, toward the rocky shore of Eris. The bombs exploded behind her, finishing off what was left of her submarine.

She found her rhythm quickly, swimming strongly toward shore, breaking through the waves. It was five miles to the beach. A long swim in open, choppy ocean, but she was strong, the all-time record holder on the Alliance obstacle course. The swim took her back to her training, when everything seemed so clear and her talents so valued. Every second stroke, she took a breath, and she could see bombs dropping in front of her now, too, exploding all over Eris Island. She herself must be inside the killing zone, she realized, but a lone swimmer was, at least for the moment, a lower priority target. As she powered through the waves, she felt indestructible.

Pete looked cautiously out the window as Carlson's crew was swarmed by drones.

At first, the drones assessed the immediate threat, bombing Carlson and her men. They threw themselves to the ground, but there was nowhere to hide on the rocky bluff. Bombs fell all around them. They were close enough that Pete could see them screaming, but he couldn't hear them over the constant roar of the exploding bombs. Some of the Typhon crew rolled into the crevice, driven either by gravity or by an instinct to seek some kind of shelter.

Simultaneously, a formation of drones headed toward *Polaris*. Pete saw Finn wince as the first bombs struck his ship. They poured their bombs onto the boat, then formed a beeline back to the island to reload. The *Polaris* held up bravely as bombs poured onto her, but eventually the top of the hull cracked, and smoke poured out as more bombs poured in. The drones were in a frenzy.

And then, suddenly, *Polaris* was gone, replaced on the ocean surface by a black slick of oil and a layer of bubbles as the ship's air banks cracked and exploded.

The drones returned their attention to Eris Island.

They began targeting the pallets of bombs, which exploded with such power that the concussion almost knocked the men down in the control tower. What glass remained in the windows was shattered. Pete covered his face with his hands and felt flying shards of glass cut his knuckles. Alarms went off in the tower as bombs dropped close by; Pete saw one indicator saying that the main tower door was breached, compromised by a series of nearby blasts. But the tower itself stayed safe as the drones focused all their energy on targets outside the ten-foot radius. Pete noticed, fascinated, that the drones were prioritizing the larger pallets of bombs first, then going after the smaller ones. The island was soon blanketed in explosions.

Pete saw a smoke cloud in the distance, on the south side of the island. His heart sank as he realized that the old buildings of the medical detachment were being destroyed. Whatever remained of the group's quest for a cure was being bombed into shreds.

It was over quickly. Soon, the island was overflowing with quick-moving, unarmed drones. Pete could practically read their primitive little minds. They were without bombs, with no chance of rearming, having destroyed all their own munitions. They quickly went into self-destruct mode.

They all picked targets, what few structures were left on the battered island, and flew perfect swan dives into them. Only the ten-foot circle around the tower was safe. Some drones flew into the sea as well, spotting some target of opportunity, a piece of flotsam from one of the sinking submarines.

It took thirty minutes before the bombs stopped falling. It seemed much, much longer as they sat and listened and absorbed the sound from a thousand bombs through the broken windows. Pete remembered reading about artillery barrages in World War II that had gone on for days. He didn't know how men could ever endure that kind of noise for so long without going insane.

His ears rang so badly that it took him a minute to realize it was over. He stood up slowly, and McCallister did the same.

Outside the windows, the island was smoking from a thousand craters, large and small. But no drones flew overhead.

The quiet was breathtaking.

"Everybody OK?" said Pete. He stood all the way up, carefully.

"I'm all right," said Finn.

"Me, too," said Stewart, although Pete could hear otherwise in his voice. The old man didn't get up.

"Admiral?" Peter walked to him.

A dark patch of blood spread across his uniform. "I don't think it's anything serious."

"Are you shot?"

"I don't think so," he said. "Broken glass. Hurts like the devil, and lots of blood, but I'll be fine."

Pete looked closely into the admiral's eyes, looking for false bravado. While his body was bloodied, his eyes were steady and calm. Considerably calmer than Pete felt.

"Freeze!" Hana Moody suddenly burst through the door. She rapidly trained a pistol from Pete and the admiral to Finn, and back again. Her eyes stopped briefly on the admiral, confused by a stranger in admiral's shoulder boards. Incredibly, Pete saw in her eyes deference to his rank. Her weapon looked foreign; Pete realized she must have scavenged it from one of the dead Typhon marines.

"Jesus Christ, Moody, how did you—?"

"I rushed to the door of the tower. Stayed pinned against it while you got the drones to do your dirty work."

Her soaking-wet clothes were torn, her face dirty and bloody. As loud as it was inside the tower, Pete couldn't imagine what it must have been like on ground level during the barrage.

She steadied the gun at Pete, but hesitated to point it at the admiral. "You're all prisoners of war," she said.

From the other side of the tower, Finn laughed out loud. "Our war is over," he said. "You can put that thing away."

"You've betrayed the Alliance," she said. "And I'm going to see that you pay for it."

Finn then did the one thing that guaranteed the most viscerally angry reaction. He laughed at her.

With a guttural cry of rage, she fired. Her aim was off, perhaps due to unfamiliarity with the Typhon gun, and she hit Finn in the shoulder. He spun to the ground with a grunt.

She trained the gun on Pete, the only man now standing in the tower. "Have you got anything to say?"

"I'll do whatever you want," said Pete, trying to exaggerate the panic in his voice. "But we've got to help the admiral!"

Her eyes darted to Stewart. "What's wrong with him? Who is he?"

"He's been hit!" said Pete, trying to add to her confusion and doubt. "They shot the admiral!" He knelt down as if to aid him.

As he did, he reached in his pocket.

Moody looked away, just for a moment, to the graying admiral covered in blood. Maybe she thought he could be her ally, a supporter of her crusade for the Alliance. Even wounded, he was the portrait of high-ranking dignity, with his gray hair and weathered face. Maybe she thought Pete and Finn had taken him prisoner up there in the tower. Whatever she thought, his presence was enough to distract her for just a moment. It was long enough for Pete to withdraw his nine-millimeter pistol, and fire a shot.

He hit her in the thigh. She spun around even as she was trying to raise her gun, but Pete fired again, this time hitting her square in the chest. She stared at him, stunned, eyes wide open, but still on her feet, still with the pistol in her hand.

Pete stood, took a moment to aim, and fired a third shot, into her chest.

She fell to the glass-covered carpet of the tower floor, dead.

CHAPTER THIRTY-ONE

They waited a full day in the tower, watching the drones trickle in and kill themselves on the island. They ate a little from the well-stocked bunker in the basement beneath the tower, slept a little in the two cots, taking turns on watch upstairs. They dressed the wounds of the admiral, picking out the pieces of broken glass that had lodged in his chest and scalp. Finn's wound was more serious, but the bullet had exited his shoulder cleanly, and they dressed and bandaged him as best they could.

They dragged Moody's body onto a landing in the stairwell, for lack of a better place, and covered it with a green tarp that barely covered her.

At sunrise, Pete wandered upstairs to find the admiral staring out at sea.

"Anything?" he said.

"No."

"Think we should venture out?" said Pete.

The admiral nodded. "It's probably safe now. Haven't seen a drone in hours."

He turned and leaned against the console that still glowed green with the shortened radius that kept them safe from any drones that might still be alive. "But now that we've got a second," said the admiral, "let me ask you a question. Why are you here?"

Pete had to think for just a minute. While his memory had come back, it was still hazy, as if operating in a lower gear. And so much had happened. . . .

"They sent me here," he said, "because of the flu."

"Is it that bad?"

"They say it is," said Pete. "So here I am."

"They evacuated all the doctors a few weeks ago . . . it was entirely classified, of course. I managed to stay behind while they left. I figured they were taking the vaccine with them."

"They didn't survive the trip. So they sent me."

"Sent you to stop one epidemic . . ."

Pete raised his hands to indicate the airfield, scattered with the wreckage of a thousand drones. "And I stopped another."

"Maybe you'll stop both," said the admiral. He reached under his coat and pulled out a thick manila envelope that he'd been hiding. "I went down there and looked around after the medical team left. Found this on a desk—pretty sure somebody wanted me to find it."

"What . . ." said Pete, as he took the envelope.

Across the front of it, in large red letters, it read: THE CURE.

The three men made their way out onto the island, explored on foot. The drones had performed well until the very end. No structure was still standing except the control tower, protected by that green electronic circle that Pete had inscribed around it. He'd left it there, just in case, and the three men kept a wary eye on the sky. But Pete had a feeling that all the drones were gone, the word spread by dancing drones and self-destruct sequences under way all over the Pacific.

They came upon the bluff where Carlson had made her last stand and scrambled to the top.

A number of weapons were scattered across the bluff. Finn picked one up.

"Grenade launcher," he said. "They almost got us with this."

Pete bent down and picked up two bandoliers. "Are these the grenades?" They looked like very large shotgun shells, each with a bulbous nose.

"They are," said Finn. He took the two belts and counted up the remaining shells. "Twenty-two left," he said. He put the belts across his chest. "Let's see what else they left behind."

"Over here!" said the admiral. He was at the edge of the bluff, pointing down into the crevice.

When the waves ran out of the space between the bluff and the island, they revealed a grisly sight: almost the entire Typhon force, their bodies broken and twisted. Pete saw movement and thought for a moment that someone had somehow survived. Then he realized that the bodies were covered in thousands of tiny crabs, busily consuming their dead flesh.

"Let's drag Moody's body out here with them," he said, remembering how she had treated his friend Ramirez.

On the other side of the island, they came over a rise to the remains of a low-slung building that still smoldered.

"What's this?" said Finn.

"The medical research facility," said Stewart. "What's left of it."

They climbed a hill, from which they could see water in all directions. Waves crashed on the south side of the island,

and seagulls dived around them. Each time a gull's shadow crossed the ground, Pete caught himself flinching.

"Now what do we do?" said Finn.

"Everybody will realize soon that the drones are gone," said Pete. "There are people that have been waiting for this moment. To seize the island."

"Will this end the war?" said Stewart.

"It's been over," said Pete. "I'm convinced. Both militaries have all been driven underground and underwater for so long; they're decimated. Nobody wants to fight anymore. Nobody has for a while now. I'm sure there will be negotiations, bad intentions and good, but the war is over. We just destroyed the only weapon system that was still functioning."

"Will they call us traitors?" said Finn. "Saboteurs? For destroying it all?"

"No one needs to know," said Pete. "Both sides were here; now both sides are gone. We'll say they destroyed the drones while fighting each other. I'm the expert on drones, I'll explain how it's possible."

"Will that work?"

Pete sighed. "It's close enough to the truth. I can live with it."

The men thought that over for a minute and continued to look at the sea.

"So what now? We stay here and wait for somebody to come get us? What if the enemy gets here first? What if it's another one like Carlson? Or Moody, for that matter?"

Pete shrugged. "I'm not sure we have any choice. We're stranded."

"Maybe not," said Stewart.

He led them down a path to a small inlet on the rocky side of the island. A heavily reinforced concrete shelf hung over it. "Come on," he said.

The admiral was surprisingly spry given his age and his injuries. Pete had to help the wounded Finn down the path.

At the rocky edge of the water, they could look into the dim pen to which Stewart had led them. Inside was a perfectly white Navy cutter.

It was pristine. The water lapped gently against the hull. Black X's had been painted against the side.

"We kept one here for additional trials with the drones," said the admiral. "We never needed to use it because the drones worked so well right out of the gate. But it's a perfectly seaworthy boat, with two full tanks of diesel fuel and room for all of us." Pete noticed a large tank against the back of the bunker, and pointed.

"Extra fuel," said the admiral.

Finn walked over to the boat and pulled himself with his good arm up the small ladder that led to its deck. He had a huge smile on his face.

"Admiral, I'll be your XO."

"No, you be the commanding officer," said Stewart. "I've been thinking about retiring."

They spent two days carrying all the food they could from the tower to the boat: powdered milk, powdered eggs, canned vegetables, canned beans, and hundreds of tiny boxes of cereal. Whatever the impact of the war, thought Pete, the Alliance's Frosted Flakes production had remained strong throughout. On the way back, they each carried a five-gallon plastic container of diesel fuel and positioned it in the control room.

They also practiced with the grenade launcher that had been salvaged from Carlson's team. The thing was supremely well designed for war: tough and easy to use. With no instructions of any kind, all three men were soon shooting it accurately, until they were down to the last six grenades. They judged Hamlin to be the best shot.

That night, they decided to rest, and leave at dawn.

The sun was coming up as Finn started the twin diesels. They had tested them out the day before, and they required some minor work. Pete could see pure pleasure in Finn's eyes as he worked on some last-second adjustments, his shirt off.

"You just going to stand there while I work?" said Finn.

"I'm an aeronautical engineer," said Pete. "Can't help you."

Finn rolled his eyes. "Well, you're second-in-command now."

He gave a hand to Stewart to help him on deck, and then Pete untied the two lines that held the boat to the small cleats inside the pen.

"What will we name her?" asked Finn. "A ship needs a name."

"How about *Polaris*?" said the admiral.

"No," said Pete. "That boat was unlucky."

"You got a better idea?"

"*Pamela*," said Pete, without hesitating, and they all nodded in agreement.

"Are we sure there are no drones out there?" asked McCallister.

Pete nodded. "As sure as we can be. They must be self-destructing all over the place by now. And all of the ones within range of the island have probably made it back by now and self-destructed."

"Who do you think will get here first when they realize the drones aren't a threat anymore?"

Pete shrugged. "Not sure it matters. We'll make sure there's nothing left of value here. For either side."

Finn turned a switch, and the little boat's diesels roared to life. Pete could feel the power in the rumbling in his feet. Two plumes of black exhaust shot from the stacks as Finn gunned the engines slightly, and ably pulled the boat out to sea.

As they exited the pen, the bright sun almost blinded them.

"At this point in my career, I never thought I'd command a surface ship!" yelled Finn. Pete was hauling in the lines.

"Think about this," said Pete as he worked. "You're probably commanding the largest surface ship in this ocean."

"I might make admiral after all," said Finn.

He revved the engines slowly and pulled away to the leeward side of the island, the side that went hard against the control tower, right by the bluff where Carlson and her men had died. Finn cut the engines, and Pete made his way to the aft deck. The grenade launcher was waiting for him.

"Close enough?" shouted Finn from the bridge.

"Should be," said Pete.

The deck undulated slightly in the calm water, something Pete hadn't practiced for. He lifted the launcher to his shoulder, aimed it at the tower, and waited too long to shoot. The grenade went wide. It exploded impotently on the ground with a spray of gravel.

"Nice shot," said Finn.

"That doesn't help," said Pete. He raised the grenade launcher again, and exhaled deeply.

He pulled the trigger again, and the grenade arced gracefully into the air. It went right through the middle of one of the broken windows; they could actually hear it land with a thump on the carpeted floor. There was a pause—then an explosion. Glass and smoke shot out of all four sides of the tower, followed by orange flames and black smoke as the diesel fuel ignited.

"Well done!" said the captain.

"Let's do one more," said Pete, breaking down the launcher and reloading it. "Make sure there's nothing left in there."

When they were done destroying the tower and all traces of what had happened inside, Finn gunned the engines and swung the bow toward open ocean. They surged forward and starting cutting through the waves instead of riding on top of them. Pete leaned against the aft railing as the boat accelerated. Behind them, Eris Island shrank into the distance. A dolphin jumped exuberantly in their wake. For the first time since he'd awoken on the *Polaris* with his memory erased, Pete smiled.

A FEW NOTES ABOUT TECHNOLOGY

One of the nice things about setting a book in the future is that any outlandish technology can be excused as artistic speculation. I've written two submarine novels set in (more or less) the present, and I can assure you that submariners, while a generous and enthusiastic group of readers, do hold me responsible for the smallest technical inaccuracies. So I welcomed the idea of writing a book set in the future, because it seemed to offer me unlimited ability to make technology do what I wanted it to do. That being said, I tried to ground this book's technology in reality wherever possible. The age we live in offers many technological marvels, many of which require no embellishment by an author to make them soar.

For example: the Robobird. This anti-seagull weapon exists, a wing-flapping replica of a hawk (the company also makes an eagle) used to scare away seagulls and other offensive birds. There are several videos available on the company's website, clearflightsolutions.com.

The big drones in the book required a little more embellishment than the Robobird, although we are clearly now living in the age of drone warfare, and advances in capabilities and tactics are hard to keep up with. The leap to make the drones purely autonomous, rather than directed by a "pilot" on the ground, doesn't seem like it would require much of a technical leap, but rather one of doctrine. Many of us are squeamish about the killing done on our behalf by drones now; taking humans out of that decision is still some time away. But for some of the mere physical specifications of the drones, the actual dimensions of the thing, I borrowed from the ScanEagle, a drone made in a joint operation between Boeing and Insitu. The ScanEagle has been flying for the US military since 2005, and just like the imaginary drones in this book, it has a wingspan of 10 feet and a length of 5 feet. It weighs just about 40 pounds, and can carry a payload of up to 7.5 pounds. It can soar up to 19,500 feet at speeds up to 80 knots. So while my drones certainly are the product of my imagination, they aren't too far off from a drone that has been flying over the world's trouble spots for a decade. More details can be found at http://www.insitu.com/systems/scaneagle.

Degaussing, the process of reducing a submarine's (or a surface ship's) magnetic signature, is a very real thing. I have been through it myself while serving onboard the USS *Alabama,* a Trident submarine. The degaussing range I went through, however, was very much above the surface of the water. And the Soviets really did build a fleet of titanium submarines to avoid this problem.

Submarines really do manufacture their own oxygen, and their own water, from the sea that surrounds them. Ocean water is boiled and the vapor collected to desalinate it. And in the oxygen generators, high-voltage electricity is used to pry the H_2O molecules apart, giving the crew its oxygen. When I reported to my submarine, these processes, along with nuclear power, seemed to me to be the most magical, the most Nemoesque part of submarine engineering, and they still do. Which is probably why I find a way to work them into every book.

Escape trunks are very real. There are three of them on a Trident submarine, and Trident sailors spend a day or so learning how to operate them. They then spend the rest of their sea tours learning how to prevent accidents and fight casualties that might ever require such an escape. This training has a sense of urgency because no one expects the escape trunks to really work—the depths that modern submarines operate in are simply too great for this kind of egress. I once heard a chief say there was a secret procedure somewhere for using the escape trunk as a jail cell—submarines have no brig. I never saw the procedure myself, but if we had ever needed to lock someone up, this probably would have worked as well as anything.

There really is a surface-to-air missile designed for submarines to use against their nemesis, the helicopter. It is made by a German company, Diehl Defense, and was originally designed to work aboard the German Type 212 submarine. It doesn't appear to actually be deployed aboard any operational submarines, but videos are available on the company's website. The MOSS is real, too. The acronym stands for "Mobile Submarine Simulator."

The Dyce Laboratory for Honeybee Studies at Cornell is very real, and looks much like I've described it here. And while it may sound like one of the most far-fetched things in the book, the "waggle dance" is also real, and is an amazing, wondrous method of communication between bees that scientists are still deciphering.

Eris Island is, alas, entirely imaginary.

ACKNOWLEDGMENTS

Thanks as always to my most dedicated editors: my parents, Ken and Laura Tucker.

Also thanks to Pete Wolverton, editor of my first novel, who remembered me and sent this project my way.

Finally, thank you to Brendan Deneen, a great editor and a great storyteller himself. This was the most fun I've ever had writing a book—let's do it again soon.